THE ABSENCE
OF SOUL

American-English version

AMANDA TWIGG

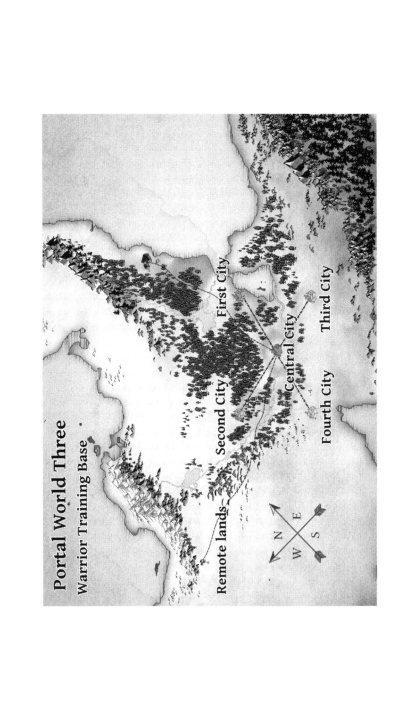

Army Ranks

- **Senior Ranks:**
- Chief Warrior
- Chief Warrior Elect
- Warrior First
- Warrior Second
- Warrior Third
- Warrior Fourth
- Specialization/City Chief
- **Basic Ranks:**
- Citizen - birth to eighteen years
- Cadet - in soldier training (three year course)
- Soldier - on completion of soldier training
- Warrior - on acceptance into Warrior Hall
- **Sub Grades**
- Trainee - applied to Warrior and specialist ranks
- One-bar - basic level achieved/not always awarded
- Two-bar - competent level achieved
- Three-bar - expert level achieved

Chapter 1

Landra dawdled outside her father's command room clutching a summons. Any training session with Chief Hux promised pain, and the timing of this one couldn't be worse. Rather than knock, she traced a finger along the woodgrain door she knew was there, but her gaze slid beyond, as if seeing through glass.

Shelk. So, now I see through wood?

This had only happened once before, so she dismissed the vision. Better to return to her room now rather than face Father and expose her flaw. No punishment could match the disgrace of having magic. She took a deep breath and pulled her tunic away from her chest. By narrowing her eyes and refocusing, she brought the door back into view. The sight of blessed woodgrain calmed her Soul, giving her the chance to gather her thoughts.

What would a soldier do now? Not run, for sure.

Her heart craved a Warrior's future, one where she competed in the championships, traveled the six cities, and looked for love. Magic didn't fit in with that, so rather than submit to fear, she bunched her fist and knocked.

"Enter."

Inside the room, oversized wooden furniture and an equipped combat area reflected her father's personality, and slippers by a chair made this look like his home, but his armor-clad figure looked suited for war. He might be Chief Warrior Griffin Hux, commander of six cities, but she still thought of him as Father.

"Fight me," he said, pinning her with a terrible stare,

Woah. No "nice to see you, daughter." Just "fight me."

He moved to the mat's center and sank into a fighting stance. Ceiling lights bounced pink rays off his battle spikes and highlighted the gold twists in his Warrior-length hair.

For all her denials, Landra couldn't hide from magic. She might not be seeing through doors now, but aura sight was her constant bane. A glow surrounded her father, shrouding him in turbulent shades. *Deep blue, almost black. Is that temper? Fury?*

"What are you waiting for, Landra? Fight me."

The threat-like challenge sped her drumming heartbeat. An empty stomach, over-trained limbs, and a flimsy tunic weren't any preparation for this. She stood to careful attention and considered her next words. "Father, have I done something wrong?"

A nerve twitched in his bristly cheek. His gold-flecked eyes gave nothing away, but his readied muscles offered a warning. He surged forward, slamming her to the floor and chasing the air from her lungs. His arm trapped her neck, and he pressed home the hold.

"It's Chief Hux in here. And tell me, daughter, have you done something wrong?"

Can't breathe. Stop. She kicked her legs as panic took hold. This wasn't training. It was an attack. No amount of arguing with Trainer Winton warranted this beating, leaving magic as her only possible crime. Years of suppressed fear bubbled up. *Discovered now? Shelk.*

"Father, I—"

"Show me some spirit, girl. Make this a fight."

As Landra's vision blurred, she pushed on his arm. An unexpected release allowed air into her lungs. She curled over her belly and spluttered as Father rolled to his feet and resumed his battle crouch. He swished the blade in menacing sweeps.

"Good!" he said. "Now, show me what you can do."

Good? I nearly died. Is that what he wanted? Magic-cursed soldiers earned temple demotions or exile, but a flawed Chief Warrior's daughter was different. Her existence could provoke a leadership challenge or civil war. Would he remove her to save the base? *Every day of the week.*

She rubbed her throat and eased to her feet. Father darted forward again and swiped his pink blade across her bare arm. Her hand flew to the wound, and she gasped. The cut wasn't deep, but blood squeezed through her fingers and her skin burned. Angry red lines spidered outward from the gash, sensitizing her body and turning her dread into outrage.

A magic blade? Oh, Father, the irony. D'you know what you've done?

"Stop staring," he said. "That cut's barely bleeding."

Landra wanted to protest, but the curse of having visions was hers alone. Father could no more see the weapon's magical tracks than he could view her aura. She licked the red liquid from her fingers, and a hot, metallic taste seared her tongue. The sensation made her fury soar. *Not my fault.* She dropped into a fighting crouch, ready to battle. "Let's fight."

"At last."

"But it's not fair. You have a knife."

"Take it, then." He wasn't offering the blade; she had to fight for it.

She circled, her gaze locked on the weapon. "I'm a citizen. You can't expect me to match Warrior training."

"You won't if you bellyache. You might not be cadet age, but I've paid tutors to hone your skills and harden your fists. Show me what my credits have bought and take the knife."

That again.

Father's bulk, reach, and experience outmatched her own, but her peripheral vision took in a weapons display where locking clips hugged five swords and three knives to the wall. Faking left and dodging right, she sprinted toward them across the mat. He read the move and intercepted. He tackled her off the mat and rolled her over the desk, sloshing a half-downed mug of scute into the air.

Before she could recover, he followed up his move, ramming her back into a bookcase and trapping her hand beneath his knee.

"It's against combat rules to leave the mat," he said.

"So is drawing blood."

He pinned her throat with the knife, and its magic burned her skin. Any more pressure, and her blood would gush. Had it really come to this? A hysterical laugh escaped, and she sucked in his scute-laced breath. At least he had to get drunk for the battle. It didn't help her mood.

"Fight me," he said again.

Why? To justify the kill? Saliva dried in her mouth. She longed to be cherished, but her father's muscled body pressed against her chest, offering something darker. It wasn't fair. She didn't deserve this.

Enough!

Landra drove a knee into his groin and watched his agony register.

Is that what you want? Are you happy now?

His leg shifted, and his face boiled. With the space it gave her, she twisted free. A leg sweep unweighted him, and she chased him down to the floor.

That's for all I've endured hiding my flaw. You've no idea.

She set her teeth to his thumb knuckle and crunched. His fingers sprang open, and she snatched the knife.

And that's for making me fight.

She darted back to the mat, set her stance, and rolled the knife between her palms. Her aura tumbled around her hands in violent swirls, and her shoulders heaved. "Now, I'm ready."

Father sagged back to the floor with a sigh of inevitability.

"Get up. Let's do this." She beckoned him back with the knife tip. The weapon's bone handle sat perfectly in her hand, sending a rush of energy through her body. The fight hadn't been her idea, but she would see it to the end.

Her father climbed to his feet and shook his head. "No, that's enough."

"Enough of what? Are you coming back to the mat or shall I fight you there?"

"Neither. We're done. I've seen what you can do."

Frustration fueled her battle rage, making her fingers tremble around the knife handle. "You wanted me to fight, and now I'm ready. All you've seen is scrapping. What's the matter? Doesn't my style suit your image of a Warrior? I thought you wanted me to prove my worth."

He leaned back to rest against his desk and pressed a hand to his ribs. "You already did."

Landra was sure she hadn't. "I broke the rules. I fought like—"

"Like you wanted to survive?"

"I brawled. I can do better."

5

"You don't need to do better."

Uncertainty rolled Landra's stomach. Her father had calmed too quickly, and his aura had settled into a uniform shade of blue. She'd been fighting for her life, and now he'd just stopped.

He lifted his gaze to capture her attention. "Look at the knife."

She eyed the blade's unnatural gleam of power. A carved Warrior image on the handle tugged a memory loose.

"It's the Collector, Landra. A symbol of office."

Images of Father wearing the knife to his investiture flitted across her awareness. What did that have to do with the fight? A host of possibilities surfaced—all of them impossible. "I…" She couldn't make sense of her father's words.

"Believe it, Landra. Taking the knife completed the succession rite and sealed your future. One day, you will become chief." He tightened his pose and offered a grim salute. "Congratulations on your promotion, Chief Elect."

"But… But…"

What about my magic?

Chapter 2

If it wasn't for the early morning stomp of boot heels outside her door, Landra might have logged the previous night's events as a scute-induced dream. Her small room hadn't changed, with its basic furniture and a rail of uniforms acting as a backdrop to her citizen's life, but she sensed the unusual activity heralded change. Snuggling in bed and scrunching her blanket to her chin, she sought out the familiar paw-shaped knot in the ceiling's grain. Floating pink threads obscured the shape but at least the wood hadn't disappeared.

She hadn't slept. How could she? The job Father had inflicted on her was beyond her capabilities and didn't make sense. Of all the possible reasons for her late-night battle, leadership succession had been the furthest from her mind. Hadn't her brother been groomed for that role? Then, there was her magic. If she understood how it worked, maybe she could control the visions. They were becoming more troublesome—just when the need for secrecy had grown.

A paper appeared through the gap under her door.

Different. Wrong!

She glared at the offending message and then swung her legs from the bed. Stiff muscles locked her body into a sheet of pain, and her head rattled like her brains were loose.

Woah! Did I age ten years in my sleep? Got to see Medic Gren.

Balancing her pained body, she shuffled across the room to glare at the intruding paper. Even the chief's daughter had to collect mail from the scribing hall's notice board, so a hand-delivered message felt wrong, right down to her bones. She set her doubts aside and considered the duty Father had tasked her to perform. It didn't matter that it was a mistake. Things would be different now.

She eased down to retrieve the note and felt the wafer-thin, recycled paper of a newsletter. The championship candidate pool had grown by twelve, a section of ring thirty-two had closed for repairs, and Chief Hux's inspection of the Warrior guard was set for midday. Of the four rank changes listed, one Templer was scheduled to take the exile train to the remote lands.

That's trouble. Temple bods won't like that.

Before she could consider the implications, her touch found a second, thicker paper below the top sheet. She pressed it to her nose and sniffed, marveling at the fresh smell, but her soldier practicality was offended by the extravagance. Chief Hux's precisely penned script marked the sheet.

- First siren - sword training (apartment armory)
- Second siren – history (apartment library)
- Third siren – SEE ME!

Anyone accidentally seeing the schedule would think it an average morning for Landra, with a combination of soldier training beyond her rank, studies, and a reprimand. She knew it was more and took his personal summons to mean that he meant to go through with his plan. Third siren felt like a long time off, so she decided to catch a word with him before duties started.

With a good amount of wincing and groaning, she struggled into a standard blue training tunic and pants, sharp enough to satisfy Father but practical enough for her scheduled sword session. Her rash from the Collector smarted where the ridged web pattern stood proud of her skin, but there was nothing to do about that now. Before choosing a jacket, she forced herself to consider the knife.

She leaned her belly against a disused planter that ran the length of the room and peeked inside. A pink gleam leaked out from one edge of the cloak she'd used as a cover, as if the Collector refused to be forgotten. Clearly, the knife couldn't stay there for any inspection officer to find.

Why didn't I take dispensation to keep my room private? But she knew why. She'd wanted to be one of the soldiers— normal. Now, that decision was biting her in the ass, and normality was gone. She buckled an old knife strap over her complaining shoulders and slotted the knife into the sheath at her back. She'd take the shelking thing to Father, and he would know where it should go. After slinging on a loose jacket, wriggling the knife into a good position, and fastening her buckles, she yanked the door inward. A guard facing into the corridor and occupying the full height of the doorway blocked her exit.

A Warrior. Careful.

The hair gave him away. Landra couldn't wait until she entered Warrior Hall, so she could start growing her hair. It was a symbol of power and experience every soldier aspired to wear.

She guessed the dark curls draped down this guard's back must represent twenty years of growth—a seasoned Warrior and member of the elite guard for sure. The array of achievement ribbons on his ceremonial cloak proved it. She tried ignoring his Warrior blue aura, but its wavy edges demanded her attention. Few auras had such ill-defined limits, and her gaze kept tracking its amorphous patterns.

"Excuse me, sir," she said with a small cough.

"Stay inside," he answered over his shoulder, allowing her to see the ranking insignia cut into the shorter hair above his right ear.

What the…?

This wasn't just an elite guard. Four lines cut below a "W" identified him as the Warrior Fourth, and the addition of an "R" marked him as a ranger. There was only one Warrior Fourth, but seeing a ranger in the city was even more of a rarity. The freedom to wander the six cities and remote lands was an intoxicating temptation. So, when this man could travel anywhere, why was he outside her door?

"I have to go out," she said.

"Sword training's not until first siren. You can leave ahead of time to grab breakfast, but not yet."

Landra stared, shocked that the Warrior Fourth knew her schedule. She had expected changes to her life but hadn't guessed how quickly they would take hold. "Hux Hall is my home." Her face heated. "Are you ordering me to stay in my room?"

"Yes."

Yes? What am I? A child?

Landra suspected this loss of freedom constituted her first sacrifice as chief elect. An ache stiffened her back, reminding her that it was the second. She'd already sacrificed her fit body, even if that was a temporary inconvenience.

"I need to leave at once. I'm Chief Hux's daughter."

The guard gave a salute to two soldiers marching down the apartment's narrow corridor before he spun around. The dark, weather-roughened skin showing above his scraggy beard conveyed no emotion, but the short sword strapped to his chest told Landra that he was on Warrior duty. His work-worn uniform looked well below inspection level, contrasting with the crisp, clean ceremonial pleats of his cloak.

"I know who you are. And it still baffles me how you escaped the Junior barracks before cadet age. No one else gets to live at home with family. And here I am, not even cleaned up from my stint in the remote lands. I don't know what I did to deserve babysitting duty. Maybe I pulled a low assessment score or maybe our new Warrior Second doesn't like my face, but I'm stuck here with you, so I'd appreciate some quiet."

Landra's face burned. "I'm not a child, and I can look after myself."

The guard's face twisted into a smirk. "I hear you can scrap, but it takes more than that to be a soldier. And at least one person thinks you need protection." He glanced down the corridor in the direction of Chief Hux's command room.

"That's because …"

Landra bit her lip. Chief Hux had sworn her to silence, and she wouldn't divulge her secret at the first chance. "I need to see Chief Hux now."

The guard edged forward, using one hand to push her back into the room. "That's not possible," he told her, before closing the door.

"I—"

Shelking bastard!

Landra stood there, mouth gaping. Gaining respect from Warriors was going to be tough. After staring at the door's wooden grain for too long, she yanked the handle. It wouldn't budge, so she banged on the panel for several minutes before it opened.

"I have urgent business wi—"

"Having trouble?" Dannet appeared in the doorway.

"No! Yes. What are you doing here?"

"They dragged me back from the cadet academy this morning."

She flung her arms around her brother and squeezed. Their auras touched, and the familiar smell of fighting leathers and machine oil soothed Landra. She didn't let go. She couldn't. This was her safe place, next to her brother.

"Steady on, Lan. Are you trying to hug the breath out of me?" He nudged her away and peered into her face. "Are you all right?"

"No." She wanted to tell him everything.

"I know what you mean. They didn't give me time to eat before escorting me out of Cadet Hall. I've never seen such tight security around the apartment. Bexter came back with me, and I didn't think they were going to let him in with all this fuss."

All this fuss? Could this be about my promotion?

A glance at Dannet convinced her that not all the trouble was over her new role. If the news was even out. If he knew that he'd been passed over as chief elect, she was sure his mood would be different.

"Maybe this will cheer you up." Dannet handed her a palm-sized wire cage with a purple bead at its center.

"Why?"

"I know you like puzzles, so I made you a trick ball."

She didn't have time for toys and set it down. "No. Why are you back early?"

Dannet's eyes widened. "Haven't you heard? Everywhere is on lockdown." He glanced back to the door. "Putting Warrior Fourth Thisk on guard seems a bit extreme, though."

She couldn't argue with that, even knowing her changed status. Her brother's half-story surged her frustration. "What's going on? Why is security tight?"

Dannet ran both hands over his short hair. His rounded face and big eyes looked stricken to stillness. "I really thought you would know, Lan. A Templer tried to assassinate Chief Hux, and now Warriors are snapping at everyone. They're seizing swords from harmless citizens, freezing accounts in the tally halls so no one has credit to eat, and searching children. It's awful. They sent all the first-year cadets away and put a curfew on Templers. I was escorted home."

Landra absorbed the news but could only focus on one fact. "A Templer did what? Is Father hurt?" She tried to fit this information together with the previous night's events.

"He's fine. It was a priest who dressed up in soldier uniform and joined the Warrior Hall candidate tour. The fool pretended to cast a Soul spell, dancing around in circles and everything. Then he slashed Chief Hux in the ribs with a dagger."

Landra's empty stomach danced. "How can you call him Chief Hux at a time like this? He's our father."

"Have to. It's an academy rule."

Not one I'll do well with. " I saw today's newsletter. The incident wasn't reported."

"No, and it won't be. As far as I can tell, they're trying to keep it quiet. How they'll manage that with the Warriors so edgy, I've no idea. Every citizen with a hint of Templer blood is being questioned. The assassin's already on the exile train, and more Templers are likely to follow. This could start a purge."

Dread rattled through Landra's frame as she stared at her brother's warm blue aura. Back when she was a twelve-year-old with emerging visions, hiding her magic had seemed wise, but now it left her with no one to turn to for advice. She didn't like keeping secrets from Dannet, and now she had two. Agitated dots mottled his aura in a display of anxiety, and she didn't want to land more grief at his door.

"Landra! I want to tell you something."

His serious tone and use of her full name caught her attention, and she tilted her head back to look up at his face.

Bigger. Older. Don't go away again.

He dragged his sleeves down over his wrists and pulled his lanky frame to order. The cadet uniform fell into crisper pleats than usual, and his boots gleamed as if he'd polished them for a week. He sucked in a deep breath and stiffened.

"Landra, I think Chief Hux means to announce me as his successor," he blurted, and air rushed out of him in a relieved sigh.

Her mouth sagged open. The Collector suddenly seemed too large and pink to stay hidden beneath her jacket. Her brother's upturned chin and glinting gold eyes betrayed pride, and she swallowed hard, trying to choose her next words. "Why do you think that?"

"It just makes sense. If something happens to Chief Hux without a deputy in place, the leadership goes up for grabs. I can't see the Warrior Council letting that happen. I came through the concourse. The ceremonial plinth is half-built and the ceiling is covered in Warrior colors. They're getting ready for a promotion ceremony."

Oh, Dannet.

A mixture of guilt and dread rooted Landra to the spot. She stared, barely knowing what to say. "You can't know Chief Hux means to name you."

Dannet puffed out his cheeks. "True, and I know what you're thinking. He might choose his Warrior Second. Tasenda's a good woman and a great fighter, but I can't see this position going outside the Hux family. We've ruled the base since before homeworld Templers exiled us here. I don't think he'll break with tradition now."

Landra coughed. "I wasn't thinking of Tasenda."

"Then who?"

Her stomach churned. She wanted to tell Dannet her news. She wanted to give him the Collector, but Father had already rejected him for the post of chief elect. "Surely, you don't want to become chief. It's not a normal life."

Dannet sighed. "It's not that I want the position, Lan. Honestly, my investiture as chief elect will come as a relief. I've grown up knowing this day would come, and waiting's been the hardest part. At least now, something is happening."

Landra rubbed her lip. Once Dannet's width matched his height, he would have the look of a chief, and he wanted to rule. She wished Father was here to sort out this mess.

"I have to see Chief Hux before breakfast," she said.

"Is that all you have to say? I thought you'd be more pleased."

She stared at her brother. His gold-flecked coloring was all Hux, but his mouth turned down at the corners rather than up like Father's and his broader forehead gave him a

Fourth City look. Still, she could visualize him strutting through the halls in the gold-fringed chief's robe.

Why didn't Father choose you? It would have been better all around.

"All of your achievements make me proud," she said. Dannet didn't deserve deceit, and she knew right then she would share her secret.

Before she could speak, the door swung open.

"Time for food," Thisk said.

"One moment, sir." Dannet reached across to tug Landra's collar high. "No need for anyone to see that bruise," he said in a soft voice by her ear. He wet his thumb and rubbed it across her brow.

"Ow!" The pressure enlivened pain. *From the Collector's handle.* "Don't make it bleed." She tipped her head aside to avoid the question shining her brother's gold-flecks eyes. He would have one truth today, but it couldn't be now. Not in front of Thisk. She darted out into the corridor under the guard's judgmental scrutiny.

Her appearance was shoddy and showed signs of her illegal fight with Father, but there was nothing to do about that now. At least she looked better than the Warrior Fourth, and she could sort it out later, along with speaking to Father, visiting the medic, beginning her new training, and, above all, talking with Dannet. Her life as chief elect was starting to look busy.

Chapter 3

Shouting from the food hall reached them while they were still in the corridor. Landra picked up her pace, Dannet matched her stride, and Thisk followed like a shadow. They turned into the communal area to find it unusually deserted—with empty benches, washed-down tables, and dimmed lights. Pink aura light gleamed from beneath the kitchen door, but the shouting had stopped.

Landra's heart pounded louder in her ears than the clanging cogs of the homeworld clock, which hung on the wall. "What happened?" she asked.

"Who knows?" Dannet crossed to wind the clock's mechanism.

"Is it really useful to know the time according to the turning of a planet in the distant sky?" she asked. "This is hardly the..." She'd been going to say time.

"It's a wonderful piece of machinery, Lan. If it ever stops, the settings will be impossible to calibrate."

It wasn't something Landra could worry about. The atmosphere felt wrong in the food hall. She touched a solitary sandwich, which sat like a blemish on the cold food counter.

Hard, old, and…

"Barthle's pastries!" She said.

"What?" Dannet asked.

"I can't smell Barthle's pastries. I've woken up to that smell for as long as I can remember. Didn't realize until now. This place isn't right without it."

"Mist-rotten shelk!" Barthle screamed from inside the kitchen, accompanied by the sound of crashing pots.

Thisk stepped between Dannet and Landra, his sword drawn and his mouth working as if he were rolling a pea over his tongue. "Stay here," he said, his aura roaming in wavy patterns. He pushed the kitchen door open.

"What d'you want?" Chef Barthle's deep voice growled. Thisk ducked beneath a flying pan.

"There's no food," Barthle said, storming out of a second rotating door. He left it spinning on well-oiled hinges. Dark smudges covered his cheek, stretching up into his hairline and partially obscuring his insignia. He'd abandoned his work tabard, showing off more stains on his under-uniform. The blazing blue of his aura matched the furious gaze he turned on Thisk. He slid his attention over Landra and let his focus settle on Dannet. "Hey, boy, you were always good at tinkering with machines. My oven's down and the water's colder than a remote land glacier. Can you fix it?"

Thisk puffed out his cheeks and rammed his short sword back into his chest sheath. "Is that all this is about? I thought something was really wrong."

"Wrong? Of course something's wrong," Barthle said. He waggled an angry finger at Thisk until he noticed the Warrior's hair insignia. "With respect, sir. Do you know I had to send the early shift to ring sixty-four food hall, and it's a good thing Chief Hux is in a meeting. I've not missed taking him a hot breakfast in eighteen years of service." He turned to Dannet again. "Can you help, boy?"

"I'm a second-year engineering cadet, sir. Not qualified yet."

"Well, you'll do for now. A fancy engineer is on his way, but only the mist knows how long that will take."

"I'll give it a go," Dannet said, but Landra recognized the uncertain twitch in his cheek. "Come with me?" he whispered to her.

They followed Barthle into the kitchen and had to skirt around a chef support worker who was retrieving strewn bowls from the floor. Another chef cadet stuck firmly to his work bench, eyes pinned on the fish he was gutting as if it held the answers of the mist. Of the four work counters, one with a metal surface sat askew from the wall, and the pink magical glow blossomed from behind its casing.

Barthle waved his hand at the misplaced unit. The whole system went down, so there's no hot water or heat for cooking. Unless it gets fixed, we'll be on cold rations and scute."

"Sounds good to me," Thisk said, picking up a carrot. He bit off the end and relaxed against the wall.

"Well, it's not," Barthle said, unable to contain his frustration.

"Not sure what I can do, Chef Barthle, but I'll take a look." Dannet crossed to the unit, tugging Landra along by the sleeve. He lifted a pan off the stove. "We need to move these." Once Landra had helped him clear the surface, he set a flat palm over the metal surface and twisted dials.

"It doesn't take an engineering education to try the on switch," Barthle said.

"No, sir, but there's a procedure."

Landra often forgot how young her brother was

because he'd assumed a fatherly role during Chief Hux's absences. Just now, his teen-blemished skin and wide eyes made him look even younger than his nineteen years.

"Can you do anything with it?" she whispered.

"Probably not. I'm a good engineer, but this isn't my field. Come around back with me while I take a look."

Dannet squeezed behind the counter and crouched, but Landra hesitated at the limit of the pink glow until he tugged her down. Prodding a decaying tree root that coiled on the floor, he pulled a face. "This stuff's rotten."

She watched her brother scrape blackened tendrils from the long rods which filled the cabinet. A whiff of rotting vegetation met her nostrils and the remaining fronds fell away, leaving dirty scars on the metal. Beetles scattered and scurried down the rods.

Landra's face twisted in disgust. "Is it infested?"

"More like decrepit. These dead tree roots are the power delivery system and should connect with the heat rods."

His aura pulsed like a speeding heartbeat, but it couldn't match pace with Landra's rhythm. Sections of the vegetation glowed with a similar signature to aura light. The vision wasn't useful when she needed to focus on Warrior skills for her new role.

Dannet poked at the coils. "I can't fix this, and a qualified engineer won't do any better. There's not much in the system with moving parts. I think it's more of a problem with the magical energy flow."

He lifted one of the weighty coiled roots, and Landra flinched at an aura spike. She traced the power along the tree root, which emerged from a hole in the floorboards. Magic flowed in a pink stream along the coils until a decaying section of fibers blocked its progress. Everything beyond the break was blackened and dull, allowing magic to spill out.

"What will you do?" she asked.

"Don't know. Only a Templer can salvage this. Just as well the problem's confined to the oven." He glanced up to the lights clasped in wooden claws on the ceiling. "If the damage reaches further, all Hux Hall power will fail. It could take out an entire sector.

"Do many systems rely on magic?" she asked.

"Most. Warriors might have ruled here since our exile to this world seventy years ago, but priests still wield some control. Chief Hux can't banish them completely because we need their magic.

It was a sobering thought. Dannet dropped the coil, and Landra jumped back when the impact exploded brighter light into the cabinet. Her aura edges tattered from the surging power breaching her limits. She tugged her brother's arm, because he sat amidst the energy swell, scraping dead growth from the rods as if nothing were wrong.

"We need to get out," she said.

He didn't move.

"Now." She dragged him free. "You need to let Barthle know about his oven."

"If I must," he said.

She didn't envy him the job of delivering bad news to an enraged chef, but the power was still mounting inside the cabinet and they needed distance. With them barely clear, a snap of energy rocked the oven, blowing out a ball of visible light and puffing smoke into the kitchen. Landra staggered sideways, coughing.

"What did you do?" Barthle stormed toward the pair. "You blew up my oven!"

"I didn't. I…" Dannet stumbled away from the blast and spluttered. He shook his head and tapped his ear.

Barthle waved his hands toward his precious oven. "Just look at it."

"I can't think what happened," Dannet said.

Landra knew what had happened. She'd seen the power grow in the broken root until the fibers couldn't hold it any longer, but she couldn't let Barthle know that. The chef picked up a tenderizing mallet and loomed over Dannet, fury in his eyes and temper flashes streaking through his aura. It wasn't fair. Her brother had never claimed to be a qualified engineer, and the accident hadn't been his fault. She stepped in front of Dannet, and Thisk positioned his large frame between Landra and Barthle.

"Stand down," Thisk ordered, more command in his voice than Landra had ever heard from her father. It looked as if the chef would take the Warrior on until a whoosh of the swing door signaled the engineer's arrival.

A small woman marched in, pinched lips in her pixie face and three bars hatched across soldier tracks in her ginger hair. The addition of an "E" identified her as an engineer.

Barthle ground his teeth, but his aura settled from furious lines to angry bubbles. "At last!" He turned on the woman. Three engineer support soldiers, one Templer, and five guards followed her through the swinging doors to gather at her back.

Landra stilled, her gaze settling on the Templer's red robes and the T-specialization insignia cut into his hair. He posed tall and serene, as if unbothered by the heavy soldier guard or the swords they levelled in his direction. Flowers decorated his chest-tall staff, but his aura barely differed from those of the surrounding soldiers, with only thin slivers of pink differentiating his Soul from theirs.

Her breath caught. *Do you see me, Templer? I see you.*

His aura didn't waver under her scrutiny. He opened his robe to reveal practical engineering trousers and boots of deep red. "May the mist protect you," he said, offering his upturned palms in Landra's direction.

She flinched from his spreading aura.

"Nothing to fear, citizen," one of the guards said. "We've got this shelking Templer under tight control. If he so much as twitches, I'll run him through."

"Exactly," Barthle said. "There'll be no mist worshipping in my kitchen. We've no need of homeworld religion here."

A weak smile tugged at Landra's mouth. Seeing the abuse directed at the Templer, it didn't look fun. Who would choose that life?

Thisk pushed her toward the door. "Time to leave." They regrouped in the food hall.

"Well, that was an eventful breakfast," Dannet said, a strained laugh playing like music beneath his words. Despite his nervous outburst, his young face had already relaxed into its natural lines. "I don't know what I did wrong in there."

"You didn't do anything," Landra said, with enough certainty to invite Thisk's regard.

A pair of Hux Hall scribes appeared through the corridor entrance. "Where's the menu?"

"No menu. No food," Thisk said. "Head to ring sixty-four food hall if you want to eat."

One look at Thisk's insignia sent them scurrying away.

"Shall we follow?" Dannet asked. "I'm starving."

"You can do what you want," Thisk told him, but his grip on Landra's jacket suggested she had no such freedom. He tipped his head toward the practical base clock that sat below the world clock. An almost empty light bar showed that first siren was moments away. He marched her to the exit.

"I'll catch up with you later," she called back, twisting her head to grin a goodbye.

Dannet stared after her, bafflement forming lines around his eyes. She knew how strange it must look for the Warrior Fourth to be guarding her every move, but there was no way to explain right now. *Later. I'm going to tell you about my promotion, and everything will make sense.*

Dannet was the one problem she could solve.

Chapter 4

Standing in the armory, Landra felt hungry and weary beyond reason. Worse, she'd not seen Father, so the Collector was still cradled in the sheath on her back. There'd been nowhere to leave it.

She didn't want to face Trainer Winton, but he hovered before her, a sneer twisting his long face. It was the only crooked thing about him. His clipped hair and Fight Trainer insignia were etched with geometric precision, and his loose slate blue outfit fell in even pleats. His aura showed the fewest fluctuations of any she'd seen, like a reflection of his rigid personality.

"Reporting for sword training, sir," Landra said.

"Hmm! Yes."

"Am I late, sir?"

No excuse would be good enough—not her schedule change and certainly not that she was running on a Warrior's timetable. Winton would take that as a fabrication. She stretched her shoulders and fixed her gaze on the mirror. The reflection of vacant training mats, untouched towel stacks, neatly stored weapons, and empty targets let her know there'd be no commotion to hide behind today.

"You're just in time," Winton said, like arriving with no minutes to spare was an offense. He crossed to the door and set the reserved sign in place. That should have meant he had her to himself, but the door opened and Warrior Fourth Thisk strode in.

What d'you want, ranger? To see me beaten in battle? Humiliated?

From the contempt he'd displayed earlier, she couldn't make sense of him wanting to watch her sword work. Winton gawped before gathering himself and finding a slick salute. "Good morning, sir. Are you looking for Chief Hux's command room? It's down the corridor, next door on the left."

Thisk returned the salute with less precision. "No. I've time to spare, and it suits me to watch this session." His bass tone made the words an order rather than a request.

Winton's face flushed, but he recovered quickly. Landra didn't think his ramrod back could stretch taller, but somehow, he found a little more height, as if proud his work could be of interest. She was less pleased. Convincing any soldier of her suitability as chief elect was going to be hard enough. Managing it with a sword in her hand was likely impossible.

"Please take a seat, sir," Winton said.

Thisk ignored the invitation and leaned against the wall beside a knife target. He folded his arms and smiled at the trainer, making the action a command to proceed.

Winton hovered a moment longer before tracking in a circle around Landra's position. She stifled a sigh. *This won't go well.* Her hair was too long, making its gold flecks blend into short streaks, and the single diagonal line of her insignia was indistinct. To round off her shortcomings, swelling distorted the roundness of her face above the cut on her brow and dirt from the oven had tracked onto her jacket. She wasn't certain what Father expected of her as chief elect, but she guessed a reprimand wouldn't be good.

Winton narrowed his gaze. His scrutiny roved over her uniform before settling on her hair. Air whistled through a gap in his teeth. "You're in time for training, Citizen Hux, but maybe you should have taken longer. That hair insignia is a disgrace. When did you last have a trim?"

Landra wondered why she'd doubted the petty man would choose to flaunt his authority in front of the guard. Cadets got away with one day's overgrowth in the academy; Her brother had told her as much. Besides, Thisk looked a mess. *Bet you won't say anything to him.*

"I was due for a barber's visit at second siren, sir, but my schedule was changed at the last moment." *A feeble excuse.*

Winton nodded. "Mine too. Training a citizen this early seems very odd." His gaze flickered to Thisk, but his tone betrayed that he blamed her for the inconvenience. "Why has this happened, citizen?"

"I don't know, sir," she lied.

"Demerit for Citizen Hux," Winton said, chalking a line against her name on a wall board.

Not fair!

"May I ask why, sir?"

"A second demerit for Citizen Hux."

Landra's contrived pose collapsed then snapped back into place.

"The first was for a poor turn-out," Winton said, one of his tidy eyebrows lifting, "and the second's for your insolent tone. Now, unless you want to go for a third, I suggest you show more respect."

A new edge to the trainer's pettiness warned her to silence.

Father's not going to like this. Not one bit.

"That's better." A smug twinkle highlighted his grey eyes. "Now, let's train." He removed his jacket, hung it on a peg, and selected a plain sword from a rack. Returning to the mat, he swung it around his fist in readiness to work.

In that moment, Landra realized the true extent of her folly. All heat left her face. The Collector still rested comfortably on her back, and there was no way to remove her jacket without putting it on display.

If you see the weapon, will you know what it is? She was sure Thisk would recognize the knife, and the consequences didn't bear consideration. Tugging her jacket down at the waist, she crossed to the rack and examined the swords. Her hand trailed over the weapons, pausing above a light-weight weapon with a decorated guard and a pink-tinged blade.

"Not that one, Hux," Winton warned. "Don't you recognize an elite weapon by the color of the blade? Only Warriors are allowed those."

She'd known that, of course, and had only been admiring the weapon.

What would you say about the knife on my back?

The Collector could have been a set with the sword, but this wasn't the time to admit owning an elite Warrior weapon. She ran her hand over the remaining hilts, judging them on function over beauty. Pulling a simple weapon free, she swished the blade in a testing sweep and grimaced as its weight pulled on her injured muscles. Hefting a sword in mock battle was going to hurt, but she joined Winton on the mat and assumed a classic fighting pose. *Maybe inspiration will follow.*

The trainer's eyes widened to show white ringing his

grey pupils, and his gaze slid over Landra's uniform like it was yesterday's slops. His top lip curled into a snarl.

"You've always struggled to meet my standards, Hux, but at least you've shown me some respect. Until now! Tell me, citizen, are you planning on doing me the courtesy of removing your jacket?"

An icy chill raised the hairs on Landra's neck, and she couldn't fathom why keeping the Collector safe on her back had seemed a good idea. Part of her wanted to show the blade to Winton, just to prove her worth. Her sensible side knew it was a horrible idea, so she ignored the trainer and held her pose.

Winton's mouth fell open. "Do you think beating me is so easy?"

"No, sir," Landra said, but the tilt of her head betrayed inner confidence. If she was going to best any experienced soldier, it would be Winton. Submitting made life bearable, but his predictable style made him an easy target, even with a sword.

The trainer readied, his sneer showing an even line of teeth, but his eyes flickered to Thisk.

Want to impress the Warrior, Winton? Well, you're out of luck. I need to prove my worthiness as chief elect, so don't expect me to fold.

"Feet wider, head up." Winton edged sideways.

Landra turned to his movements, checking her style until she was sure it was perfect. Winton struck first, sneaking in low and thrusting his sword beneath her defenses. In Landra's head, the counter move was fluid. In reality, her sore limbs locked, mid-action, giving Winton the advantage. He swung his blade, whipping the sword from her grip. He shouldered her to the ground, adjusted his position, and brought his weapon tip to bear over her face. "Hah!"

Shock snatched Landra's breath as she stared up at the

ceiling's lights. On any other day, he could never catch her with a basic move, and his smug grin was infuriating. She gulped a lungful of air and rolled out from beneath the weapon, but pain tightened her chest.

Focusing on injuries won't help. She blanked the agony from her awareness and dived for Winton's legs. The unorthodox move surprised the trainer, and he toppled into a recovery roll. Before he could stand, Landra lurched forward and stomped on his sword arm, pinning it to the floor until his hand sprang open. As the sword released to the mat, similarities with the previous evening's fight were impossible to miss. But this wasn't Chief Hux, and she wasn't fighting for the Collector.

The trainer's aura paled, signaling her chance for victory. She straddled his body with blood pounding in her ears. A world of consideration passed in that moment. Her father's orders for secrecy were paramount, but an inner urge overrode his directive. *Finish him.* She pulled the Collector from its sheath and pressed it against his neck.

"Hah!" she echoed.

The warm handle enlivened Landra's spirit, and the glinting blade excited her to battle readiness. Her aura deepened and enveloped the blade until their glows pulsed to one rhythm. Winton had goaded her for too long, and she'd now bested him in a fair fight. She searched for respect in his eyes and waited for the euphoria of victory to set in, but his contorted features shocked her to stillness. She held still with the knife pressed to his neck, but as she stared at the carved handle, her mind reeled. The absurdity of using the Collector struck her like a Warrior's blow.

Stupid, stupid, stupid. Why? She couldn't fathom why she'd used the Collector at all, and her grip on the knife relaxed. Winton's aura shrank to the faintest line around his body.

You're afraid. Oh shelk. What did I do?

Her head lightened and she started to release her grip, but a pull on the back of her jacket forced the action.

What?

She looked up, struggling. The Warrior Fourth had her by the jacket collar, and he hauled her up until only her toes touched the floor.

"Allow me to help," he said to Winton.

The trainer waved him away and climbed to his feet. "I don't need any help." He recovered his sword, dug the tip into the mat, and leaned on the hilt for support. "I tempted the girl into that move and was ready to counter. You shouldn't have interfered, Warrior."

The guard smiled. "My name is Warrior Fourth Thisk. I realize that you have matters under control, but it's clear that Citizen Hux poses unique difficulties as a student." He raised a bushy eyebrow and widened his grin until white teeth shone through his coarse beard. Landra squirmed in his grip.

The temper lines smoothed out from Winton's face. After a moment's consideration, he nodded. "She certainly is trouble, but what am I supposed to do? She's the chief's daughter. I can hardly go whining about her performance."

Landra's mouth fell open but the tightening grip on her jacket stemmed her protest.

"I'm glad we agree," Thisk said. "I may be able to help you with this problem. My posting to Hux Hall is for an entire training cycle. It seems sensible for me to take over Citizen Hux's training from here."

Landra stilled and held her breath, barely believing she'd heard right. Warriors never trained soldiers below the Warrior trainee rank.

Winton rubbed his shaved head, his jaw sagging. His

glare drilled Landra, letting her know she would suffer for this embarrassment. "I really don't think she is worth a Warrior's trouble."

Landra wriggled again. "I think—"

"Don't," Thisk said, pulling her higher so her feet dangled. "Thinking doesn't appear to be your strength." He turned to Winton and fixed a wicked glint in his eye. "Some people believe I am capable of making decisions about who is worth my trouble. I know it's an honor to train the chief's daughter—and I must admit you've done a good job—but Citizen Hux is a difficult case. She needs specialist handling from here."

Blood rushed to Landra's cheeks. "I'm dangling from your fist. I can hear you."

"I'll get to you in a moment."

Winton dithered. "But…," he stuttered to silence, and his shoulders bowed in defeat.

"Good. It's decided. I want this armory cleared, so you are dismissed." Landra saw her chance to escape and kicked her legs, trying to stand.

"Not you, Hux." Thisk wrapped her jacket around his fist for a better hold.

Winton hesitated, obviously wanting to argue with the order. He shot a worried glance in Landra's direction, but his scowl showed more concern for his reputation than her safety. "I'll need official reassignment from Chief Hux."

"Of course."

"And…" The trainer fell silent.

"Leave your weapon by the door. I'll replace it before I leave." Winton glared at Landra as if she were to blame for his embarrassment and dismissal. He moved slowly to gather his jacket and then set his sword against the wall. As he opened the door, he speared her with a final accusatory glance full of mean intentions for when their paths crossed again. She groaned at the prospect, but neither soldier noticed. The door thudded shut, and Landra heard her own heavy breathing in the new silence.

"Now," Thisk said. "Explain."

Chapter 5

Landra wriggled, and the Warrior released his grip, allowing her to drop to the floor in an inelegant heap. The surprise impact screamed pain through her sore body, and she squealed with shock. She huddled there for a moment as Thisk bolted the door. He turned back, and she squirmed under his scrutiny. A questioning glance replaced his previous disinterest, but she wasn't ready to give answers. Excuses and arguments raged through her thoughts as she eased to her feet, only to flee when she faced him.

Ranger Warrior Fourth Thisk stood apart from his comrades like a vagrant at a wedding. His boots folded into weathered cracks where smooth polish should gleam, and dust clung onto his uniform. He was a man of action rather than a parade-ready soldier, but his substandard appearance didn't lessen his commanding aura. This was a man to be obeyed.

The looseness of his aura boundaries was something she'd never witnessed before, but she'd never met a ranger. Patrolling the remote lands and acting as Father's eyes in the dangerous terrain required a unique spirit. Wildness didn't lessen a ranger's authority, but it did foster unpredictability, and Thisk's feral temperament glinted behind his dark stare.

"Ranger Warrior Thisk, may I ask why the fourth in line to the chief's position wants to train a young girl?"

Thisk swung his cloak over one shoulder, showing off the Warrior-blue lining. He placed one hand on his short sword and fixed his wild stare on Landra.

"Am I the fourth? That might be my ranking, but without the Hux name, I might as well be hundredth in line."

Landra squeezed the Collector, her heart thumping. *He knows. What now?* His words could only mean that he recognized her knife's meaning and that she'd moved ahead of him in the line of succession. Excuses formed in her head for when she faced Chief Hux. His one instruction had been to keep the promotion a secret.

"What do you want?" she asked.

Thisk leaned on one hip. "Bold! Disrespectful!" He snorted. "I want to know what gives you the right to carry an elite weapon, Hux, and what makes you worthy of being my chief elect."

Nothing. I'm a fraud. Worse, I'm flawed. She swallowed, unable to answer. Taking the Collector from her father didn't seem like enough. "You'll have to ask Chief Hux about that."

"Really?" Thisk said, incredulity making his pose collapse. "So, it's true. A young girl, untried in the championships and with no leadership experience, is to be my chief elect. Tell me, Landra Hux, what makes you special?"

He'd guessed her promotion, but he hadn't believed until she'd confirmed his suspicions. *Why did I speak?* Then she remembered that he'd demanded a response, just as he did now.

"Nothing makes me special," Landra said, fully believing her words.

"Did you steal the Collector?"

"No!"

"And what was that nonsense with your trainer?"

Thisk looked ready to fight, but Landra didn't relish the prospect of battling a deposed Warrior with no blood-bond, so she replaced the knife in her sheath. "I made a mistake. I don't know what came over me."

Thisk snorted again. "Maybe it was the Souls of your ancestors."

"I…" Landra hadn't any idea how to respond. Surely, the Warrior Fourth couldn't believe old-world Soul magic still thrived. He'd already teased out one secret too many. *This feels like a trap.* His aura showed none of the lighter blue shades that accompanied her own flaw, so he was Warrior to the core. Either he was calling her out, or he'd listened to too many guard-room stories.

"Sounds like magic nonsense to me. I make my own decisions, stupid as they may be. I'm probably just tired and hungry."

"Probably." He scratched his ragged beard.

Divert him. Confuse him.

"Does Chief Hux know you favor magic?"

"Woah!" Thisk said. "Don't exile me yet. I've no more Soul magic than the next soldier. That doesn't mean I deny its presence on base."

"Really?" *Father, have you sent this man to test me?*

"I'd rather just train as a Warrior." It felt like the truest statement she'd said all morning.

A smile quirked the Warrior Fourth's mouth. "As would we all." He unclipped his cloak and hung it on a peg. The flowing material carried as many award ribbons as her father's cloak did, but its shorter length made them pack tighter together. He drew the short, fat sword from his chest sheath and took up position in front of Landra.

"We're going to fight now. Remove your jacket and offer me the respect you should have given Winton."

Train… or fight? There was no way out of this, so she unbuckled her jacket and draped it over a bench. The Warrior stepped close enough for his smell to fill her senses —worn leather mixed with... *What is that? Not the laundered scent of ranking soldiers who visit Hux Hall.*

Thisk poked his tongue out, as if tasting something sour, and then teased her collar aside with his sword tip. "Bruises? Illegal fighting?"

"No!" Landra said, tilting her chin up, but she recognized her lie at once. There was nothing legal about her encounter with Chief Hux. She caught a breath, deciding some events needed forgetting. "Not really."

"Good, because I'd hate think my future leader is stupid." A rumble came from his throat. "We're an army with no war to fight, Hux. We won't survive by turning on ourselves. A future leader should remember that."

Landra couldn't blame the Warrior for his outraged expression, but she saw no way to gain his respect.

He rolled his sword over then clasped it in preparation. "Now! Shall I kill you and finish this nonsense?"

Ah. It hadn't occurred to Landra that Thisk might want the chief's position enough to kill. He even had the power to make it look like an accident. She thought she should react, but her calm demeanor held. The fluid edges and gently swirling shades of Thisk's aura were the signs of a man at peace rather than one about to commit treason and murder.

"You disagree with my appointment as chief elect, then?" She kept all emotion from her face.

Thisk held still, his dark eyes gleaming with amusement. "Of course. There's no way you deserve the honor." He stood up and relaxed the sword to his waist. "But that's irrelevant. I'm a Warrior in the Jethran army and loyal to Chief Hux. It's clear now why I was put here. I have no interest in protecting a young girl. My chief elect, however, that's a different matter. And maybe, one day, you will deserve the title. Did Chief Hux give you a date for the announcement?"

Hope bubbled up in Landra. He actually considered her future worthiness a possibility. This wasn't Father who desired a Hux succession or her brother who thought everything she did was both hopeless and wonderful at the same time. There seemed like no point in hiding the details now that he knew so much.

"Just before the championships. I have a sixty day training cycle to prepare."

"Good, that gives us time to get you ready to compete."

"I… My scores are nowhere near the qualifying level, sir, and I'm too young to enter."

"Irrelevant," Thisk said. "The chief elect gains automatic entry, regardless of age. If the announcement comes before competition starts, you'll be expected to participate. Everyone will want to see what you're made of."

Terror, excitement, and disappointment warred within Landra. She'd longed to enter the annual competition since watching her father take the title more than ten years ago. Yet, she had expected her inclusion to be a final prize for years of effort. Having the opportunity given to her because of a title, rather than merit, felt dishonest. Her reaction went unrecognized by Thisk. He adopted a formal pose with his sword across his chest.

"Landra Hux." He met her gaze, looking every bit a commanding officer.

Her stomach fluttered. *What are you doing, Thisk? You look like a date proposing marriage.*

He tipped his head in a small bow. "I, Dolan Thisk, Ranger Warrior Fourth of the Jethran Army, pledge my duty of protection to you, Chief Elect Landra Loni Hux, and I will train you to lead."

Holy mist. That's not a statement. It's an oath.

She wavered, not knowing how to take this change in fortune. He made the chief elect role sound more important than training as a Warrior. She supposed it was, and if the Warrior Fourth was prepared to follow Chief Hux's orders in this matter, what place did she have in doubting the decision?

He raised his sword again. "Train."

Landra picked her sword up, rolled it over in her hand, and brought it back to readiness. The moment outmatched any dream she'd had of becoming a Warrior, and the impending fight felt more real than any training session she'd had with Winton. Her heart pounded, and the thrill of battle thrummed through her body, agitating the patterns in her aura.

Thisk groaned. "You can ditch championship posturing. I'm not judging you on juggling a weapon or the smoothness of your roll. I'm teaching you to survive."

She firmed her grip on the sword just before Thisk made his first move. His blade swung quicker and with more force than Winton had ever managed. She tried dodging, but her muscles cramped again and her body screamed with pain. She'd barely moved when Thisk's flat-sided blow smacked into her side. The impact collapsed her to floor, and she crunched around her belly. *More bruises. Ow!*

Peering down, the Warrior spiked his sword tip into the mat next to her head. "Hmph!"

She stared up at her new tutor, unable to speak. After a long consideration, he replaced his sword in its chest sheath.

"I've never trained a soldier before, and it's clear I have lessons to learn. You're no use to me like this. Eat, see a medic, and meet me back in the library at second siren. I'll be taking all your lessons from now on, and it's time for a history lesson."

Landra's eagerness ebbed at the prospect of academic study. She'd read every book in the Hux Hall library, twice, and her current assignment was a repeat of previous work. "Shall I bring the books I've been working on?"

"Gods of the mist, no. Our history lives, Chief Elect, and it's about time you learned that. You're going to need warm clothes."

Without explanation, he left her on the training mat, writhing in agony and staring after his departing form.

Warm clothes? What the shelk?

Chapter 6

"Good day, Citizen Hux." Cadet Baylem greeted Landra outside the armory. "I'm to accompany you until second siren."

"Baylem?"

Baylem held her pose a moment then eased the tension from her shoulders. Her smile puckered dimples into her rounded cheeks, and her light aura brightened. "Sorry, Lan. Warrior Fourth issued the order, so I took this as official soldier business."

"Don't," Landra said. "The Fourth is just... Well, I don't know what he is, but be yourself. I've had enough disruption today without my friends going strange."

"Glad you said that. Everything's topsy-turvy. Half the guard is missing, and Barthle's stomping around his kitchen clattering pots loud enough to hear back on Jethra. Don't go near the food hall if you value your life."

"Too late. I tried for an early breakfast."

"And you're still alive? Wow! Huxes are tough. Did you work out what got him riled?"

"A fault in the magic power supply."

"Yuck! Nasty stuff, that magic. Don't tell anyone I'm saying this. Official line is that Templers and Warriors work together, right? But I wouldn't put it past priests to interrupt the supply out of spite. If you ask me, the Warrior Council should rip out the system and start again. There'd be no need to keep the temples open, and we could exile all the priests. Wouldn't that be sweet revenge for when they kicked us off the homeworld?"

Landra couldn't disagree, despite the creeping fear that it could signal her own end. She considered sharing news of the assassination attempt but flattened her lips into a thin line. If the incident wasn't public knowledge now, sharing it with Baylem would make certain of it being city-wide gossip by evening.

"What's our schedule?" Baylem asked, clapping her hands together. "We could try the food hall again. I hear Dannet went back there with Bexter." A mischievous twinkle glinted in her bright eyes.

"Too much to do." Landra buried her disappointment and set off down the corridor. "It's a trip to Leo's and the showers for me." The movement spasmed pain through her chest and stole her breath. "Besides"—she stopped to lean on the wall—"no one should see me in this condition."

Baylem hung close, nodding at passing soldiers to stem their attention. "Tough training," she said to a willowy scribe who paid too much notice.

"Thanks," Landra said after the scribe moved along.

"I can see you're battered and there's a story there, but I won't ask what happened and Bexter won't care."

"What do you mean?"

"Surely you've noticed how he is when you're around. His back stiffens like a sword's rammed beneath his jacket."

"Don't be stupid. He barely notices me."

"Oh, he notices, Lan, but he wouldn't dare make a move. I mean, you're the chief's daughter, and he doesn't want to end up on charges or ruin his career."

"Why does my father make a difference?"

"He just does. I'm exactly the same around Dannet. I want to talk to your brother but just..." Baylem wriggled her body and sighed.

"Dannet?"

"Of course, Dannet. He's become quite a soldier since going to the academy. Basic training's broadened his shoulders in a very attractive way." She opened her hands wider than Dannet's shoulders had ever measured and grinned. A plea shone from her eyes.

"Stop!" She couldn't think of anyone considering her brother in that way. For her own part, she liked Bexter, but if the cadet found her unapproachable now, how would he feel when she was chief elect? That was another problem for later. She continued her pained stride toward the barber shop, and Baylem fell in line beside her without question.

The *tic, tic* sound of Leo's clippers met them before they reached the open front of the barber shop. As they turned in, the sight of Bexter sitting in the barber's chair made Landra trip over nothing and stumble into the room. Leo's clippers paused, Bexter squinted up at her with as much surprise as she felt, and a waiting Warrior shot her a glance. She elbowed Baylem to hush the girl's nervous giggle.

"Sorry," Landra said, trying to avoid glimpsing her reflection in the wall mirror.

Too late.

She saw her ragged hair, red cheeks, and a sweat-patched training tunic. It was hardly an appropriate look for chief elect duties—or impressing a handsome cadet.

"Take a seat," Leo said. "I shouldn't be long."

If she hadn't needed to smarten up, Landra would have made an excuse to leave. "Thank you." She squirmed into the closest chair.

Staring at Bexter was unavoidable; his broad features and broader chest drew her gaze. His dark hair and green eyes were attractive by Jethran standards, but it was the purity of his aura she found most alluring. The deep blue shades formed an even edge around his form and pulsed to a deeper color in time with a steady heartbeat. Landra experienced most aura limits as a barrier, but Bexter's hues invited her into his space.

"This worked out well," Baylem whispered.

"Shush!" Landra looked away from Bexter and stared through Leo's lighter aura to the wall beyond. The barber's shades jumped and twitched in time with his clippers as he danced around the cadet. He trimmed the hair short then swapped his clippers for an insignia marker to etch a ranking design.

A nod from him made Landra realize she'd been staring. Thankfully, Bexter had his head tipped sideways, so he hadn't noticed her scrutiny. After returning Leo's nod, she focused on an instructional wall poster from Chief Barber Vernon.

The clippers silenced, and Bexter removed his protective cape. He stood up and brushed a few rogue hairs from his jacket before coming to attention.

"Two-bar cadet." Leo picked up a badge with diagonal lines for rank and two more hatched lines for second-year status. It matched Bexter's hair design perfectly.

Landra stared at the floor, thinking to give Bexter a

chance to leave without further embarrassment. Polished boot caps came into view, and warmth from the cadet's aura enveloped her body. She looked up. Had he ever stood this close before?

"Citizen Hux, Cadet Baylem," Bexter said.

It sounded official. She gathered herself and did a quick assessment of her condition. A definite whiff of sweat rose from her uniform, and she felt as if every bruise and ache showed. Conscious of his flawless grooming, she surged to her feet and tugged her jacket straight. Baylem came up at her side, barely able to contain her excitement. For all the girl's three extra years on Landra, her immaturity often showed through.

Poise, Baylem. Please don't embarrass me.

"Good morning, cadet," Baylem said.

"Will you join the group training at third siren, Landra?" Bexter asked.

It was an invitation, but she wasn't sure of its meaning. Was he offering general courtesy, as all soldiers who resided in Hux Hall were automatically invited? Or was he looking for an excuse to talk? Baylem had hinted at his interest, but the transition from childhood friends to something more felt impossible. Not that he'd been her friend. He'd practically grown up with Dannet and much of the boys' childhoods had involved finding ways to escape her company.

"I've been given a heavy schedule for today, but I always try to attend the session."

Does that sound like an acceptance, a refusal, or like I'm brushing him off? Shelk, I don't know.

Bexter's spine straightened, and Landra realized he was nervous.

"I'll be there," she blurted, determined to find a way to make her schedule fit around the training. The cadet rewarded her with a careful smile that could have mistaken for politeness, but a deepening richness in his aura left her in no doubt of the invitation's nature. His aura grew, spreading toward her in a clear indication of interest, and her own blue shades quivered in response. Excitement rattled through her as she started planning how to make herself presentable.

"I'll see you later," Bexter said, his green-eyed gaze lingering on her face a moment longer than casual politeness dictated, and then he was gone.

Landra's thoughts raced. She shared a grin with Baylem, but inside, she was dying. The relationship needed to develop before her chief elect announcement or she might seem unobtainable. *Easy, right?* Sixty days should be enough time.

Chapter 7

Landra returned to her room before second siren. She showered, changed, and was in possession of a numbing salve from Medic Gren. The salve came with a bed rest instruction. Part of her knew the doctor's order overrode all commands, but bailing on the Fourth didn't feel like an option. Still, how hard could a history lesson be?

Thisk arrived early and dismissed Baylem from the door.

"Weren't we supposed to meet in the library?" Landra asked.

The Warrior waved her question aside. "Is that what you're wearing?"

Landra compared her citizen-blue jacket with the Warrior's mottled brown and green outfit, realizing her miscalculation. He'd cleaned up and trimmed his beard, but woolly linings bulged above the tops of his boots, a fur hood topped off his double-layered cloak, and the fingers of his padded gloves dangled like a bunch of Barthle's hung sausages. If his aura had been even, it would have barely shown beyond the thick garments, but his blue, irregular outline protruded beyond his bulky clothes in several places. His hands glowed with a shimmering azure, as if the gloves couldn't contain his essence.

She tried not to stare. "Where are we going?"

"Above."

Landra nearly couldn't find her voice. "Above? I—"

"I'm guessing you've never been."

"I've barely been out of the Hux Hall apartment. There's rarely a need."

"You're in for an experience then."

Her mouth fell open. She hadn't ever thought to visit the overlevel. Most soldiers never went outside. This wasn't a safe history lesson tucked away in the library, and it was as far away from bed rest as possible. "Isn't it dangerous?" she asked. "I heard a guard was mauled by an animal, and two maintenance soldiers died in a lightning strike last cycle."

"Is that the gossip? The overlevel's fine at this time of the year if you know what you're doing. You scared?"

He was the second ranking Warrior to question her courage in two days, and she examined her feelings for hints of cowardice. Her hands were dry and steady, but her heart set a charging pace in her chest.

Is that fear? No, it's excitement.

A trip to the overlevel offered more chance to step up to her chief elect duties than any amount of hours in the library. A smile spread across her face.

"I'm not afraid, but Father will be annoyed with me if I die."

A glint of amusement creased the dark skin above Thisk's beard. "I believe his anger will come my way, so let's make sure you stay alive."

"What about my history lesson?"

"I told you, citizen, history lives in our world if you

know where to look. I'm searching it out and taking you with me. Or you can sit at a table in a wooden box, surrounded by books."

His aura animated in time with his words, as if roused to action, and he swept from the room without checking to see whether she followed. Landra stared after him, a host of questions racing through her mind.

Are you giving me a choice? Will my clothes be warm enough? Am I supposed to bring the Collector?

The thud of his boot heels faded, and she came to the shocked realization that he wouldn't wait or come back, so she stuffed the medic's ointment in a pocket and dashed out to the double stroke of second siren.

She careened along the accommodation corridor, rounded the corner at speed, and bumped into a Tally Hall soldier who stood beyond the bend. The willowy man's tally slates cracked to the floor, and an annoyed flash emblazoned his aura.

"Sorry, sir." Landra bent to gather the pieces. She thrust the fragments into the soldier's hands, gave a fast salute, and then darted away before he could demand an explanation.

"Demerit, Citizen Hux," a scratchy voice yelled from behind.

Why does everyone know my name? Shelk.

Her undignified flight attracted more stares. She spotted the Warrior's dark curls disappearing through the main exit, and approached the checkpoint as if on a battle-field charge.

"Accompanying Warrior Fourth Thisk," she barked at the guard.

She recognized the two-bar soldier from his relaxed frame and passive features, but his flickering aura glowed with rampant curiosity.

"Departure of Citizen Landra Hux," he shouted as he unbarred the door.

"Shush, Hesson! I don't want everyone knowing my business."

She charged through the exit wanting to explain, but there was no time. Her dramatic departure would make the evening's gossip over a jug of scute, but there wasn't anything she could do about that, so the worry faded from her thoughts.

She emerged into the clamor of base activity and spotted Thisk's bulky frame in the narrow corridor. He plunged into the throng of soldiers on the main thorough-fare without a backward glance, so she scrambled after him like a flustered attendant. Shift change had brought an unusual number of soldiers into the ring sixty-two corridor, and melded blue auras reached from floor to ceiling. After a steadying breath, she slipped into the stream of marching soldiers and looked for her tutor.

Where are you, Thisk?

Bobbing, dark curls amongst the mass of shaven heads helped her locate the Warrior. His mottled cloak clashed with the throng of blue uniforms, helping her to track his route. She tried catching up, but his stiff march was hard to match. Soldiers moved aside to create a gap for his passage, only to close ranks behind him and block her way. One offered Thisk a passing salute, and he gave an official nod of recognition without pausing.

Landra zigzagged through disgruntled soldiers wondering if this was what Father had intended. He usually forbade her from roaming the city unsupervised, so she wasn't certain whether to feel adrift or liberated. The Warrior's dark silhouette against the main concourse glow made her slow. She caught up to find him leaning against a wall. He cocked his head toward a door outline in the wooden grain, scowling as if she'd lost a championship race.

"We're going through here," he said.

The camouflaged door matched one she passed every day in Hux Hall. Her home's unused entrance barely warranted recognition anymore, but this door grabbed all of her attention.

Outside. It really goes outside.

Thisk pressed a gloved hand to a subtle mark on the wall, and a panel swung away. Landra sucked in a breath as a leak of cold air nipped at her cheeks and inky darkness chilled her Soul. The Warrior crossed the threshold with calm indifference, and blackness swallowed him. Heart thumping with determination, she gave herself up to the gloom. Coldness enveloped her form, immediately penetrating her jacket to raise the hairs on her arms.

Why didn't I ask you more about this history lesson? Why didn't you tell me more?

Her uniform could have coped with dips in the library heating system, but it couldn't hold back this chill. Folding her arms across her chest for warmth, she waited for her eyes to adjust to the dimness. Small dots of emergency light knots came into focus, and Thisk's aura shifted about the small space like he were an underlevel ghost.

"Best move before you freeze," he said. "You'll find extra clothes at the back of the shaft."

Landra checked her bearings. A tree trunk grew through the shaft's center, and her gaze slid down the wrinkled bark to where it disappeared through the floor. Her shuffling feet moved dried leaves from the base, and she saw cracked bulges in the flooring planks where the trunk's girth exceeded its allotted hole.

Old. She placed a hand on the bark. *Is this your history, Thisk?*

"Get a move on," the Warrior said.

She shuffled around the trunk until the rear wall came into view. A ladder stretched from floor to ceiling, nestled between a rack of weapons and shelves of folded clothes.

Overlevel's up there," Thisk said. "It's exposed to the world, so it's colder than the devil's mist. We all live inside the midlevel, like a soldier sandwich, and the underlevel's below." He stamped his boot heel on the floor next to the ladder.

Landra didn't have time for this. She'd learned city construction with Trainer Grimwas, and her uncontrollable shivering was more urgent. She went straight to the clothing stacks and yanked a jacket free. In one fluid movement, she donned the baggy garment over her uniform and sighed as mist-blessed warmth silenced her clacking teeth. Tension eased from her body and she rolled her shoulders, stretching against pain the cold had awakened.

Thisk lurked a few strides away, his dark eyes lost in the murky light, but the weight of his judgment settled on her like he was a council judge.

"Why leave these clothes here?" she asked.

"If you'd spent more time in the junior barracks, you'd know."

Another dig.

"I'm not responsible for my upbringing. "My mother died when I was four. I'm sure Chief Hux did what he thought was best."

"I'm not criticizing the chief." Thisk rammed a hat on her head and let the flaps fall over her neck and ears. "I'm stating a fact. These shafts are evacuation routes, so most soldiers practice escape drills through here. The supplies are lifesavers for anyone heading out in a hurry."

"Oh, I didn't know."

"No reason you should. You have guards assigned to

escort you out if there's trouble, and they do enough drills for everyone."

She mulled over that concept, never having realized how her existence differed from that of other soldiers. Thisk made Winton's tough training sound like pampering. She yanked down a heavy blue cloak with a fleecy lining, wondering if the Warrior would object to its dark blue hue. He ignored her to sort through a bulging rack of weapons, so she swung it around her shoulders, feeling its heavy weight settle on her back and its hem swish against her calves.

"Couldn't we have left through the Hux Hall shaft?" she asked, poking her hands through convenient holes to fasten the cloak buckles.

Thisk sighed. "Do you always ask this many questions?"

"I… you're my tutor now. I thought—"

"Fine! Hux Hall's shaft serves fewer soldiers, so it's not as well stocked. And the sentry is impossible to stand down. Those guards are drilled to stay at post come fire or flood. I figured you didn't want everyone knowing your business, and the lad on this exit was happy to take a break."

Landra suspected a quiet exit through the Hux Hall door would have raised less commotion than her chase down its corridors, but it wasn't her place to comment. She stomped her feet into warmer boots without a word. Thisk settled a bow and quiver on his back and swung a bulging sack over one shoulder.

"Wh—" She stemmed the question and craned her neck as the Warrior climbed the ladder. At the top, he levered a locking plank aside and thumped on the trap door. The dust of years drifted down, but the panel didn't budge until a second strike jumped it outward. He heaved it over, and icy wind raced in circles around the shaft, whipping the leaves into a frenzy.

Landra raised an arm to shield against the invading brilliance from above and squinted at the Warrior's disappearing form. He temporarily blotted the light. Then he was gone.

Not again. You didn't say to follow, but maybe that was implied.

Stuffing an extra knife into her cloak, she prepared to abandon her city. She climbed toward the brightness, barely understanding why anticipation quickened her breathing and overrode her fear.

A bright, crisp day welcomed her at the top. She planted her feet on the wooden roof, covered her eyes from the sun she'd only seen in drawings, and sucked in a lungful of fresh air. A familiar odor rode on the current, and she tried to identify its source. Thisk came to her side and recognition dawned. The same scent permeated his clothes, and she knew this was his world. He smelled of the outdoors.

He flipped the trap door, and it thudded closed with a jostle of leaves. "The guard will lock that from inside."

"Lock it? How will we get back to Hux Hall?"

"We won't. Not today."

"What? This wasn't part of the deal." She knew she shouldn't shout at the Warrior Fourth, but containing her alarm proved impossible. This place was worth a visit, but staying for any length of time felt like an invitation to death. "I have to go. Chief Hux wants to meet me and… I've got jobs to do."

Thisk ignored her disrespect in a way Winton would have never managed. "There is no deal. We're not bargaining, and your jobs can wait. Besides, Griffin left the city."

Landra's jobs couldn't wait. Explaining her promotion

to Dannet might save for tomorrow, but Medic Gren wouldn't accept her absence. Missing training with Bexter seemed unimportant by comparison, but her chest hurt with disappointment.

"I'm only a citizen, so it's not up to me to miss the meeting, even if Chief Hux isn't around. I have to obey rules."

"Really?" Thisk snorted. "I look forward to watching you follow rules. Are you going to do that now?"

Her mouth gaped at his smirk, and his grin stretched wider.

Insufferable man.

"Look at me, Hux. I'm a ranger Warrior operating outside of the city, where Jethran standards are of limited use. If the chief wanted you to follow rules, do you think he would have put me outside your door?" He spun about and marched toward the tree before Landra's shock had time to register on her face.

Not obey rules—ridiculous!

She stared at the back of his mottled cloak, trying to comprehend his meaning. Surely, this couldn't be the man Father had entrusted with her care and training. She stormed after him to where the tree trunk rose out of the city roof.

"What does Chief Hux expect me to learn out here?"

Thisk scratched his beard. "Not sure. He doesn't know we came."

"What?"

The trap's locking bar slid into position from below. She twisted her cloak tight around her shoulders, trying to calm her anxious breaths and form her next question.

"What do you think I'm going to learn from freezing my butt off up here?"

Thisk only shrugged.

You don't know. Shelk! How could this happen? Father, what did you do to me?

"You're supposed to have the answers. You're my tutor."

"I told you. I've not trained anyone before."

Landra's mouth opened, but the Warrior's raised hand silenced her protest.

"Look, Hux, reading from books isn't worth our time, but I can show you the world you're destined to command. Isn't that worth something?"

From outside its walls?

She refused to take the blame for missing her meeting with Father. Thisk's reckless behavior would go in her report, and the Warrior could bear that punishment. Gren was a different matter. Defying the doctor would pull a demerit for sure.

Her head throbbed, her gut ached, and her body locked with stiffness, but she had learned one lesson already. She would never underestimate the recklessness of Warrior Fourth Thisk or the dangers of a history lesson.

Her gaze turned out to the world that she saw for the first time. Right now, she would willingly swap the vast, inhospitable expanse for a training session with Winton—and she wouldn't even complain.

Chapter 8

"Eyes here." Thisk pointed to two target-sized plaques pinned to a tree trunk.

Landra reset her expectations to cope with the turn of events and honed her gaze on the Warrior's finger.

"This top diagram shows the four outlying cities, plus Central City here." He pointed toward the map's center.

She'd never seen map view, so maintaining a show of indifference was tough. "Aren't there six cities?"

"New City was built after the maps were drawn, but it's way out between First and Third," he said, waving across the overlevel toward the distant forest.

She peered over the rooftop's curved fences and dotted trees, trying to pick out a city skyline in the expanse beyond. A green forest stretched toward distant foothills, and mountains rose on the horizon, their uppermost caps swathed in fog and snow. There was no sign of civilization.

Rumors suggest her mother had been lost in that wilderness. Her secret hope of a reunion died. Even if the woman had survived, finding her in that vastness would be impossible.

"Citizen!" Thisk snapped. "Pay attention."

"I am."

He raised an eyebrow. "This detailed map below shows Central City's midlevel."

This could be interesting. She examined the circular diagram and recognized several reference points. Hux Hall, the main concourse, and Cadet Hall were listed by name.

"We're here." He indicated to a sword emblem, which marked their position in relation to the geography below. "If we're parted, head for the nearest tree. Not the tall firs beyond the city limits, but these leafy trees with silver trunks rising through the roof. They all have shafts."

Landra only heard one word. "Parted?"

"It's a precaution. I'm not leaving you."

"Good to know." An anxious knot squeezed her stomach. Thisk had already marched off twice and she had to believe he might do it again, but this training was Father's will at work, so she had to deal with her situation.

"If you knock and identify yourself, a sentry will let you in," Thisk said. "But avoid that if you can. Turning up alone will cause a scene and make a stack of paperwork. Now, let's move out."

The Warrior set off along a fence line and Landra followed. He couldn't have taken more than a hundred strides before he threw his bag to the ground. "Here."

"Here? What's here?"

"The place we test you," Thisk said.

He dropped his bow and quiver, and he swung off his cloak. The fabric snapped in the wind, so he secured it behind a fence. Drawing his sword, he stabbed the blade tip into the ground. The planks underfoot resembled indoor flooring, but this wood looked toughened. It refused the blade's bite.

"Prepare," he ordered.

Landra stared at him, barely able to see his eyes between the fullness of his beard and the brim of his hat. "You want me to fight?" She swayed in the wind.

"Not fight, Hux. I might bend rules, but there's been enough law breaking for one cycle. We're going to train."

Her gaze roved over the barren expanse, windblown leaves, and Thisk's menacing form. "Here?"

"It's the perfect place to hone your skills. If our army engages in war, you'd better hope it's outside; otherwise, we're fighting amongst ourselves or enemies have breached the city. What better place to test out a new leader?"

He raised his sword in readiness. Once set, the gale didn't budge his solid frame. The loose sleeves of his thick shirt slapped against his skin and wild wisps of hair fought free of his hat.

Landra took a deep breath. She relished training, but this was the second peculiar battle she'd faced in as many days. As she unbuckled her cloak, the flaps flew backward over her shoulders, allowing the cold to penetrate her jacket. Shudders ran through her body to awaken her aches, but she faced the Warrior.

Would it hurt to challenge me when I'm prepared?

Thisk planted his feet and held his sword, sun rays bouncing off his pink-tinged blade. Landra sighed with relief that she'd not brought a long weapon. Her damaged muscles weren't ready to support a heavy blade. She discarded her gloves, despite her stinging fingertips, and reached back for the Collector. Its handle bit like ice against her tender skin.

Avoiding this seemed impossible. She took up her own guarding pose and waited for Thisk to make a move.

The Warrior stared at the Collector and bellowed out a rich laugh.

Insulting. She throttled her knife handle and ground her teeth. Winton had never laughed at her efforts. How embarrassing!

"You're not much of a thinker, but you've got guts. I'll give you that," Thisk said.

She bristled with affront but held her position. *Stupid Warrior. I might not be able to outmuscle you, but I bet I can I outthink you.*

She held still, refusing to make the first move. Thisk wheeled the sword in his gloved hand before dropping the blade to his side.

What now? She relaxed.

"No, hold your position." He pushed her knife arm back up.

She snapped into the pose, and he left her there.

Bruised and cold, the stance required more concentration, physical control, and mental strength than she possessed. She held the knife outstretched until her muscles twitched.

Thisk circled her, examining every nuance of her stance. He nudged the blade a little higher. "Here," he said. "This is the first position of the hethra, one of our oldest fighting styles. It's taught in Warrior Hall and should never be sloppy."

Burning pain shot up Landra's back and into her arms. "I can't hold it!" Shaking overtook her, and the knife slipped from her grip. Thisk caught it by the handle before it touched the ground.

Impressive.

"It takes years of training to enter Warrior Hall and even more to perform elite moves," she said. "Surely, the hethra disciplines are meant for seasoned Warriors."

"If you carry an elite weapon, mastery of elite techniques is essential. I'm not asking you to perform complex fighting moves, Hux. Just the first knife position."

He hoisted his own blade into horizontal stillness above his head and set his body into a perfect stance. "Do you think the hethra is about muscle mass?"

"Of course."

"Hardly."

"That's easy for you to say. Your arms are wider than my legs."

"Every soldier reaches a limit, Hux. The art of the hethra is to keep the body working longer than the brain believes it's possible. A soldier's darkest moments can offer the greatest opportunity against a weak-minded opponent. Accept the pain and focus. I won't teach you advanced fighting techniques until you have some understanding of this skill." He closed his eyes and relaxed his body. His aura roamed wide, but its shade settled into a blue pool of calmness.

Landra raised the Collector again to match his stance. "Can this help me qualify for the championships by right?"

"Some things can't be rushed. Most third-year cadets struggle to make the grade, and you're a citizen rank. Why the hurry?"

The answer came as easy as her next breath. "I watched Father battle to victory when I was five. I've wanted to be like him ever since. Is that an exiling offense?"

"If it is, we'll both be training in the remote lands tomorrow. You have the heart of a fighter, but you're pushing too hard in the wrong direction. Save your energy for battles you need to win."

"This is important. How much respect will direct entry bring me?"

"Your chief elect rank will bring respect."

Landra wasn't sure that was true. "Won't I be a target for any soldier wanting to prove a point?"

"You're a target anyway. Plenty of soldiers carry grudges against the Hux family. Oppressed priests would destroy you in a breath, and soldier factions believe the chief pays Templers too much consideration. Then there are Warriors who will see you as an obstacle to the chief's position. Your life may be short once the promotion's announced."

Might as well paint a target on my back. Landra's stance tensed, and her focus broke. Her arm dropped again, and she groaned. The Warrior's mature frame showed the usual wear associated with fighters in their fifth decade, but if he chose to attack for real, she had no adequate defense. "Are you a risk to me?"

Thisk opened his eyes and met her gaze. "Everyone is a threat. Never think otherwise." He nudged her arm up but dropped his own sword to his side. "Now, let's do this. If you want my respect, learn the hethra."

"It sounds like Jethra."

"Of course. It's a homeworld skill."

He elevated her arm above her head into an even more uncomfortable position. The blade wasn't heavy, but she was weak enough to feel the strain. Clammy heat suffused her body, and a whiff of sweat rose from her uniform.

The Warrior watched the blade tip, as if waiting for failure. She tried to keep it steady, but pain rocked her body and squeaking noises escaped her throat.

Embarrassing. Don't fold.

"More angle at the knees." Thisk clipped the back of her legs with his sword hilt.

A grimace twisted her young features, and beads of moisture broke on her cheeks. It was like he was forcing her to fail, but she sank lower and braced again.

"That's better. Hold it there."

The blade's tip wavered.

Thisk stepped close enough for his breath to brush her cheek. "You've weakened quickly, but this is the point where the hethra comes into its own. Now, visualize walking through the midlevel and tell me what you see."

She wanted to shout at the Warrior, but she wanted to impress him more. "I…"

"Just do it."

An image of a Central City concourse formed in her thoughts. "I'm looking down a main causeway, watching a unit heading toward the next city."

"Good."

Landra settled into her daydream, enjoying the notion of joining the departing soldiers. She submitted to the vision completely, ignoring the obvious expansion of her aura. "The transport station is dark. There's never enough power to run the pod. It will be a long march for the soldiers through the tunnel beneath the tracks."

"Can you smell anything?"

"Sweat," Landra answered. She wrinkled her nose, realizing the odor came from her own reality rather than her visualization. The slip allowed pain to intrude. "No, that's not the smell," she added quickly, latching onto elements of her vision again. "The walls stink of varnish. I think they've had recent work."

"You're doing well. Now, look back."

Landra turned.

Thisk forced her straight with a firm rap on the cheek. "In your mind."

The contact reawakened her attention, but she focused on the exercise, obscuring her pain. "That's toward the City Center and Warrior Hall." She pictured the tight-curving corridors of ring ten. "I want to travel the cities before I go there, maybe even to the farthest edge of New City." She buried the thought, recognizing it as yesterday's desire. Wandering the cities had no place in the life of a chief elect.

"Who else is around?"

"Only strangers." It wasn't quite true. She suspected the characters were drawn from memory. "There's a work detail waiting for entrance to the overlevel."

"How do you know where they're going?"

Landra's eyes wrinkled. "They're wearing weather protection uniforms and maintenance kits. Maybe the power's out. One's wearing a Templer robe, so there could be a problem with the magical power supply." She tilted her head to a sudden noise.

"Do you hear something?" Thisk asked.

"Music." She rolled her neck and hummed to the tune, discovering that joining the melody eased her pain. The song filled her awareness, bringing more serenity than she'd known for a while and clarifying her vision.

"Hux. Hux!"

Thisk jabbed his sword hilt beneath her ribs, forcing a gasp to rise from her belly. It exploded in a puff of white vapor before her eyes. She creased forward. The Warrior stood before her, surface blood reddening his cheeks above his beard.

"What was that for?" A burst of agony erupted into her consciousness and stole her breath. "Agh!" In her dream, she'd been enjoying a bubble of stillness. Now, she recognized the bite of the wind and the burn of her limbs. Her stomach heaved, but she swallowed back vomit, refusing to humiliate herself in front the Warrior.

"Humming is against regulations," Thisk said. "Pull back and find your image again."

"That's all I did wrong? Father expects me to break

rules, but you hit me for humming?" She yanked the shirt away from her sodden body.

"I never said you won't be disciplined. Now, resume."

She glared at Thisk but set back into position, less inclined to please him but more determined to show her strength. It was excruciating, so she sank deeper into her imagination. Dannet and Bexter were wrestling in the armory, and Winton watched. The trainer's narrow face displayed stiff rebuke.

"That's good," Thisk said. "Now, let the magic take you."

Chapter 9

The Collector slipped from Landra's grasp, and she danced back from the falling blade. "Magic?"

Agony pressed her to her knees, but it couldn't overshadow her outrage. She'd worked hard to hide her aura sight, and now Thisk had forced her to indulge the magic. It took three painful breaths before she could repeat her accusation. "You were teaching me magic?"

"No! I was teaching you the hethra."

"But it's magic?"

Thisk clenched a fist around his sword hilt. "Not exactly."

"How can you be so casual?"

"Don't glare at me, Hux. This old-world skill is still taught in Warrior Hall."

"It doesn't matter what they teach back on the home planet," she said. "In this world, I..."

How could she explain her fear without divulging her visions?

The Warrior's beard rippled above his grinding teeth.

He retrieved the Collector and approached Landra, deep anger glinting in his dark eyes. "I can't teach you magic because I don't know how. What I can show you is the Warrior skill of accessing power from Soul-laden artefacts."

She glowered at her knife hanging from the Warrior's fist. Its Templar properties weren't a surprise—she still had the magical rash it had left on her arm—but she'd never intended to use them. "I can't do this."

"It was going well before you dropped the knife. I think you can."

"That's not what I mean. Earning respect is hard enough. If it gets out that I trained in magic, you can forget my promotion. There's not a soldier on base who'll follow me."

"All Warriors know the nature of elite weapons." He waved the knife handle toward her face. "Now, resume."

"Does Chief Hux use Soul magic?" Resentment festered in her gut.

"Shelk! What's wrong with you, girl? Of course he uses magic, just like you."

The accusation shifted her world and terrified her to stillness.

"We all use magic every day," Thisk said. "Otherwise our city would be a frozen, dark tomb, and all our people would be dead to the mist. So, yes, Griffin does use magic, but, truthfully, he never had a good connection with the power or a feel for the hethra."

"I don't believe you."

Cold anger formed lines around the Warrior's eyes, and his fists rolled into balls. "Who are you to call me a liar, Hux? You might have a title, but underneath, you're just a homebred brat." He stormed to where Landra stood. She tensed, expecting a blow, but instead of raising a fist, the Warrior lifted her hat flap and rammed the weapon home into its sheath.

"I'm not saying the Collector didn't come to life in his hand, but he never connected with the magic and the blade burned out of control. Shelking near cindered through Warrior Hall when we trained. Is that enough truth for you, Chief Elect?"

She blanched at the condescension wrapped around her title. She'd been so consumed with her new predicament, she'd forgotten herself. "I never heard that before."

He glowered but his aura settled. "Griff didn't like to use the Collector after the incident. I guess he's relieved to have passed the knife along."

"To me!"

"Yes, to you, so deal with it, citizen. Now, resume."

Landra's hands shook with fatigue. She wanted to apply more salve and go home, but she'd already worn Thisk's temper ragged.

"Sir?"

He stared, challenge in his brown eyes. "What?"

"I have more bruises than the ones you can see."

The Warrior's teeth clamped, and his withering stare tracked up her body. "That happens when you fight illegally. Do it again, and you answer to me, cadet."

Cadet! Did he really call me cadet?

Yes, sir."

The Warrior retrieved his cloak. "You came to me exhausted, and the hethra takes a toll. More so up here. We'll try this again later. Hunker down and get some rest."

Weariness tugged at Landra, making her body too heavy to remain upright. Shivering rattled her limbs, so she wrapped her cloak around her body and curled up in the shelter of the fence. The few leaves beneath her bottom provided no padding. She wriggled to find comfort that wasn't there.

Thisk leaned against the fence, his intense stare taking in the expanse, and his large fist gripping his sword. "You know, Hux, soldiers aren't normally allowed to challenge my orders. That's another thing you'd have learned in the junior barracks."

She had questioned him, she knew. Was this place stripping her of all sense? Winton would have had her on report and doing double duty for less.

"I'm sorry, sir."

"Don't be."

Don't be! What sense does that make? She glanced sideways and lifted her hat flap to check out his expression. Serious lines wrinkled the bridge of his nose, but no hint of jest twinkled in his eyes.

Are you giving me permission to challenge your orders?

This was the Warrior Fourth, but he used magic. He was wild but respected. He had struck her for humming, but she needn't be sorry for challenging him. Much as she liked puzzles, she doubted he posed a solvable problem.

Where did my ordered life go?

This shabbily dressed Warrior, not fit to pass inspection, had taken her far from her destined path. In their short time together, he'd called her a brat, citizen, chief elect and now cadet. CADET!

That naming showed more respect than Winton had ever sent her way. On this day of pain and new demands, she found a purpose to drive her performance. It grew inside her, pushing out all other thoughts. She feared the Warrior's unpredictability, but his small recognition had fed her hunger for approval.

Her head sagged to her knees. The spot wasn't warm

nor restful, but the sleep that had eluded her in the night found her immediately, as did her dreams.

A clacking sound disturbed her strange rest. She was fending off a worm-headed animal in the nightmare, and her weakness condemned Mother to death. She recognized her mother's ill-defined form by a feeling rather than by her blurry features, heightening the emotional trauma of the loss. Now, an image of the beast with a frozen limb hanging from its mouth set in her memory. It crunched down on the bone in time with the sounds.

A hand clamped her mouth, and panic from her nightmare bled over into reality. Her eyes widened, her heart raced, and her hand grabbed for the Collector. All weariness had fled, and she was ready to fight.

Chapter 10

"Felland!" Thisk hissed in Landra's ear.

She stilled against his touch and glanced out. A hefty four-legged beast lumbered along a far fence, snuffling through leaves. Its dappled fur resembled Thisk's cloak and its powerful legs culminated in fat paws, but when a terrified rodent scuttled away, the beast extend a long claw from its soft pad. One swat speared the escaping rat, and the felland curled around its prey, sinking pointed teeth into its flesh.

Landra's chest heaved from the scene's similarity to her nightmare. The beast's orange aura rippled with satisfaction as it devoured the prize, but each of its breaths sucked the fur tight around its bony frame. Even from this distance, the definition of its ribs showed starvation that the small rodent wouldn't redress.

The wind direction shifted and the beast raised its head, blood-stained teeth bared. It sniffed the air, and the rumble from its throat carried on the breeze.

"Shelk, it's caught our scent," Thisk said. "Stay here."

He jumped up, sword in hand, and ran down the fence.

Once he'd left Landra a good way behind, he faced the felland and waved his arms. "Yah, yah."

The animal turned on the warrior and pressed into a hunting crouch.

"Yah, yah!" Thisk shouted again, but now he raised his sword in readiness.

Landra watched in horror. Thisk looked focused, but no matter how he controlled his features to calmness, his buried emotions fluctuated his aura in an anxious display of thrashing azure hues. His uncertainty compounded her own terror. She huddled in a ball to watch the scene, like a wind-frozen statue.

The felland crawled toward Thisk, its belly dragging along the city roof. It paused a short distance away, eyes fixed on its prey. The Warrior's equally intent stare matched the focusing of his aura, and his raised blade held firm. Landra gasped, realizing his calmness came from the hethra. She couldn't begrudge him the magic for this.

The cat's swift spring erupted without warning. Thisk's sword met the animal's leaping form and squealing carried loud on the wind, but the felland didn't stop its attack. It was small, Landra realized, difficult to spear, and had sneaked inside the Warrior's defenses. His blade had pierced its shoulder, but the injury only enraged the animal to a more desperate attack. It wrapped its body around Thisk's trunk, its teeth bared and its raking claws slashing through his cloak and shirt to the flesh beneath.

Landra's body moved before her brain engaged, and she squeezed the Collector. Pain masked by terror, she climbed to standing, not knowing whether Thisk would expect her to remain still, join the fight, or run. The beast might be hurt, but its strong aura burned with plenty of fight.

"I'm coming!" She burst into a run as she charged

toward the battle. By the time she reached Thisk, a frenzy of fur, teeth, and claws had enveloped him. His unwieldy sword couldn't touch the animal now it was hugging his chest, but he gripped it in a tight squeeze to stem its attack.

The Collector of Souls hung in Landra's hand, and she made the final charge with it thrust forward.

"Agh!" she screamed, as she plunged the knife into the fight. The frantic battle made targeting the animal difficult, so she stilled for a moment, tracked the felland's movements, and then struck. Her blade hit the beast more by luck than skill, and its yelp of fury carried on the wind. The felland twisted in her direction, and she saw into its green eyes. Their auras touched, and the shock of its predatory spirit, desperate hunger, and terror overwhelmed her own thoughts. She snarled and crouched, ready to battle like a beast, but Thisk intervened.

He slashed his sword again, this time swiping the felland from Landra's path. The animal's raw, uncensored fury pierced her, but another knife-sweep from the Warrior sent it sprawling. She recognized surrender in the animal's aura before it ran. As it scampered away, blood trailing in its wake, Thisk sank to a knee and clutched his chest. She bent to attend to him.

"Kill it," Thisk hissed.

"What?"

"Kill the felland. Quick, before it gets away."

"It's bolting. We're safe."

Thisk's insistent, dark gaze backed up his order, so she stood and set her stance for a throw. She lifted her knife and stalled at the sight of blood staining the pink blade. She'd not registered fear during the fight, but now her fingers trembled. Her breathing stilled as she targeted the animal. Reluctant to kill a fleeing beast, she froze in position, and the felland limped away. Its aura had dimmed, and she recalled its emotions. Its wild, ruthless nature drove its actions and it needed to eat. How could she blame it for that?

"Throw," Thisk bellowed, but she sheathed the Collector and dropped her arm.

"It's too far away."

"Damn you to shelk, Hux. Do you ever follow orders?"

Landra turned to the Warrior. His gritted teeth shone through his thinned lips and wild beard. Blood oozed through the slash marks on his shirt.

"Are you going to be all right?" she asked.

"I'll be fine. Rather I would have been fine if you'd killed the felland."

"It couldn't do us any more harm."

"No, and now it can't do us any good, either. Tell me, citizen, are you hungry?"

A raging demand churned Landra's stomach. She'd thought it had come from the beast, but now she recalled how long it had been since she'd eaten. "Yes."

"Well, you can stay that way because you just let our dinner wander off. And don't think you did that animal a kindness. No felland should be this close to the city. Winter's coming, and it should be migrating to its southern hunting grounds now. The incoming ice will kill it, even if it manages to survive its injuries.

She stared after the animal, but it had disappeared into the distance. Her stomach squelched with hunger. "Didn't you bring food?"

"No. Did you?"

"I wasn't expecting to stay up here."

The Warrior leaned on his sword and eased to his feet. "Maybe there's more than one lesson here, citizen. Don't let your dinner escape, and prepare for the unexpected."

"How can you prepare for the unexpected?"

"It comes with experience," he said, easing his cloak from his shoulders. He pulled the slashed shirt fabric away from his chest and scowled at blood that welled through the material. "Seems like it's time for your third lesson. How are you at setting bandages?"

None of Thisk's lessons seemed useful for a chief elect, but she said nothing. She didn't think there was enough experience in the world to deal with the unpredictable Warrior. He changed her rank from moment to moment, as if it reflected his satisfaction with her performance.

How do you prepare for someone like that?

"We need to retrieve our belongings first," Thisk said, sheathing the sword on his hip.

Landra went to support his arm, but he shook her away. They staggered along the fence line to where their meager items nestled in the leaves. An uneasy silence settled as if the gulf between them was too huge for either of them to know what to say. Thisk found his sack and dug out a fresh shirt. He never winced, but flares of deeper blues spotted his aura. "I have some salve," Landra said.

The Warrior eased off his slashed top and gritted his teeth against the cold. One shallow cut split the greying hairs on his chest, but two raking slashes and a bite mark cut deep into the muscle of his left arm.

He eased himself down, and Landra knelt beside him.

"Wouldn't we be better tending to this in the midlevel?" she asked.

The Warrior glared. "What salve do you have?"

She rummaged the pot out of her cloak and handed it over. Thisk examined the label for several seconds before removing the lid.

"You saw a medic today?"

Landra sucked in a breath. She'd crossed the Warrior

Fourth enough for one day, so this had to be the truth. "Yes. This morning."

"It's a strong treatment. Did Gren clear you for training?"

"No, but… I thought we were going to have a history lesson."

"Oh, citizen, you really do have a problem with rules, don't you?" He rubbed the clear ointment into his wounds. "Tear my shirt into strips." He nodded at the tattered garment.

Landra slotted her knife into the slash marks and ripped down the fabric. Thisk took the strips from her and bound them around his arm and chest. There was no discussion about his method, so if this was a lesson, he was expecting her to pick up bandaging skills from watching. He groaned when he reached the fabric strip around his back but stopped Landra from helping with one glare. As he shrugged his cloak over his bandaged body, his aura finally settled.

"Why did you join the fight when I ordered you to stay away?" he asked.

I thought you might die.

"Because I didn't fancy going back to the midlevel alone," she said. "I hate paperwork."

Thisk didn't smile, but warm azure shades rippled through his aura. His colors had taken on a more even pattern now he was warm, making him seem likely to recover. She shivered, only now registering that she'd truly feared he might die.

"You're not a very good chief elect."

Landra's imposter feelings returned. Thisk appeared unaware of her confidence dip and continued to glare.

"What should I have done?" she asked.

"You should have kept yourself safe."

"I was worried you might—"

"Society would cope without me. Another Fourth can be appointed without disruption."

"So I was supposed to leave you to deal with that alone?"

"Yes. A chief elect is another matter. Your death would damage the peace treaty your father is working hard to secure. Our existence is fragile, Chief Elect Hux. We can't afford to lose you."

"I couldn't let that thing maul you."

Thisk grunted. "Like I said, you're not a very good chief elect. You're too nice."

Too nice. Nice! What does that mean?

Landra opened her mouth to argue, but no words came out. She didn't feel nice. She broke rules and was argumentative. How could that be nice?

Thisk laughed at the outrage widening her young features. "I could have said worse."

"Well, you're not a good tutor," she said, and the Warrior's bellow of laughter made circles in his aura. "I never claimed to be."

"And I never claimed to be a good chief elect."

"Do you still want to eat?" Thisk asked from nowhere.

Stupid question. Landra's stomach ached with emptiness. "Of course."

"Well, you're in luck."

The Warrior cocked his head to a distant fence, and she followed his gaze. More than a dozen black birds perched there, silhouetted against the lowering sun.

"How's your shooting?" he asked, picking up his bow.

Landra's scores were hopeless, and the Warrior nodded at her defeated expression.

"Just what I'd expect. I guess it's time for your next lesson."

Chapter 11

Landra considered the flock of birds.

"Keep still," the Warrior said. "Gliders are jittery creatures. You'll scare them away."

They didn't look jittery as they rested and spread their
wings toward the sun. Occasional wind gusts set them to
flight, but they settled quickly and preened their feathers
back into position.

"Just one will give us a good meal." He offered her the
bow. "They're surprisingly meaty."

"Barthle's pie is on the menu tonight," she said.

The Warrior shook the weapon at her, jagged, inky
lines animating his aura. "We're not going back to Hux
Hall and I'm injured, so this is down to you."

However much he controlled his face and body, Landra
saw emotions painting tracks in the colored shape
surrounding his form.

Frustration? I know the feeling.

She shut off her protest and accepted the bow.

"If you've never been to Third City, I suppose you've
never used the animal pens for target work." It's another

thing that should have been covered in basic cadet training."

At eighteen, she was shy of cadet age, but this training didn't match Dannet's tales from the academy anyway. Despite her pain, she'd started to enjoy her overlevel experience. She didn't want it to end, so she assumed her position without a word.

"Steady," Thisk said.

I'm trying.

Eyeing the gliders, she contemplated killing a live target for the first time. She'd slashed the felland in battle but hadn't taken the kill throw. Now, these gliders looked content, as if their bellies were full. It was more than could be said for her churning guts, so she accepted the arrow Thisk offered.

"Animals move and adjust to their environment," he said.

She remembered Winton reciting the same line from a manual but was certain the trainer had never killed a bird. She pulled off her gloves with her teeth and stuffed them into a pocket. As she assumed a balanced stance, Thisk wandered to the fence and folded his arms.

Guess I'm on my own.

This felt like a test, so she nocked the arrow, focused, and drew the bow string until her fingers touched her cheek. Winton had taught her this, but tension locked her limbs and tightened her grip as never before. She recalled her breathing exercises, and after several gasps, her spirit calmed and her body relaxed. Awareness of her cold, aching limbs and the drastic turn her life had taken faded from her thoughts. There were no doors to see through here, and she started to relax. She concentrated on the bow's polished wood and the birds.

Go for the nearest one.

Closing her eyes, she listened to the wind. As her breath stilled, she opened her eyes and aimed. The release felt smooth, and her fingers fell away as she watched the arrow speed to its target. The birds rose in a frenzy of clacking sounds, and her missile arced over the fence into clear air.

"Shelk!"

"Try again." He handed her another arrow.

"I thought my aim was good."

"Live birds are different from base targets, even if you've trained on moving marks. Creatures are unpredictable, and there's wind."

Landra considered his words before nocking the second arrow. She raised her bow and followed the same routine. This time, her arrow sprang toward its target, and she held her breath for longer, willing it to strike true. The gliders took flight to avoid the missile and then settled back closer to Landra's position, as if in taunt. The one she'd targeted preened its feathers, unconcerned.

"This is harder than I thought." She dropped her head.

"It takes some getting used to. Give it one last try. I'll shoot one down if you miss this time. I didn't bring many arrows, and I'm too old to go hungry."

Landra ground her teeth. Despite her little time with the bow, she'd studied the techniques and couldn't see why hitting a bird should be difficult. She began her routine again but held her set position as she planned her next move. An idea formed.

"Clack clack!" She mimicked the glider call. The birds rose in answer and flew towards her. She tracked the nearest one until it hung for a moment, silhouetted against the sky. Her release was smooth, but at the last moment, the bird dropped into a dive, allowing the missile to skim past its body.

Landra didn't want to face Thisk's disapproval.

Not good enough for a chief elect.

The bird circled her head and she couldn't bear the taunt, so she reacted in the way she knew best. She pulled a knife from beneath her cloak and tracked the glider to judge its speed. Now that it was close, she saw a faint yellow aura ringing its form. That gave her something to target. Her arrows had deviated to left in the wind, but her knife was heavier. Still, she calculated a small compensation, waited for the bird to hover, and then drew her arm back, ready to throw.

"No!" Thisk shouted.

Landra's arm was already in motion, and she hurled the knife skyward. She wondered at how time could slow. It seemed too long before her blade reached the bird, but it struck home and she knew the gilder's death moment by the frittering of its aura. The lifeless carcass plummeted, leaving the yellow patch of aura light still in the sky. It held together for a moment then dissipated on the wind.

"Yeah!" she cheered, exhilarated by success and unable to keep the triumph from her face. "Did you see that? I hit the glider."

Thisk stood tall, staring at the point where the bird had fallen. Without a word, he turned his attention to Landra, furious eyes glaring out of his bearded face.

Tense limbs, raging aura lines—fury. Oh shelk! What did I do now?

"I would have stopped, but I was already throwing when you called out. I need to eat as well, and I'm better with a knife than a bow."

"I can see that."

The Warrior's clipped words came laced with anger.

She'd downed the target, even if it wasn't in the way he'd wanted. Pleasing him seemed impossible. He wanted her to make decisions when it suited him, but how was she supposed to know when that was?

"Do you think the Collector of Souls is a toy?" he demanded. "That weapon came from the homeworld and has been handed down through generations of leaders. Its significance to our people can't be measured in credits."

His anger suddenly made sense. "Warrior Thi—"

"You've thrown the knife at a bird in a fit of arrogance over perceived failure. I don't expect you to have mastery over every skill, Hux. Each day's ability is merely a new starting point in your development. I would have taken the shot. Now, the Collector is somewhere on the overlevel. What if the bird had managed to keep flying and carried it to the remote lands? It could have been lost to our people forever. It's clear that you have no desire to carry the knife, but its importance to our world is far greater than the petty desires of one spoiled citizen."

"Thisk." She pulled her knife from the strap at her back and waved it. "That wasn't the Collector of Souls. I brought another knife from the shaft stores. The Collector is here." The weapon gleamed magenta in her grasp.

Whatever the Warrior had meant to add, the scolding died on his lips. He stared at her knife, visibly trying to calm himself.

"You wanted me to throw it at the felland. How is that different?"

"The felland was already injured and couldn't have taken the knife away," he said, regaining control of his tight fists. Fury still roiled through him as he gazed up to the point in the sky where the bird had been before it plummeted. He stared for a long time. "That glider was moving and a good distance away. How confident were you of making the strike?"

Landra shrugged. "I've made tougher targets but not moving and in this wind. Still, I was more certain to hit the thing with a knife than an arrow."

He chewed his lip. "Clearly! Still, every resource on our world is valuable, and my rebuke over risking a knife stands. Luckily, whoever taught you to throw did a good job. You have a solid knife arm, and that was a good shot."

Is that a compliment?

"Thank you."

"You don't get the credit, cadet. If Winton taught you to throw, then he deserves more respect."

"Winton's more of a sword man. My instruction came from the chief."

"Of course," he said, as if everything made sense now. "But Winton must have drilled you."

Landra's first instinct was to say no. The trainer had offered little encouragement, reported slight infringements that were overlooked in cadets, and drilled her relentlessly in tasks until they matched manual standards. Soul-destroying as it had been, she realized his regime had honed her skills. Distance gave her a new perspective.

"He worked me hard and gave me solid soldier training."

"Really? I'll look forward to you demonstrating solid soldiering skills," he said, rich sarcasm oozing from every word.

And back to the insults.

Before she could object, he pointed to the fence where the bird had landed.

"Collector or no, that knife needs retrieving. Step to it, cadet, and bring the bird before it's scavenged. I'm hungry."

Chapter 12

Landra kicked the leaves, but a stained fence panel gave her a clue to the bird's position. She followed the stain down and rummaged in the leaves below until her boot snagged on something solid. Nudging the glider's limp, black shape from the leaves, its uninjured appearance made her wonder if it had died from shock rather than any wound. So much for her knife skills. She preferred not to touch the bird and nudged it again with her boot until it rolled over with its head lolling to one side.

Seeing death up close froze her to stillness, but her mind raced and her aura swirled before her eyes. Dreams of her mother's death intruded again. Moments ago, the bird had been sunning itself, and now it was gone. The speed of its passing made life seem fragile in a way she'd not considered before. The wind still blew and the sun shone, but the bird had stopped.

There are worse ways to die. Inevitably, the experience took her to the place that had troubled her for a long time. *Did someone shoot you with an arrow, Mother, leaving your body limp like the glider's? Or did you fall sick?*

Ignorance left a hole in her life, and she didn't have enough information to fathom its shape. Dannet refused to speak of the incident, and rumors only spun her imagination into darker places.

What were you like, and how did you die? Did you love me?

"Cadet!" Thisk's voice carried to her on the wind.

She pinched the glider's feet between her fingers, avoiding the sharp talons, and was surprised by the jointed firmness beneath her gloved grip. The bird swung in the wind, emitting an echo of life that quivered her aura. It swayed lifelessly as she kicked the leaves in search of her knife. Luck favored her, and one random leg sweep uncovered the weapon. After replacing the knife beneath her cloak, she set out at a quick march toward the Warrior.

Thisk had arranged his gathered twigs on a round tin from his pack and was adding thinner brown wisps of dry vegetation from his pocket.

"Put it there." He cocked his head to a bare patch of roof. He took a small stone from his pocket and trapped a clump of wispy tendrils against it with his thumb.

Landra watched in silence, her mother's memory hanging around like a ghost at her side. The Warrior struck a tool against the purple stone, and small light flashes shot from the contact. The glow died, so he struck again.

"Shall I find a bigger rock?" she asked.

"No need. This Soul bead carries plenty of power, despite its size."

"Soul bead?" she said, stepping back. His use of the artifact wasn't surprising after all he'd said about magic. She wondered where Father had found this soldier. His loyalty to Warrior-kind was questionable, and he'd obviously spent too long roving the remote lands alone.

"I guessed you might have a problem after that fuss

over the hethra. I was hoping to light the fire before you got back, but the wind's giving me trouble." He hunched over his working hands to shield the spark from the breeze but without any luck. "Give me the Collector."

It sounded like an order. She removed the knife from its sheath and let it hang by her side. The weapon was more than just a knife. She knew that. It came with a world of problems and was never intended to be shared—or to strip meat from a carcass. Her fist squeezed tight around the handle.

"Now."

She proffered the knife, and her perception shifted. Would it be a bad turn of events if he kept the Collector? True, he had issues, but he was infinitely more capable of carrying out the chief elect duties accompanying the weapon.

Thisk locked her gaze with his own. "It can't be passed along," he said, as if reading her mind.

"Chief Hux passed it to me."

"Did he? If he simply gave you the knife, then he broke with tradition."

"It wasn't exactly a gift." She rubbed her bruised throat.

"Ah! That explains a lot. Are you inviting me to fight for the Collector, Chief Elect Hux?"

Can I? If you take the knife in a fair fight, will the responsibility pass to you? It was a tempting notion, and Father couldn't complain if she lost the weapon in a legitimate challenge. Still, if the chief had wanted this responsibility to go to Thisk, it would have been easy to arrange. She stopped torturing herself with doubts and accepted the inevitable.

"Not today, Warrior Fourth."

"I thought not. But I only want to borrow it."

He yanked the knife out of her grip and repositioned

the vegetation on top of the Soul stone. With a sharp snap, he dashed the Collector's blade against the pebble, and incandescent pink sparks sprayed from the contact. A singing tone accompanied each strike. Landra's sensitized aura quivered with each blow, and her mouth gaped. The reverberating ping clashed against her senses and made her skin tingle.

Stop! Please, just stop.

"Is breaking an heirloom better than losing it?" she asked.

The Warrior struck the Collector against the stone again, his aura swelling in time with the blow, and a smoldering odor rose in the wind.

"Thisk! If you break that, I might as well take myself to the remote lands now. Taking a snapped blade back to Chief Hux would be..."

Unimaginable.

He waved her concern away. "Homeworld weapons are stronger than they look, and the colored metal creates better fire. The built-in magic makes it burn hotter and longer." Sparks flew in searing pink streaks from the Collector, and the tinder burst into flames with a pop. He dropped the wisp pile onto his twigs, and unnatural pink fire grew up around the wood.

Landra couldn't have been more horrified if the Collector had sprouted wings. Seeing Thisk deliberately utilize its Soul power was too much to bear. She wasn't afraid that Thisk would expose her flaw. Her sick-filled throat came from fear that he would encourage her to grow it.

"Does my father know what you do?" He glanced up at her, appearing to consider. "Maybe, but I don't think so. Some soldiers are more sensitive to the Soul than others. He might not even be aware when magic is used."

"But you are." A world of accusation edged her words.

"There you go again, trying to banish me. I might have learned a few tricks on my travels, but that doesn't make me a Templer."

The fire roared, and Thisk offered her the Collector back. She hesitated for a moment before accepting the weapon. It surprised her that the Warrior had made Fourth, and she wondered if Chief Hux would let him keep the rank once she reported. If there was any part of her that appreciated his ideas, she buried it deep. Others might be able to dabble in old-world skills, but holding a strict soldier line was her way only to avoid discovery.

She slid her eyes shut and dared to consider the knife. Its lifeless handle sat in her palm, carrying no noticeable warmth or thrum of power.

Father carried you, along with generations of our family before. Shouldn't I feel that in the blade?

She sensed nothing. Returning the knife to its sheath on her back, she fell into a moody silence.

"Everything good?" Thisk asked, as he plucked the bird.

She tried for an angry face and pierced him with her most vicious stare. "No. My life's more tossed around than one of Barthle's salads. How can anything be good?"

She settled into a snug ball in the shelter of the fence. Peeping over her knees, she watched him gut and slice the bird, spear chunks onto his sword, and then wedge the sword tip high enough into the fence so that the flames licked the meat. He stoked the fire into a greedy inferno before settling down to gaze into the heart of the flames. It seemed like he'd forgotten she was there.

The moment was peaceful, despite the whooshing wind, snapping fire, and muffled vibrations of a siren below. Swathed in padded clothes, she felt comfortable enough to reflect. The vivid colors here sparkled brighter than in the midlevel, like her father's strong aura when he was stirred to anger. The rich sky color matched the mid-blue shade of a two-bar's uniform rather than a deep Warrior hue. She knew this place was dangerous, but the freedom of outside held an attraction.

"Warrior Fourth Thisk?"

He jabbed the fire, but a new stiffness straightened his spine. After a moment, he fixed her with an intent brown-eyed stare.

"Yes, Chief Elect Hux?"

She gathered her courage. "Did you know my mother?"

A crease appeared at the bridge of his nose. "Does that have a bearing on your training as chief elect?"

"No, but I've been thinking about her recently. Do you think she died from an animal attack? Because I heard she used to work in the remote lands. A visiting cadet told me and…" Her words dwindled away.

"This is hardly appropriate, Hux. I'm here to train you. At least, I think it's what I'm supposed to do." He scratched his bearded cheek. "The mist knows why this job fell to me. I'm hardly suited, but here we are. As for anything else, it's not my place to say."

Landra sighed. "Really? Because it doesn't seem like it's anybody's place to tell me what happened. After all these years, visiting cadets know more about her death than I do. I've imagined it happening in so many ways."

The Warrior stared into the fire.

"Warrior Ranger Fourth Thisk, as chief elect I am asking you to tell me what happened."

He chewed his lip, considering, and then suddenly relaxed. "Oh! For a moment, I thought you were going to give me an order. Then, I might have had to answer. If you expect to command, Hux, polite requests aren't going to work. You need to make decisions and give orders." He pulled the sword from the fire and examined the charred meat.

"But if my mother patrolled the remote lands, maybe—"

"Forget it," Thisk said, steel in his voice. "I did know your mother. Loni Hux took the Warrior's run, so if you're thinking of finding her living in the remote lands, forget it."

The Warrior's run? The ceremony for desperate soldiers who wanted to end their lives in one last battle? The Warrior's route to suicide? You left me for that?

Landra couldn't breathe.

Surely Thisk was lying, but why would he do that? The suggestion hit her harder than any body blow. It had to be a mistake. Even considering the possibility forced tears to well, and she stiffened her face to hold them inside. He didn't deserve the satisfaction of seeing her pain.

"That's not true," she said.

Thisk kicked the fire, sending cinders twisting off on the wind. "Oh, really? You think you know more than me? I see uncertainty twisting you in knots, Hux. As chief elect, you need to focus on our society's future, not the past. So, I'm telling you, by my Warrior's Oath, I worked the run that day and saw your mother on the path. She died in the city on that day. Move on."

Landra felt as chilled in her guts as she did in her toes. She couldn't look at Thisk. Of all the ways that she'd imagined her mother dying, she'd never considered this form of abandonment or cowardice. Another excruciating agony made her shake. "You worked as a Warrior on the run? Did you kill her?"

"No! No. She wouldn't have put me in that position. I'd

guarded a couple of her engineering expeditions to New City. We lost touch, but I knew her well enough."

"But if she'd come your way, you would have struck her?"

Thisk paused. "If she'd come my way, I would have performed my duty. It was her right to ask that of me." His words grated, making him sound older than his true years.

Landra couldn't hold back her tears any longer, and they streaked warm down her cold cheeks. "My father allowed this?"

"It isn't my place to say."

Her tears erupted into sobs.

He gave her a hopeless look, as if he didn't know what to do with her. "Fine. The chief wasn't in charge then, so he had no official power to stop her. I don't know what went on between them or why she chose the run. Loni was a fine soldier and as strong-willed as they come. If things had been different, she might have been chief."

"Really?" *That's news.* "Different how? Was having children a problem?"

"Forget the self-blame. Loni took motherhood in her stride, but the council would never let her rise to the top spot. Engineers are too valuable a resource to waste on leadership."

"Too valuable to be chief?"

"What use is a leader without a world to command?" Thisk said. "More systems turn off every day, and we have to find new ways to live on this rock."

"If she was so valuable, why did they let her do the run?"

Honest bafflement furrowed the Warrior's weathered brow. "I don't know but if she'd made up her mind, I don't think Griffin or the council could have interfered. They respected her wishes, and so must you."

Never. Landra relived the betrayal with every breath, but Thisk was relentless.

"Griffin took you and the boy out of the junior barracks straight after her run and has kept you close ever since. Many soldiers think too close."

"Like you?"

"I did say that, but I'm only the Fourth."

Landra wanted to rage at the Warrior, but none of this was his fault. She'd wanted the truth, and he'd supplied it without censor. Now, she wanted to shout and scream, but she choked it all inside. Vague memories of leaving the barracks came back, but no one had ever mentioned her mother's death. That news had come later. Pain welled inside her, and she exploded in another sob. Thisk sighed and turned away to stare into the fire. The wavy edges of his aura thinned and fluctuated, as if her emotions unsettled him. A wonderful smell rose from the cooked bird, and she resented its intoxicating aroma. How dare something smell so good when she felt so betrayed? She couldn't remember her mother's touch or the lilt of her voice. She'd lost her long ago, but now her treasured image had been destroyed too. She wanted to kick the fire to cinders, but instead she hugged her knees tighter. Thisk ignored her outburst, and she was grateful for the space. If the Warrior thought emotions made her weak, that was his problem. He'd been there when her mother had died. Maybe he could have stopped it. He was the nearest target for her anger, and she didn't care about his opinion anymore. She sat clenched tight until he served up the food.

The bird was the most delicious meat she'd tasted and, at the same time, the most gagging. They finished it quickly, drank water from Thisk's bottle, and cleared away like a storm was coming. The Warrior whisked up his belongings and set out toward the heart of Central City, where a copse of treetops rose through the midlevel. He spared no look to see if she followed.

Landra glanced back at the Hux Hall shaft then scrambled after him. She joined his march, which was both forced and silent. As the trees neared, she dared to ask, "Where are we going?"

Thisk didn't look at her to deliver the news.

"The temple."

Chapter 13

The direct path to ring seven took less than ten minutes to reach, and Landra still hadn't gathered her thoughts when they arrived at the shaft door. She'd avoided temple visits for so long it was hard to know what to expect. Sweat moistened her palms inside her gloves.

"Do we have to do this?"

"No, we can go home," Thisk answered.

"Great."

"But I won't trust you as chief elect if we do."

He stamped his boot heel on the trap door.

She sighed and sank inside her cloak, waiting for the panel to open. Almost at once, it swung over and crashed to the roof. A guard's head and sword tip peeped out from the hole. "Identify yourselves."

"Ranger Warrior Fourth, seeking permission to enter," Thisk said. "Returning from overlevel duties with my apprentice."

"Yes, sir."

"Apprentice?" Landra asked, once the guard had disappeared.

"It works for now."

They clambered down the shaft and deposited their outer garments in a laundry crate. Landra's citizen uniform was more creased than she liked, but stripping in front of the Warrior wasn't going to happen. She flattened her uniform fabric and brushed her used hat over her boots.

Thisk settled his dark curls over his insignia and set his sword on one hip. The weapon looked ready for action rather than a display of power, but if this was an attempt at anonymity, Landra judged it would fail. His uniform held the dust of years and couldn't fail to attract attention, but it wasn't his clothing or the insignia badge pinned to his collar that would give him away. The ranger carried himself like a man who expected to be obeyed.

She watched him firm and darken his aura as if he were adopting a different character, and she wondered if he knew what he did. *Not likely.* His free-flowing colors had rippled unchecked on the overlevel, but now they condensed to a hard-edged ring around his body, like uneven armor.

"Stay close and don't talk to anyone," he said as they emerged onto the concourse.

Landra clamped her mouth so tight she had to breathe through her nose. They passed

a darkened pod station and made their way down a gentle slope, where a smattering of red robes broke up the soldiers' blue uniforms.

"I thought there'd be more Templers," she whispered.

"You won't find many out here. Most have their movements restricted to inside the temple."

He gripped her shoulder like she were a runaway child, but the control was preferable to him marching off again, especially here where she felt misplaced. As he nudged her farther down the ramp, a tickling sensation crawled over her skin like swarming ants.

Something's wrong. Dread—fear. What the….?Not my own.

She shuddered, panic suddenly cramping her heart. Nothing made sense. Thisk's aura crowded her space, battering her Soul with agitated fluttering. A flash of red robes headed for them, and the Warrior's apprehension rattled through her as clearly as if it were her own. The grizzled ranger, who could survive the planet's worst and wasn't against using magical artifacts, found something so unsettling about Soul practitioners that he would rather be elsewhere. Anywhere.

So, it's not just me. Why did we come here, Thisk?

She couldn't ask. The Warrior's purposeful stride didn't betray his feelings, but his aura broadcast his distrust unchecked. She couldn't help admiring his outward bravado.

The red-robed figure closed in, skimming by as if they were invisible. His face hid beneath a baggy hood, but a brush from his wan blue aura flashed more awareness through Landra's consciousness than she wanted. His thoughts were… No, not his thoughts. These were her thoughts now.

Tyrants, the lot of you. Die, soldiers. Die.

Landra absorbed the vile hatred into her Soul, taking the bitterness and resentment as her own. And here was Thisk: powerful, dominating, and the enemy.

Kill!

She reached for the Collector.

Stab him. Plunge the knife into his heart. Watch his blood drain to the floor and the light dim from his eyes. Quick.

The Templer kept walking. One stride, two strides, and he disappeared into the crowd. His violent thoughts went with him. Landra stemmed a squeal as the murderous impulse drained away.

What the shelk?

She brushed her wayward hand over her scalp and slowed her heavy breathing. The Collector still sat in its sheath, and a glance up at the ranger sensed no recognition of the terrible assault she'd been about to commit.

Her aura ranged in swirling threads, and it couldn't be left that way. *This is dangerous. What if it touches another Soul? What if…? Take control.*

She sucked in a breath, as if to draw her aura close— useless. Echoes of the alien emotions still haunted her memory, and the trembling reached her fingers. *Do something.* On impulse, she recited a math problem to shut out invading thoughts.

Two times one equals two. Two times two equals four.

Her aura responded to the logical reasoning by settling into orderly patterns. She found some peace. As she mentally chanted, her aura's surrounding colors folded in and bound tight to her frame, giving her a chance to breathe. She glanced up at Thisk, but another snatch of his distrust wafted over her.

Two times three equals six. Peace. Oh, Thisk, is this mutual fear and hatred you wanted me to see—feel?

"I've seen enough now," she told him, but the Warrior guided her to the back of a snaking queue, which led to the temple.

"Hardly," he said. "This is your chance to face the fear of magic, soldier. I had thought to spend a night in the local flop shop. Now, I'm thinking to get this over with. We'll go inside the temple and be on our way."

"What? No. We can't go inside."

"No?"

Landra was already facing her fear, and it was more

terrifying than she could have anticipated. Her squeezing chest couldn't take any more.

"Aren't you afraid?" she asked, her question daring him to lie.

"Odd question, soldier. I thought you'd pegged me as a temple lover."

Landra couldn't admit to knowing his emotions and groped for an explanation. "Everyone fears Templers a bit," she said.

"There's some truth in that, but this is like the hethra. During training exercises, we convince our bodies to work when our minds say we're done. The same control can be accomplished with fear. We only know courage when our fear is greatest."

No lie. Another lesson. Just what I need.

She took in the scene, wondering if she had the guts to follow this through. A robed woman and child stood in front of them, and the temple's closed doors loomed ahead. Library drawings hadn't prepared her for the size of the panels or the intricacy of their etched artwork. A Templer staff adorned one side, a Warrior's sword the other, and intertwining flower etchings decorated the remaining wood. She had to admit that Thisk had opened her life up to more new experiences in one day than she'd encountered in all her time at Hux Hall.

In the shadow of the great doors, a smaller panel opened and a soldier emerged. A Templer at the head of the queue disappeared inside, and everyone in line shuffled forward. Landra didn't want to move.

Living on the edge is exciting, but there has to be a limit. She had one strategy for handling the burden of her magic. Secrecy was her armor, but now she wondered whether to tell Thisk her secret. If he knew, he might take her home. He might also look at her with fear, and she couldn't bear that thought. With each step closer to the door, her mind changed. As one boot fell, she prepared herself to confess all. On the next stride, she convinced herself to silence. *Shelk. Two times four is eight.*

With the door only a few steps away, the Templer child in front pushed his hood back, openly displaying a flourish of blond curls, which stood out shockingly against the red of his small robe.

"Get that child's hair cut to regulation length," a one-bar soldier said in passing. "You might not care about exile, but it's not fair to take a youngster with you."

The Templer woman grabbed the boy's hand and flipped up his hood. "Yes, sir. Stay with me, Gengi, and hold my hand so you're not in the way." Her conciliatory words didn't match the agitation flashing through her aura.

Two times five equals ten.

"And enroll him in the junior barracks," another soldier added.

Landra flinched, conscious of her own home-based upbringing, but this was different. The woman might have accepted a temple posting, but forcing that life on a child didn't seem fair. The child looked about seven, but his aura swam with the milky blue shade of a newborn. It was pale and fluid, unlike the deepening shades Landra saw in barrack-bred children. A barely perceptible shake of Thisk's head ordered her to silence, and his hand clamped tighter on her shoulder.

The next time Gengi bounced his ball, he missed the catch and it rolled away. He slipped from his mother's hand to chase into the crowd. As much as he darted past soldiers and scurried between their legs, moving feet just nudged the ball farther away from his grasp. As he ducked through the crowd, his hood fell back again to reveal his blond curls.

"What's this?" a soldier demanded.

"Temple brat," came a reply.

"What's he doing loose?"

"Needs a whipping."

Jeers rose from the crowd, and attention fell on Gengi. His Templer mother hovered at a distance, her blue aura whirling with terror. Landra expected her to run to the child and was shocked to see her frozen. This woman, who'd been bold enough to flaunt her beliefs with the color of her robes and the cut of her son's hair, wasn't prepared to dive into the mob to save her child.

An older soldier with a full three bars cut into his insignia crunched his boot into the boy's ribs. A high-pitched yelp reverberated around the concourse, and a responding cheer from the crowd urged more violence. The soldier set his heavy boot to the boy's back.

Landra was no Templer lover. The priests disrupted city life at every turn, openly disobeyed the law, and had tried to assassinate Father, but she couldn't condone abuse. The guard pressed his weight through his boot, and outrage exploded in her like an overlevel storm. Gengi was a child, and any concourse guard could have set him right with a gentle warning.

His Templer mother posed as still as the door's illustrations, terror and hatred etched onto her set features, but her swirling aura raged, as if ready to explode.

Two times six equals twelve.

Another kick fell and Landra started forward.

Thisk's tightening grip halted her progress. "No!" The intensity of his order reached Landra's bones. "Stay here." He marched into the crowd, using his bulk to forge a space through the incited onlookers. "Stand down."

The three-bar soldier lifted his boot, ready to kick again, but a glance up showed him the looming blade of

Thisk's sword. "Woah! What's the problem, guard? I'm just having a bit of fun with the boy."

"It's the Fourth," a keen-eyed soldier shouted.

Thisk's curls covered his hair insignia but his collar badge displayed his rank. A hushed chant ran through the crowd like a passing whisper. "It's the Fourth," one soldier said to the next until silence fell.

Landra watched all color drain from the three-bar soldier's aura. His wide face paled until the insignia tattooed onto his naturally bald head stood out like a branding on his sallow scalp.

"Warrior Fourth, sir," he said, gathering himself to awkward attention. "I didn't realize you..." His words dwindled away as the futility of them sank in. "I was just having some fun, sir. Temple brat's not supposed to be wandering the concourse."

"The boy wasn't breaking the law. Unlike you," Thisk said. "What's your name?"

"How can you say he wasn't breaking the law? That hair!"

"Is legal within the temple district. I asked for your name, soldier."

A better view opened up for Landra as soldiers eased away for fear of discipline from the Fourth. They eyed him warily, and she realized her own developing relationship with the Thisk was different from theirs. He was her protector and guide, and she wasn't sure whether to be grateful or insulted. Her ambition had always been to be a respected soldier.

Gengi huddled on the floor, clutching his side and sobbing so loudly that his Templer mother found some courage and scuttled forward. Thisk snatched his head to the movement, furious eyes staring out from his bearded face.

"Woman, make sure the boy sees a medic," he said. "Then enroll him in the junior barracks. It was foolish to be on the concourse with tensions so high. You're lucky I was here."

"Yes, sir," she said with a bob, but her respect wasn't convincing. She dragged her son up by the arm and scampered away with him safely tucked in the crook of her arm. Her path took her to the front of the temple queue, and it only took a short discussion with the gatekeeper for the door to open. The pair disappeared inside.

Thisk turned his attention back to the soldier. "I asked for your name." The Fourth's clothes might be plain and worn, but power radiated from him, and Landra saw it bloom in his aura.

"Dermot," the soldier answered, reluctance tracking a faint slur into his voice.

Thisk regarded him, as if measuring his worth. "That will be 'Soldier Dermot, Ranger Warrior Fourth, sir.'"

No one present could have denied Thisk's intent. He would have respect or take action. Maybe both. If anyone had thought the bothersome incident would fade away, they knew better now, and a tense silence descended on the scene. It rippled outward until the concourse stilled into an expectant hush.

Boot scuffs against wood disturbed the tableau as a rotund soldier bumbled up to the scene. His tight-fitting guard uniform put him in charge of the concourse, but Landra suspected that his was a disciplinary posting.

The guard stopped short of the scene, rubbing his shaved scalp and staring through large eyes in disbelief. "Wha—"

Thisk raised his free hand to stop the man, never taking his stare from Dermot. "Hold there, guard. I'm handling this."

A defiant flash flickered in the three-bar soldier's mid-blue aura, but he kept it from reflecting in his ice blue eyes. Landra wondered if he would defy Thisk. An awesome power radiated from the Fourth, and true anger swirled in his aura, making its unformed edges reach out to Dermot in tongues of blue light. If the soldier chose to fight, she sensed Thisk's sword would fall in the name of justice. He had the strength to dispense punishment, and his rank gave him the right. She held her breath, waiting to see how the encounter would unfold.

Dermot straightened to a more respectful pose, and the raging glint from his aura grew to a seething swirl. He tightened his pose, but his stare looked through Thisk, as if focusing on something beyond.

"Soldier Dermot, Ranger Warrior Fourth, sir," he said.

The address drew some steam off Thisk's temper, but he held his formidable pose. "Guard, take him to the cells on charges."

Dermot's aura slowed to grinding circles, and he found the will to silence his complaint. It was a relief to Landra. Some holes were so deep that another dig in the bottom would see you fall right through. The errant soldier gave up his sword and knife to the waiting guard and went with him, not meekly but without a fight. Thisk swayed from side to side, swishing his sword. "Anyone else?"

The crowd scattered until only a few soldiers remained. Once the area was clear, he came back to himself and re-sheathed the sword on his hip.

"Are you all right?" he asked Landra on his return.

She took a deep breath and straightened to attention. "Yes, sir, Ranger Warrior Fourth Thisk."

He rolled his eyes in exasperation and put his hand on her shoulder to rejoin the queue.

"I wouldn't normally involve myself in local disputes,

but you were going to put yourself in danger," he said next to her ear. "There are two types of temple dwellers. Some choose to be here; others are soldiers given temple postings. Both are dangerous in their own ways, and you have to know which you're dealing with."

"I wanted to help."

"Don't think to do that again. Not for any reason. Being Fourth won't protect me from your father if you're hurt in my care."

Landra didn't know what to make of that. "No, sir, Ranger Warrior Fourth Thisk."

The grip on her shoulder squeezed tight enough to make her wince.

"Just so we're clear," he said.

A contingent of priests emerged from the temple door, rousing Landra to full awareness. After a short discussion and pointing fingers, they headed straight for Thisk. A tremor of apprehension from him rocked her back on her heels.

"Leave this to me," he ordered.

"Yes, sir."

Two times seven equals fourteen.

Chapter 14

A priest with a pink-tinged aura led the approaching group. Landra cast her gaze down, but the memory of his rose-tinted shading burned in her thoughts. It surrounded his tailored burgundy robes in a way she'd never seen.

"Those Templers look like trouble," she said.

"They might be a problem," Thisk agreed.

His acknowledgement flooded Landra with relief. "I understand the dynamics between soldiers and Templers now," she said. "What more can we learn from entering the temple?"

"Me, nothing. I've visited every year since graduating Warrior Hall. It keeps me grounded. As for you, there are things inside the building that are... You need to see them for yourself, Hux."

The priest flounced up with more of a gliding motion than a soldier's stride. His thick robes swished around his ankles in heavy pleats, and a draped hood exposed the temple "T" insignia etched into the short hair above his soldier mark.

Most priests generated blue auras, like soldiers

masquerading as Templers, but the strength radiating from this man's pink-edged Soul raised Landra's neck hairs. If anyone had the power to sense her taint, it would be him.

Two times… She couldn't focus on the simple sum, and her aura whirled around her, its chaotic pattern reflecting her thoughts. It wouldn't have surprised her to find the words "Magic-flawed Chief Elect" emblazoned across her forehead.

Why didn't I guess this would happen?

She wondered what Thisk would do if she was exposed. Would Baylem still talk to her, would Dannet still love her, and, shelk, what would Father say? She imagined Winton crowing over her fall from grace and demanding exile.

What a mess.

"Thisk?" she said, but the Warrior's attention couldn't be swayed from the Templer. Squeezing her breath tight and her fear tighter, she readied to run.

"Warrior Ranger Fourth," the priest said, halting in front of them. Several robed Templers settled at his back, exhibiting the harsh blue auras and bulky frames of soldier protection officers.

"You have me at a disadvantage," Thisk replied.

Landra didn't want to look at the priest, but his presence drew her gaze like a magnet. She stared at the leaf-bound staff clutched in his poised hand. It sat inside his aura, its foliage turning inward toward his power. Daring to look into his intense eyes, she found all of his concentration turned on Thisk.

Of course. I'm too insignificant, and the priest will voice his concerns to the Fourth.

The robed man bowed. "I'm Furlew, Temple Relations Officer. May I speak with you, Warrior Fourth?"

"Of course," Thisk said, his posture and tone carrying a softness that he'd never used toward Landra.

The queue edged forward, but Furlew leveled his staff to block their progress. "If I can just have a minute. I checked the roster several times but can't find any scheduled visits for today."

Thisk's aura flared with suppressed anger, but his outward display of calmness held. "I'm on private business. My niece just turned eighteen, and I've brought her here as a treat. I don't think anyone should wait until their third academy year to visit the temple."

His easy lie seemed to relax Furlew and the Templer gave a small nod, but his gaze settled on the Thisk's sword.

"As you must know, negotiations to secure Templer rights are at a sensitive stage. That's why it's important to notify us ahead of time for any visit, to avoid misunderstandings." A frozen smile split his face, displaying crooked teeth, which still gleamed white.

Whatever this was, Landra realized it had nothing to do with her magic. Still, she couldn't relax. A green tendril sprouted from Furlew's staff, growing in a winding pattern up to the bulbous tip. Buds formed, and a tiny red bloom opened in the growing foliage. Even Thisk had to see the blatant demonstration of outlawed magical power, but his posture remained relaxed.

"Politics pass me by,' Thisk said. "I'm much happier on ranger duty."

"But everyone knows about the treaty we're negotiating with Chief Hux."

"I've been out of the city, so I guess I'm behind on the news. Is there any chance we can make an exception for a social visit?"

"Hardly," Furlew said.

"We'll keep to the path and be in and out before you know."

Despite the cordial words, tension fed through Thisk's grip on Landra's shoulder and fury rippled through his aura. As close as she was, she couldn't avoid sharing his rage. It made her want to pull out the Collector and end this now. *Two times eight equals sixteen.*

Furlew's gaze casually flickered her way and then back to the Warrior. "I'm aware of your assistance on the concourse to protect our Templer son," Furlew said, "and I do appreciate the intervention, but I must insist on official protocols being observed. If you put in a request, I'm certain a visit can be arranged for next week."

"I'll be back in the wilds by then, and it could be several training cycles before I'm back," Thisk said.

The Templer raised a skeptical eyebrow, and Landra shared his doubts. From their auras, she sensed that neither Thisk nor Furlew were being honest, and there was a limit to how long this posturing could continue. The tension would end in a fight unless someone conceded, but she doubted that would be Thisk. The Warrior pushed against the Templer's staff until it buzzed with energy, forcing another dark bloom to open.

Furlew wobbled, and red flushed up his neck and into his large ears. His startled eyes spread wide on his face. "You can't break Templer rules," he said, his tone cracking. "The treaty was signed by Chief Hux."

"I'm a member of the ruling council," Thisk said, as if that gave him the right to break any rule he wanted.

"Imagine what would happen if a Templer broke Warrior rules," Furlew whined.

Landra didn't need to imagine. She'd seen a young Templer dragged away from Hux Hall just for entering ahead of his due appointment time. As far as she knew, he'd never been allowed back. She'd certainly never seen him again. *Probably podded.*

Thisk's spine stiffened with cold anger, but he spoke with the same faked polite tone. "As Fourth, I'm involved in making rules for the entire base, including the temple. It would be useful to remember that, Templer, just so we avoid misunderstandings."

"I…" Furlew stuttered.

"Now, take the energy out of your staff. I would hate to decide that you're threatening a council member."

"I'm sorry about the staff," Furlew said, his aura wavering. "It reacts to my mood, and life for Templers is unsafe right now. I hadn't meant to challenge you, Warrior Fourth."

It was a lie. A bold, straight-up lie. Landra recognized deceit in auras, and blue lightning streaks flashing through his pink shades in a pyrotechnic display of challenge told her all she needed to know. She wanted to warn Thisk, but all of his attention was on the Templer.

"I'm no threat to you either," the Warrior said, "although I will defend myself with force. And this slip of a girl doesn't have the strength to take down a first-year target, let alone a Templer. So, are you going to let us pass?"

His grip warned Landra against the protest that formed on her lips.

"A compromise," Furlew offered. "The girl could do the tour alone."

Thisk snorted. "I promised her father to keep an eye out. She's not the sense to avoid trouble, if you take my meaning. Probably best we stay together." Despite his reasonable tone, his weather-darkened fist tightened around his sword hilt, and Landra sensed that he'd beat the man bloody rather than back down. Either the temple trip was too important to miss or he refused to be controlled by Furlew.

The Templer's lips parted into a small snarl, and his eyes narrowed. Landra felt seconds last as if they were long minutes as she absorbed the tension.

Which math sum was I on? Two times... Shelk!

"I'm not saying you can't enter," Furlew said, with Thisk teetering on the verge of action, "but you should have an instruction from Chief Hux first."

"No time."

"Can you stay at the door and watch her?"

The Warrior's glare offered no concessions, and Furlew dithered.

"I... I suppose you could go as far as the walkway bottom."

A glorious smile split Thisk's beard. "What an excellent compromise."

As he was to be allowed inside the temple, Landra couldn't see how this was any sort of a compromise, but Furlew laughed awkwardly, feigning relief. He eased his staff aside, and the residual glow faded until it resembled a polished stick again. The flower buds at its tip folded closed.

The Templer turned his full attention to her for the first time and caught Landra with a heavy, knowing look. It pressed against her senses, and she firmed her aura's rim like never before, but the instinctive reaction didn't make her feel safe.

A second passed. Two, three... Five!

Sweating. Stop!

"Enjoy your visit." Furlew dropped into the silence. She caught her breath and met his gaze. There was no sign of fear, recognition of her magic, or respect in his stare. All three absences were a relief, and a noisy gasp escaped from her lungs. An incredulous laugh bubbled in her stomach, but she gave a respectful salute as anyone bearing a citizen rank insignia should. "Thank you, sir."

The Templer fumbled an appropriate response, and his attention skipped back to Thisk. "Your niece has a Hux look."

"She's the cousin of a cousin who slept with a Hux."

Landra was too shocked at the Warrior's lying skills to be able to protest.

Furlew gave a satisfied nod and turned to leave. He scurried back to the small door, all of his earlier grace gone. His guards followed, and Landra wondered what sort of a welcoming party they would arrange inside.

"Ready for your visit?" Thisk asked.

"If I must be," she answered, "but can we swap sides?"

He glanced down at her face.

"I like my shoulder bruises to be symmetrical," she explained.

He didn't let go.

Chapter 15

They made up the gap in the queue and found themselves near the door, with only a few soldiers ahead. The next time the door opened, a sliver of pink temple light escaped. Landra heard the sound of her own breathing and knew how hard her heart pumped.

"Don't be afraid," Thisk said.

She shot a glance toward him, incapable of voicing a lie.

"Trust me on this. You need this visit before everyone recognizes your face. After the promotion ceremony, you'll only be allowed inside on official business. They restrict your movements and pretty things up. It'll be good for you to see the temple as it is."

"I'm not scared. Just cautious. Templers don't exactly like my family."

"Cautious," he repeated, an amused melody in his deep voice.

Damn you to shelk, Thisk.

The Warrior seemed intent on doubting every notion

she held about herself. He considered her an indulged, reckless child, even when he called her a soldier. To top it off, he'd said she was "too nice" to command.

I'm going to prove you wrong.

The door opened again, and a baritone voice droned a welcome.

"Keep to the path, visit the plaque, and exit quickly."

"Sounds easy," she said.

The next time the door opened, she caught her first glimpse of the city's heart. The copse she'd seen from the overlevel had its roots here, but she hadn't expected the trees to grow within the inner temple. Pink light tinged the forest of silver trunks, but the leafy tops remained hidden from where she stood. A hint of music escaped with each opening. She strained to hear the wordless melody, but a jolt from Thisk startled her to alertness. She set new caution against the tune's hypnotic effect, her heart drumming in dissonant counterpoint.

They made it to the front of the queue and the great doors loomed close enough to reach with her hand. She ran a finger through the flower design and discovered the patterns weren't all carved etchings. Living tendrils wound through the grooves, and natural buds nestled in the image.

"No touching," the door guard said, and she snatched her hand away. "Don't worry. It happens a lot. The magic calls some people."

"Not this one," Thisk said, nodding to Landra with unshakeable confidence. "She's just trouble."

The door opened again and a three-bar soldier emerged. He stuttered mid-stride at the sight of the Warrior Fourth. Gathering his limbs together, he offered a salute. "Sir."

Thisk sent the startled soldier on his way with a head flick before urging Landra through the open door. *I've a Warrior's heart. I'm not nice, just efficient. I won't answer magical calls.*

The huge circular temple chamber opened up before her. From childhood gossip, she expected to see rows of praying Templers hovering in mid-air above a concourse-sized mat. More outlandish stories told of great beasts frozen in balls of magic light. Clearly, none of the story-tellers had visited the temple.

A forest of silver-trunked trees stretched into the distance, split by twining paths.

"This is where our ancestors arrived on the planet," Thisk whispered.

It was hard to imagine what it must have been like. The tranquil temple had its charm, but she'd expected the area to be more developed. Tipping her head back to view the treetops, she saw the sparse canopy against a pink translucent shield. Stars glimmered in the dark sky beyond, reminding her of what a long day this had been.

"An invisible barrier stops the wind getting in," Thisk said, as if answering the question he thought she would ask. He tugged her to move along a perimeter path, which had a wooden wall on one side. They reached the internal face of the great doors, and he released his grip.

"This is as far as I go."

"Might as well get this over with," Landra said, staring up a main path through the trees. "Do I go up there?"

Thisk's response waited until a Templer bustled by. "Yes, and make it quick. We're already pushing our luck."

"Are you sure it's safe?"

"As long as you follow the rules. Don't mess up, citizen, or we'll both be standing in front of your father tomorrow explaining how we incited a revolution. Is that what you want?"

She ignored the question. Setting her shoulders back, she stared up the ramp to a clearing ahead.

"Don't talk to anyone, don't leave the path, visit the platform, and come straight back," Thisk said, as if he were a parent leaving a child at the junior barracks for the first time.

"Yes, sir."

She was about to step out when another group of Templers approached, armed with fierce scowls and energy-laden staffs.

"No weapons!" a woman at the head of the group shouted, her stare drilling Thisk.

"Go," the Warrior said, shoving her away.

Landra stumbled a few steps up the path before glancing back. Thisk's Warrior frame overshadowed the Templer woman, but he held his hands open in submission. After a brief exchange, he unbuckled his sword and handed it over. The sideways glance he cast Landra's way held as much command as his barked orders ever had, so she turned from the confrontation to continue her journey, her knife nestled in its sheath on her back.

Her shoulders bunched at the sound of boots on the double-lacquered wood path.

Gods of the mist. What will they make of the Collector?

She didn't look back. Didn't dare. With churning bowels, she kept her stride steady and a soldier passed by on his way up the ramp. Landra's glance back proved the Templers were still focused on Thisk. Her citizen rank had never felt more useful. As the lowest army level, she wasn't lawfully permitted to carry a weapon and didn't warrant a search. It was luck. Nothing more.

Dratted weapon. When I get home, I'm going to dump you some-where safe so you can't cause trouble.

The path wasn't long, but it was busy. Templers and soldiers walked the route in both directions. Some wore business-like expressions, while others glowed with the serenity of pilgrims. Landra couldn't differentiate priests from soldiers by their auras—only their clothes.

"The three residential floors lining the walls are for Templer use only," a scratchy, voice said.

Landra turned toward the young man in light red robes. His instruction was clearly for general communica-tion rather than an order for her alone. He stood beside a third-year cadet group, and the eager trainees attended him like excited children.

"Don't enter perimeter area or use the spiral staircas-es," he continued.

The cadets' stares focused on the space between the trees, to where their guide pointed. Landra's gaze followed to the second tier, taking in the cave-like rooms with wooden doors, connecting walkways, and spiral staircases. Templers bustled about the high paths and shuffled through attractive arches, like insects running through a nest.

She recalled her view of the wood-knot above her bed and realized how much her world had grown in one day. Thisk had been right—again.

No one should have to wait until cadet age to see this.

The guided cadet group proceeded up the ramp, so she tagged along behind. No one spared her a thought or a glance, and the rod-like tension in her back eased. Here, she was another visiting soldier—a gawker coming to intrude on the Templers' world. She didn't feel welcome, but she didn't feel threatened like she'd thought she would.

Farther up the ramp, the floor beneath the path fell

away and barrier rails bordered the walkway to prevent accidents. She leaned over the rope and saw red glowing streams of thick fluid. They sucked hungrily at the tangle of exposed tree roots and oozed into the cracks between.

"By this point, our tree roots are completely submerged in the magical power well," the guide said. "All six cities draw energy from here through organic connections. The power runs through roots, tendrils, and the very substance of our wooden city. When your lights brighten every morning, you should thank us."

"Ooh!" a cadet exclaimed.

Landra scowled at the inaccuracy of the guide's script. *Can't you see the roots sticking out of the liquid?*

"The rivers are low now, but tonight's base-wide power-down will allow our magic to replenish, ready for the demands of tomorrow," the guide said, as if in answer.

A ring popped in the river, spitting out a pink puffball. The sphere rose up and passed by Landra's head, gleaming magically to her aura-sense and exuding a berry scent. It expanded to thinness and floated away from her reaching hand. Her unfocused gaze was still tracking where it had disappeared when the guide said, "Time to move on."

She'd been daydreaming—lost—and the instruction snapped her back to alertness. Her eyes refocused, and she glanced around. *The magic really is calling me. Shelk. Got to stop this.*

She followed the cadet party as they moved off, determined to avoid another slip. *Two times nine equals eighteen. Have to keep my attention in the soldier world.* The exercise tightened her aura, but her connection with the surrounding magic remained. It was strong here.

"We're nearing the platform, so you can see our world clock clearly now," the guide said. "If you look up into the trees, you'll see the cogs draped among the branches and hanging on ropes. Unlike other world clocks, this one has six faces, all correlating to our home planet's cycles. It tracks years, seasons, months, days, minutes, and the festival cycle. To this day, our power-up and power-down cycles are based on the day facet, and one and a half of our sixty-day training cycles corresponds to a season. The festivals facet shows six separate events each year and is currently ticking down toward the gathering feast. We still observe the celebration here on base, but it is believed that the event was a time of harvest back on Jethra."

Landra had wanted to remain indifferent, but she couldn't contain her interest any longer. Thisk hadn't claimed to be a tutor, but now the wisdom of Chief Hux's choice became clear. The ranger Warrior was bold and unfettered, allowing him to show her things that Winton would never dare. She looked between the visitors and spotted the Warrior's unmoving form, standing to rigid attention with his arms folded over his broad chest. *On guard.* His solid presence filled her with confidence, and she turned to the platform, ready to face her duty. It was time to see what all this fuss was about.

The cadet group paused again, so she skirted past them and moved up to the platform's threshold to wait her turn. Ahead, a pink-robed youth with outrageously long brown hair and a milky aura, walked forward. He nodded a curt bow before the plaque and turned back to retrace his steps.

That's it? Really? How disappointing is that?

She'd expected to be exposed as flawed on her trip here, vilified by Warrior-kind, stripped of her promotion, and dumped onto an exile train. The visit to the temple's heart had been the center of her worry. Only now could she admit how deep the fear had wormed through her being. It had stiffened her joints and stifled her senses. She breathed out her anxiety and placed a boot on the platform.

An earthy smell of organic life assailed her senses and lightened her head.

Two huge trees trunks, with studded decorations, rose like guards at each side of the platform. She craned her neck to view the profuse foliage at the top. The branches arced in, twining the two living structures into an arch. "Power" was etched into one trunk and "Soul" into the other.

They're just trees. Landra repeated the mantra in her head, but they imbued the area with a sacred quality. The air hung in her throat, feeling too thick to breathe. Whispering met her ears, but when she turned to the sound, it disappeared. She thought of how the Templer had stepped up to the plaque and wondered why this felt so difficult.

Is it because of my magic or due to a lack of it? The struggle made her feel like a fraud. She was no temple worshipper come to pay her respects. She was a chief elect, come to scout her enemy so she could lead them.

The plaque was only a dozen strides away, but her approach proved difficult, with each step deadening her legs more. She spared a glance toward a seated guard, wondering if he was watching her labored progress. She needn't have worried.

He was less of a guard than any Templer, despite him wearing an old-style soldier uniform. Wrinkles grooved his skin, and bulbous swellings around his knuckles spoke of infirmity. His wizened body drooped, as if with great age, but his aura! She stared at the kaleidoscope of glorious crimson and azure hues, her leaden legs preparing to run. The blue rode rich and deep with the red swirls rippling over its surface like reflections on water. She'd never seen an aura so intense or bulky. He was obviously an experienced Templer, so his soldier's outfit made no sense.

His eyes were closed as if he slept, but the scared part of Landra wondered if he'd died. *Coward*. She cast the notion aside. Silent, so as not to wake him, she took her place before the plaque to read the message.

Her gaze fell on one word: Hux.

Chapter 16

It took Landra several minutes to absorb the full message on the inscription.

<u>By Eternal Law</u>
This temple and its people shall remain under Warrior
protection and be preserved for all time

May the Soul who lights the arch lead our people
By order of Chief Warrior, Gallanto Hux
On this day, the first anniversary of exile

Landra read it twice and then a third time. Was this what Thisk had wanted her to see? Of all her expectations, a message from her ancestor had never been a consideration. She'd imagined the plaque would bear a Templer platitude or a Soul Magic spell. It had never crossed her mind that she would read the words of a Warrior.

The message affected her on so many levels she couldn't begin to process her emotions. She ran a finger over Gallanto's name, wondering what her great-grandfather had intended. Surely, he couldn't have guessed how Templers would disrupt society; he would have never written the instruction into Eternal Law if he'd known. Why make any decree that could never be overturned? It didn't make sense.

Landra's notions about disbanding the temple were worthless now. She'd planned to develop an alternative power source and outlaw magic so the conflict could end. No wonder priests allowed soldiers onto their territory. The message secured their future more certainly than if they had the power to overthrow Warrior rule. Some of her father's questionable orders made more sense now.

She closed her eyes and set her palm to the plaque, trying to divine Gallanto's purpose. In her mind's eye, he was larger and broader than Father, like a mythical hero of old. He was as much a Warrior as she'd ever seen, so why had he given this order?

A tickle on her senses snapped her thoughts to the present, and she opened her eyes. The old soldier stood behind the plaque, a few strides away. He wore the aura of a Templer, despite his uniform, and he definitely wasn't dead.

Her hand flew from the plaque, as if she'd been caught in a guilty act. He didn't look dangerous, with his gnarled hand leaning too heavily on a stick and his stooped frame looking ready to crumble. One blow of breath would topple him. Yet his presence unnerved her.

She looked for his rank, but his long wisps of sprouting white hair weren't abundant enough to sport an insignia. He lacked the tattoo bald soldiers favored, and his collar badge was missing, making him the first rankless soldier she'd met.

"I'm sorry," she said. "I didn't see you there."

He peered sightlessly from cloudy grey eyes, but she

could have sworn that he'd singled her out from the other visitors. A chuckle shook his shoulders, ending in a coughing fit that sprayed spit across the plaque. As his shuddering eased, he turned his sightless gaze on Landra.

"I saw you," he said. "I see you!"

Landra's mouth flapped wordlessly as she tried to form a response. Confusion had obviously taken the poor soldier, but his ominous greeting sent echoes of fear through her body and a shout from behind made her jump.

"You moving or what?" a cadet said. "We all need to see the message, or what's the point of being here?"

The interruption gave her a wonderful excuse to escape, and she couldn't do it soon enough. Protocol made her stand to attention. "Good day, soldier," she said, fully intending to back away and run back down the ramp at a disrespectful speed.

"I've not seen a good day in these many years," he answered. "Do an old veteran a favor and see me back to my seat before you go, dear. I'm not as steady as I used to be, and I've tumbled once today already. This old body's just about done, seems to me."

Landra froze like an animal stuck in magic-light. *Shelk to the mist and back. Why did I speak instead of escaping?* Now she felt required to assist the man, and his claim to veteran status made her doubly obligated. She weighed that with Thisk's order to keep to the track, view the plaque, and come straight back. It didn't allow for deviations, and she was certain his instruction meant no conversations either, but she'd already broken that rule.

Rounding the plaque, she approached the veteran, but she paused at the limit of his aura rather than breach its boundary. His head wobbled in a knowing nod. Up close, the old training scars ridging his paper-thin skin were obvious, documenting a life of soldiering, at odds with his blazing aura.

"Two-bar soldier Oakham," he introduced himself.

"Citizen Landra," she offered, conscious of the furor her Hux name would cause in the temple.

Oakham lifted his free elbow in a request for help, and she moved into his space to support his arm. His aura shrank from the contact, pinching tight to his body and making the color deepen. She tightened her own aura, and the two-colored shapes buffeted against each other like swords on stone.

The old man weighed nothing on her arm and a stoop made his head dip to her shoulder, but she suspected he'd been taller in his youth.

"What are you doing here, soldier?" she asked, relaxing into her task. "A veteran like you deserves to be home, resting in the barracks."

"Home," he said, the full, round utterance conjuring an impression of contentment. Then, his entire body shuddered. "I can't go home. Anyway, my place is here, on guard duty."

"Guard duty? You mean someone assigned you this job?" She paused in her stride and looked into Oakham's glazed eyes. They disappeared into the sockets of his wizened face, and she bridled at the inexcusable misuse of the veteran. "Who gave you this duty?" she asked, meaning to report the brute to Father.

"Chief Hux, of course."

"No! That can't be true. You're confused, old man. Chief Hux doesn't abuse old soldiers."

"Oh yes, it's true. Gallanto stood right where you are and assigned me sentry duty. I remember the moment like it was yesterday. Then everything changed, and life turned to shelk."

Landra wondered if he believed what he was saying. The sooner he settled into the medical barracks, the better. She wanted to guide him down the ramp, but he looked unlikely to make it to the bottom, so she encouraged him back to the chair, thinking to bring help.

"I don't think that's possible," she said in her gentlest voice. "Gallanto died nearly fifty years ago."

"Ah!"

Oakham stooped lower and rubbed the back of his neck as if it hurt. "Is it really that long? My memory tricks me sometimes, but I still recall older times. Not that I want to. It was a sad day when my chief died, and I try to forget. The coughing illness took him. No one thought it could fell a man built like a barrel tree, but he went in less than a cycle. I think he missed Meftah too much to muster any fight."

Landra waited patiently at Oakham's side, hiding the storm of emotions raging in her Soul. *Could you have really worked for my great-grandfather?* She tried to work the numbers back, and it did seem possible.

Oakham turned his blind gaze on her again, saying, "You have his eyes and his Soul. I'd have known you were his, even if it were a hundred years from now and a million miles away."

Her grip tightened on the old man's arm, and her mouth dried. He had to be guessing. His milky eyes were too dull to take in her likeness, so she couldn't think how he'd made the jump to her identity. More than ever, she wanted to get him back to his seat so she could leave.

She contained her anxiety during the final slow steps to the chair. Turning him slowly, she supported his elbow and eased him down. As she let go of his arm, he toppled sideways, and it seemed like there would be no escape. *Too nice.* She reached to catch him. *Damn Thisk to shelk.*

Oakham rested his head on the great tree trunk and set his flat palm on the silver bark. His eyes were closed, and he took on the grey look of a man who may never wake up, yet his aura churned with life.

A faint groan rumbled in his throat. He coughed and then spoke without opening his eyes, as if drawing words from far away. "Guard duty was easier when Gallanto first gave the order. There were five of us then, so we could take it in shifts. Ballam, Clipper, and... shelk. Darndest thing, not being able to remember my friends' names. They died over the years till I was the only one left. I pledged to do this duty for Chief Hux, so I had to stay. I'm the last sentry."

Too many details rang true in his fairy tale. Landra knew she shouldn't stay to listen to his ramblings. It was dangerous and Thisk would be furious, but there was something compelling about hearing stories of her great-grandfather. If Oakham had really worked for Gallanto, he could share family details not known elsewhere. It was too great an opportunity to miss. She kneeled at his side, cautioning herself to expect disappointment. His memory was patchy and possibly untrue.

"You had a team of soldiers to protect the plaque?" she prompted.

"Not the plaque, dear. No, no. Not the plaque. That came later. Our team was here to guard the portal. Of course, we needn't have bothered. After exile, no one left on base had enough magic to work the darned thing. We didn't have to worry about escapees, and them shelking buggers on the home planet weren't about to come back to rescue anyone. We always hoped, of course. All of us had relatives on Jethra, and we thought, for sure, one of 'em would change their minds and come back. I think that's what broke us, knowing our families wanted us stranded here."

Oakham's tale offered a personal view of Warrior exiling that Landra had never found in textbooks. She felt his anger and sense of betrayal through his aura, and fury churned her gut. *Two times ten equals twenty.* The exercise helped her relax. She couldn't begrudge her people's heavy editing of history texts. If everyone shared this outrage, there would be no way to keep the peace.

"The chief scaled down the temples when he realized they weren't coming back," Oakham continued.

"Why keep them open at all?" she asked. "Was it to keep the power running?"

"Not really. The Templers stocked the well with enough magic to run the base for generations."

"So, why protect the temples with Eternal Law."

"Ah, bless him. Gallanto never gave up hope of opening the portal and going home."

"It still works?"

"Who knows?" the old man said "We've never mustered enough magic between us to find out. Never will now."

He shook his head, as if to break free of painful memories. "Anyway, enough of old-world nonsense. It's all in the past. What goes on in our cities?" He still hadn't opened his eyes, and his skin remained grey. A rattling noise accompanied each of his breaths.

Landra didn't know which of his tales to believe and became lost in wondering. The soldier broke her daydream by setting a hand on her shoulder. It wasn't Thisk's controlling grip but the tender touch of an elderly relative. His eyes opened, and his milky gaze turned on her, asking the question again. "How's my city?"

"Oh!" she sighed. "You know. Same as usual. Warriors

fear Templers; Templers resent Warriors. It never gets better."

Sadness wrinkled more lines into Oakham's face. "I'm sorry to hear that. It wasn't so black and white in my day, or I should say red and blue. Time was we were one people." His head drooped forward, and she thought he'd fallen asleep. "I always thought I'd go home," he said, raising his head as if it carried an unbearable weight. Tears tracked down his cheeks.

"I can take you home. Which barracks are you in?"

His face creased with enough pity to bring a flush of embarrassment to Landra's cheeks.

"I wasn't born on base, dear. My home is on Jethra, running through long grass on sunny days, skinny-dipping in the light pool, and growing elba trees for Mother." His shoulders heaved, and a twisted sob added more tears to his face. "She's dead now, of course, and I never said good-bye. Not properly. Not the way I would have if I'd known."

Landra gasped. Considering Oakham's age, it was obvious he'd lived when travel between the base and Jethra was still possible. Until now, homeworld tales had held almost mythical status in her mind. She stayed silent to allow him to recover.

"It's home to all of us and we should be there, but if those of us left can't work together, there's no hope of survival. Thank the mist, I've not long for this world. Seeing the end would tear me apart. I've held this line for so long and..." His words dwindled away. The old man sounded more bewildered with each revelation, yet his story came alive with more sense at the telling.

"You make it sound hopeless," Landra said, irritated at his dismissal of base life. This was the world she knew and had been chosen to lead. "We've survived exile for seventy years. There's no reason why that shouldn't continue."

"I see youthful hope in your face," he said, a futile note creeping into his words. It sounded condescending.

"What do you know, old man? There's more than a decade's cloud over your eyes, so stop talking as if you can see."

Oakham's jaw sagged open as if words would fall out, but he hesitated.

"I see," he said. "But not with my eyes."

Chapter 17

Landra had always worried she'd meet someone else with aura sight. Her nerves jangled as she assessed the implications of Oakham's words. *Can you see my magic, old man? Will you give me away?*

"I need to show you something," he said.

Digging his walking stick into a flooring panel, he levered himself up and tottered around the tree. *Tap, tap.* The stick echoed as it hit the floor. "Coming?"

Thisk was a hard man to read, but it didn't take an academy education to know he would expect obedience. She should head back now, but leaving Oakham felt dangerous. He knew too much.

She touched the Collector at her back, more aware than ever of the responsibility it carried. Her duty was to Chief Hux and the people, not Thisk. She couldn't allow the old soldier to jeopardize her position. It was unlikely anyone would believe his ramblings, but she had to be sure.

She followed him around the tree, thinking to convince him to silence. *Failing that...* Landra didn't know what she would do if her plan failed. A quick glance back showed a cadet had given up on her leaving the platform and was viewing the plaque. Pilgrims blocked her view of Thisk, and she decided that was for the best.

"Where are we going?" she asked.

Oakham smiled and linked elbows for support. "Into the pit." He cocked his head toward the platform's edge, pushed a barrier aside with his stick, and led her down a narrow path. It spiraled around a tree trunk in a downward slope, so she gripped him tight in case he fell.

"Soldier Oakham?" she said, not quite sure how to broach her concerns.

"Save your questions, dear."

Teeth grinding, she kept walking. She couldn't interrogate the man here or order him to silence. *Humor him. Gain his support.* As they descended, the *tap, tap* of his stick sounded louder than the fading music.

"One of my jobs is to check the reservoir levels," he said. "I've not made it down for years, so it'll be good to perform my duty one last time. I think Chief Hux would be proud."

She knew he wasn't referring to Father. Gallanto was his chief. It didn't seem like checking the level should take long, so she didn't argue. At the first bend, Oakham rested heavily on her arm and pointed his stick to a dark line on the tree trunk.

"The magic reached here when I was a boy. Stinging stuff, that shelking gunk. You had to watch yer ankles or it'd bubble right over the platform and splash yer boots."

His stick touched the scummy red line unerringly. Above the mark, the tree bark gleamed silver, but pitted discoloration scarred the area below. Landra thought it a wonder the trees survived. She stared in silence, her curiosity starting to ride rough shod over sense. She had to admit she wanted to hear Oakham's tale.

With a shake of his shoulders to bring him back to the present, the old man continued down the slope with his stick sounding *tap, tap.*

"I'd seen twenty summers the first time I left Jethra," he said. "Second-year cadets weren't usually allowed to visit the base, but I came over as the chief's runner."

"You were a soldier in the academy?"

"Do you doubt it?"

Oakham's red-stained aura and unnatural sight suited Templer life more, but Landra wouldn't admit her reservations. "So, you came as a runner," she said.

"Yep! Truth to tell, I was happy to escape the war back home."

His aura swirled, fitting tight to his body where their arms linked and melding around Landra's aura in other places. She couldn't tell whether it was an accident or something he controlled.

"War?" she asked. "I never heard about a war."

"Lots happened that's been forgotten or locked away. Like how Warriors were exiled for their sins."

Without planning to, Landra stuttered to a halt. If any characteristic defined Warrior-kind, it was honor. "The history books don't talk of sins," she said, not sure whether Oakham had drifted into fantasy again.

"And they won't. Not many books survived the Year Four purge, and what we have now was written by Warriors. But that's me being bitter. Truth to tell, I don't think anyone did sin."

"What are you rambling about, old man?"

"It was a difference of opinion, that's all. The Sevion race invaded our lands back home on Jethra. Warriors wanted to fight. Templers had other ideas and brokered a peace deal. Our enemies insisted on exile as part of the treaty." He took a big breath. "I think I'm ready to walk a bit more now." *Tap, tap.* His stick echoed as they rounded another bend.

Landra was torn between wanting to believe Oakham's story and fearing his version of the truth. The talk of a peace treaty resonated too closely with her present. "What was Jethra like?"

"Big. Warm. Colorful."

He stopped to point at another scummy line. "Can you read the number, dear?" Even my aura sight is failing now."

She couldn't believe how easily he admitted his magic. Rather than make an issue of his admission, she examined the tree trunk. Her keen eyes picked out the flowing script drawn onto the bark. "Seventeen, I think. It's a bit blurry."

"Sounds about right. This was the reservoir level last time I came down." He thumped his stick on the path. "Best see how far it's dropped."

Landra peered down, wondering how far there was to go. Scarred and rotting tree roots wound around them as they descended. Cloying hot air hugged Landra's skin, and a foul stench of decay reached the back of her throat and nose. Every breath sucked in hot foulness. She tried licking the taste away, but bitterness clung to her tongue.

"When I was young, children were trained in both temple doings and soldier craft," Oakham said. "Didn't matter their inclination. Take me. Was born with an aura blue as they come, my mamma said. Years of schooling and I took up some understanding of Soul magic. Even developed the sight. Not a common thing to have Soul sight, even amongst Templers of the old days."

Trying to calm her racing heart, Landra matched Oakham's slow pace, forced her breaths into long even sighs, and mentally ordered her stomach to silence. She'd never imagined a soldier would expose her secret, let alone kind, frail Oakham. He voiced his magic so openly she didn't see how to convince him to keep her secret. *It's not possible.* Sweat broke on her skin, and a traitorous thought urged her to leave him down here. *No one will find him until it's too late. Can't. Won't. Too nice?*

The oozing reservoir lapped against the spiral path a short way down from their position. Oakham tugged her toward the well's edge, and a sweet berry-fruit smell wafted up from the liquid, masking the rotting tree odor. He halted, still tapping his stick in an ominous rhythm. *Tap, tap. Tap. Tap, tap.*

Landra watched rivulets of red gunk lick hungrily at tree roots, the level swelling and ebbing to reveal a number zero on the trunk at each low tide. She didn't know what to do.

"The magic's nearly gone," Oakham said.

"The Templer guide said it fills during power-down."

Oakham tilted his blind gaze to her face, sorrow creasing his skin folds into deeper grooves. "No, it won't," he said. "We've no true Templers left to fill the well. It gets lower every day, and once it's gone, we're done.

Chapter 18

Landra wondered at Oakham writing off her world. True, there'd been power shortages. Everyone had thought it was Templer trouble. Now, she wasn't so sure. If the power ran out completely... *No heat, no light, no food. Shelk!*

She'd experienced the harsh reality of the overlevel, and that was in a warmer season. Surviving the winter cold was beyond imagination. It was hard to know what to worry about most. *How long do the engineers have to develop another power source—a day, a cycle, maybe a year?* A rebuke from Thisk seemed the least of her worries, and the job Father had set on her shoulders weighed heavily enough to make her groan.

Averting her gaze from the demonic scene, she stared into Oakham's blind eyes and his milky gaze settled on her unerringly.

"Is this what you wanted to show me?" she asked.

He sighed, a world of weariness stooping his bony shoulders. "No." He set a hand to the skin on her neck. "I wanted to show you this."

Landra's world shifted. An unworldly sensation plucked

her senses out of true, and her stomach flipped. Her vision fogged into a blur of color, and unintelligible chattering noises buzzed in her ears. She could swear she felt the smooth knob of Oakham's stick in her hand, but when she leaned, there was nothing there and her knees buckled. In a snatched moment of clarity, a host of soldiers and Templers appeared from nowhere, bustling about their duties as if nothing were wrong.

"What's happening?" she said, turning her head to bring the vision into focus. The soldiers disappeared into tree trunks, and babbling sounds formed unintelligible words near her ear. The magic berry smell hung in her nostrils stronger than ever, and vomit pooled in her throat.

"No!" she raged, hugging her belly. *This is magic.* Why would harmless, old Oakham do this? She couldn't see or feel him, but she knew he was there, orchestrating her discomfort. She flailed her arms, but the magical prison didn't respond to her physical defense. Without warning, the image froze and then fractured apart in a confusing kaleidoscope pattern that matched Oakham's aura.

Gasping, she sensed the sweat-drenching heat again, the heaving magical pool a few steps away, and the wooden planks beneath her knees. Spasms shook her body, and holding onto the foul-tasting sick in her throat became impossible. She deposited digested glider meat onto the path.

Landra wanted to fulfil Father's expectations and make him proud, yet here she was in the enemy's stronghold, vomit-ridden, sapped of strength, and uncovered as flawed. A sense of inadequacy plagued her, but she set a firm portion of blame on Thisk's shoulders. He was supposed to be her tutor, not put her in danger. *No, not Thisk's fault. Mine. Why didn't I follow orders?*

"You're fine, dear." Oakham's words came to her ears.

"Fine!" she spat with steel-hardened rage. "What did you do, old man?"

"I shared a memory, that's all. Just takes a bit of getting used to. But you saw, didn't you?"

"Saw what?"

Oakham gasped in a rattling breath. "You don't have to say. You've come too late, anyway. I don't think I've the strength to pass along the memory now. I had hoped to show someone the truth before I went, but my innards are failing."

Landra hauled herself up and glared fury at his blind eyes. Drawing the Collector, she waved it toward him. "Stay away, old man."

Her rage should have driven fear through him, but a triumphant grin spread over his face. His chin wobbled up to show tears on his cheeks. "My chief elect," he said, lifting his feeble arm in salute. "Forgive me not taking a knee, but I'd tumble into the well for sure."

Landra was more embarrassed than she could explain. "No."

"No? You're not the elect? But I've seen that knife before, in Chief Elect Sonra's hand."

"Maybe I am, but don't salute. The appointment hasn't been announced, so I'm no one. I'm a citizen rank and at the bottom of the command chain."

"But you carry the Collector, so the succession's set."

"I suppose so."

"And you saw," he repeated, with an edge of certain knowledge rather than a guess. "I could tell you have the sight from your aura. Its staining reminded me of the auras of old, but I'd given up on seeing another after all this time. Templer Denman told Gallanto there'd be another, but I never thought it would happen. And I never thought it'd be one of the Hux line with a gifted Soul."

"What are you babbling about, old man?"

"Soul memories form in our essences, as a way of storing true history. They used to happen all the time back in my day."

"Well, they don't happen now," Landra spat. "How will imposing your confused rememberings on me help anyone?"

The anger in her voice made Oakham's sunken face twitch. "My old brain plays tricks, but this isn't the same. Soul memories come from an unbreakable place. I've more than a dozen burned into my thoughts, and they've kept me going all these past years, like acts of a play. They stay true when other memories wander."

"Well, you can keep them to yourself."

"You're angry. Didn't your Soul trainer teach you this?"

Landra shook her head in fierce denial. "I never met a Soul trainer, and I never will."

The old soldier's face creased in confusion. "Never had a Soul trainer? By the mist gods of Jethra. The magic must run something powerful through your veins for the sight to come unlooked for."

"I have no magic. I'm a soldier," Landra replied, offense coursing through her entire being. "One day, I'll travel the six cities as a Warrior."

"Gallanto's Warrior pride too." A wry smile touched Oakham's lips. "I don't mean to offend, Chief Elect, and I have no worries over your Soul. It burns with as strong a Warrior blue as my chief's ever did."

"So, why are you doing this?"

"Because of Gallanto. He'd want this—told me to do it. The effort will likely kill me and I've not the strength to succeed, but I'd always hoped to die doing my duty.

Landra swayed, considering his words. Part of her

respected the Warrior honor in his plan. Another part of her longed for the relief his death would bring. She wouldn't have to worry about him spilling tales of her flaw and all the trouble his rantings would bring. *It's mean. It's necessary.* "I'll do it," she said. *May the mist forgive me.*

"Thank you, my dear," Oakham said, his tears flowing freely now. "Help me down to the path, would you?"

Easing him to the floor, Landra cradled his back against her chest. "What do we do?"

"Relax."

She had no intention of relaxing and clutched the Collector tight, planning to use it at the first sign of trouble. Instead of touching her neck, Oakham set his hand over her grip on the knife, and her mistake became clear. A connection beyond her experience formed, rocking her to the core. She couldn't move. Couldn't cry. Oakham's power well wrapped her aura with none of the frailty of the old man's body. His thoughts sunk into her as if they were part of her Soul. Another presence called, and she froze in mind and body.

Pink mist arose from the magic well, and more clumps churned beneath the path's underside. The threads floated together, spinning into a ball around Landra's blade. She stared as her knife's color deepened and a magic buzz ran through the handle. She couldn't move—couldn't fight. Sweat trickled down her neck, and her fingers trembled as she gathered her strength to break free.

"Take the memory," a voice sounded in her head.

The tones rumbled deep in her Soul, giving her no place to hide. "I won't," she said. "I can't."

"You can," the voice answered. "Save our people, child of my life. This is an order from your chief."

Chapter 19

Not Father! Not Chief Hux! Oakham trembled in her grip.

"Gallanto," the old soldier cried, making her wonder if everyone had gone on a scute-induced dream with her at the center. The depths of her Soul feared the truth. She'd felt the words more than heard them, and they were definitely Hux. *But Gallanto? My great-grandfather? That's ridiculous —stupid.* The tones had rung with Father's timbres, but this didn't make sense. Could it really be that Chief Gallanto had returned from the dead to give her a message? The hysterical part of her wondered where a ghost chief ranked in the chain of command.

The scene Oakham had used to bombard her senses wouldn't leave her thoughts. An all-encompassing ruby glow had bathed her aura, like magic afire. There'd been noise, shouting, and commotion. And a smell. Oh, that smell, like the stench down here but masked by stronger berry scents.

She wanted nothing to do with the magical vision, and distaste for Soul power entwined through her being at every level. She hated her people's reliance on its energy and how it had ambushed her life. Her silence wasn't lost on Oakham, and he sagged more in her grip.

"You don't know the trouble you've caused, old man," she said. "You just don't understand."

"I'm the last sentry. Both our past and future die with me. What more trouble can there be?"

Landra hugged him against her chest, not wanting his magical memories, but if there was a chance…

A chance of what? Shelk! How can it be my job to save our people?

The answer came with unforgiving brutality. She was the chief elect, and this was her duty. Father would agree with her purpose, she was certain, but he would never understand what she planned to do next. It didn't seem like an order from his dead grandfather would fly as an excuse.

Oakham wrapped his claw-like fingers about the Collector's handle, above her grip, and a mental connection formed. Landra didn't welcome the joining, but she didn't fight it either.

"It's a Soul memory, burned in with magic," Gallanto's voice said.

Landra closed her eyes, held her breath, and prayed to the mist. Not knowing where it would lead, she gripped Oakham tight, but she relaxed her hold on her magic. "Show me your visions, old man."

Oakham's aura melded with her blue shades, and all worldly sensations disappeared. The pain from where her knees had met the path eased, the slushy gurgling of the reservoir and the faint music from above silenced, and her vision filled with an amorphous fog. Only the berry smell stayed strong, dominating her senses to the point of nausea. Her chest released its captured breath without a sound, and she felt dull, as if trapped in a magical bubble.

"Remember, this is Oakham's memory," Gallanto said.

"You will experience events as him, sharing his thoughts and feelings. Stay in that reality."

She slid into the Soul vision as easily as entering a dream. The images formed, and Landra remembered herself as Landra in a corner of her mind, but now she was a young cadet, fit and male. She was Oakham.

Staring from the platform's edge, Oakham felt his twenty straight hours of portal duty as pain down his legs and stiffness in his back, but he couldn't miss this. Chief Gallanto needed him, so he focused on the soothing air on his skin. The arching elba trees flourished in full glory today, with their shining trunks rising to the fulsome leaf canopy. Nothing looked more wonderous than the active portal, and it felt special to be the only cadet here amongst the senior staff. The world clock…

A seventy-year-old date and spring festival reading on the clock face jangled awkwardly on Landra's senses, making her separate from the events.

"Be Oakham," Gallanto insisted, and the memory slid back into motion. *"Prepare for the next group," Chief Gallanto ordered from the platform's center, his battle-spiked uniform and flowing cloak making him look huge. His near-black silhouette stood out against the red swell of bubbling magic lapping over the platform's edge. His glorious Warrior blue aura blazed as bright as any Templer's magic glow, and his generous Soul billowed around him with streaks of deep pink patterning the rich azure hues.*

A dozen priests took their positions by tree trunks, looking more tired than Oakham felt. Their auras spread wide, encompassing their trees to lend power to the portal mechanism. With closed eyes, sweet-voiced singing, and foliage flourishing around their tall staffs, their magic bloomed with power in their swelling red auras.

Oakham's pride surged to be Gallanto's runner, and he jumped to his tasks. Clipboard in hand, he checked off the preparations. He put a tick on his sheet in the Templer box and then ran down the main ramp to the greeting party.

"Good day, Warriors," he said, offering a smart salute.

"Get on with it," Security Chief Brixon said, her face locked into an angry mask.

"Yes, ma'am." Oakham checked his list, hoping to find the relevant assignments quickly. Everyone on base was on edge, and he suspected the more aura-gifted Warriors had sensed imminent misfortune. Anxiety coursed through the base like an infecting illness, so he couldn't get this wrong.

"Medic Kelsen," he said, "there's a soldier in the next group with a medical condition. Is everything prepared?"

"I received details in advance, and we're all set, cadet. Though why they'd assign a sick Warrior to base training is beyond me."

Oakham knew the reason but couldn't say anything. He glanced up at the security detail. One, two, three, four, five, six, he mentally counted off.

"Chief Brixon, my list says we're due a double security detail for this arrival, ma'am."

"Gods of the mist, why, boy?"

"Don't know, ma'am. I just do the list."

"They're on their way, but don't you realize I had to pull them down from protecting an overlevel team? How can greeting our own soldiers need more security than that?"

"I–"

"Yeah," Brixon said. "You don't know. You just do the list."

Oakham felt the fearsome woman's simmering anger and didn't know what to say. Brixon brushed him away with a dismissive wave. A tick didn't go in that box, but Oakham didn't care. He was just a runner, after all.

"Are the billets sorted?" he asked the community officer. Holden was a small, efficient man who never got caught out. With thousands of soldiers to transport, house, and feed, he couldn't afford mistakes.

"All set, cadet. This lot's being shifted out to Fourth City, and the pod-train is waiting. I had a problem setting up credit accounts for *them, but the tally man is on it and assures me funds will be in place by the time they arrive."*

Oakham marked the box and then scribbled "CREDITS?" to one side. At that moment, the remaining security detail arrived, and he marked them present.

"With respect, officers, please can you stand aside on the small path?" Oakham asked. "We've a big supply delivery coming in this trip, so the great doors are going to open."

As if on cue, the large doors cracked apart. A single priest pushed them outward with one hand, using his magical power to move their weight. The foliage from his lofted staff twined with the door vines and throbbed with energy.

Oakham jogged back up the ramp to where Chief Hux stood. Gallanto had joined his wife and was in deep discussion. Even while engrossed, the chief noted his runner's arrival and nodded for him to wait.

The lull in activity allowed Landra to examine how strange this all felt. The dual sharing was confusing. Her identity sat tucked away in a corner of her mind, and she had no control of her interactions or emotions. They were set in a replay of actual events and couldn't change. The pause didn't last long.

"Meftah," the chief said to his wife, "does it really have to be like this?"

Chief Gallanto's wife glowed with Templer magic, her scarlet aura outshining the russet and jade shades of her gown. To a young boy's eyes, she was spectacular. Her flowing dress of living flowers wasn't meant to hide her fulsome figure, the heavy curve of her breasts, or the shapely length of her thighs. Nearly as tall as Gallanto and with the shoulders of a championship Warrior, she was every cadet's fantasy. Her close-shaved head only showed the sweet roundness of her face, and her eyes sparkled a brilliant green. All-knowing wisdom swam in their depths. The flowers of her dress wound down her arm to wrap seamlessly around the thick shaft of her staff, and a berry-magic scent wafted off her like an intoxicating perfume.

Hot, lustful urges coursed through…

Oakham's crush on Meftah matched Landra's own intense longing for Bexter enough to throw her from the memory, and the vision pixilated.

"Stay with me," Oakham said through their connection. "I'd rather not share this, but picking a memory apart is impossible. You need to see the rest."

Landra hadn't realized the Oakham of her time was here too. Now she sensed him, lurking in his own mind as she did in hers. The intrusion was shocking, and she wasn't enjoying the magical sharing, but there seemed little point in stopping now. She accepted the young man's lust as part of the memory, and the image reformed.

"Don't you think I've looked for another way?" Meftah said, touching Gallanto's arm with more tenderness than Oakham had ever seen. Tears shone in her green eyes.

"Don't do this now," Gallanto said, turning her from view and brushing the moisture from her cheek. "If this is the only way we can secure peace, we must stay strong for our people. We can't show our pain."

Meftah bit her lip and gave a hint of a nod. "This isn't good for either of us," she said. "I don't want to go back to Jethra without you."

"Then don't," Gallanto said. "Stay here."

"And who will fight to bring you home? Chief Templer Albys will close the portal for good if he gets his way, and that scene you caused at the council vote didn't help. He holds you responsible for starting the war with the Sevions.

"Those dratted leeches invaded! Was I supposed to stand by and let them take our lands? Look how many of our people they killed."

Meftah laid her flat palm against Gallanto's cheek. "No, Gall, you did what you had to do, but Albys thinks we should have negotiated sooner. The killing didn't start until our army confronted them."

"Until I confronted them! Do you agree with Albys? Can't you see the Sevions are sharp swords in feather sheaths? They sweet-talk the temple council, but given a chance, they'll turn and crush you. I'm sure of it, and who will be there to protect you when all our finest Warriors are exiled up here?"

"This isn't exile, Gall. It's a pause. Negotiations couldn't continue with you at home fueling the fire of confrontation."

"I ask again," Gallanto said, "if the Sevions turn nasty, who will protect our people?"

"We Templers have a few tricks locked up in our staffs. You know that better than anyone. If things get bad, we can use our magic, but that's not going to happen anytime soon. Bide your time, Gall. They've agreed to talk once you're here, and when we reach an agreement, we can bring you all back."

"Is that where Albys will go with the negotiations? To bring us back?"

"Of course. Never doubt that. I know he's angry about the part Warriors played in escalating the war, but you are our husbands, wives, children, and parents. This isn't exile, just a breathing space to find peace. Surely you don't want to fight if you don't have to."

Gallanto quieted, but the heaving of his broad chest showed how hard he tried for restraint. "How long do you think it will take?"

"Three cycles at the most. That's only a hundred and eighty days."

Gallanto sighed. "It will come as a shock to our Warriors. The transport order outlined off-world training without any mention of sending us out of the way. There'll be trouble when our first cycle is up and we can't go home."

"I'm sure you can handle them. After all, you voted for the deception at the council meeting."

"Don't think it means I like the solution. If everyone knew how long we'll be gone, some Warriors would refuse to come. Where would

that leave us? Our army split, unable to muster enough force to make a difference in a fight. And the negotiations would fail. Once Albys issued the order, it had to include all Warriors, including Sonlas.

Another shadow of grief passed over Meftah's face. *"Look after our daughter."*

"Of course," Gallanto said. *"At least, this way, you have a chance for a future."*

"You say that as if you don't believe you're coming home."

Oakham noticed stiffness in the chief's spine, suggesting he believed exactly that. *"I know you will try to bring us home,"* he said.

Meftah glanced over at Oakham. *"The boy's overheard everything. Will that cause a problem?"*

"He's been my runner through this entire nonsense. I trust his discretion."

"Still, he's only a cadet, and there's no need for him to stay. The exile order only applies to Warrior-class soldiers."

Oakham stepped forward and snapped to smart attention. *"With respect, Lady Templer, ma'am, my duty is to Chief Gallanto and I want stay with him. He's had me make a Soul memory of these events, and it'd be a shame to leave it half-formed."*

Gallanto looked at Meftah. *"With so many Warriors on base, it's good to have a cadet who's happy to do basic errands. We're in danger of having too many chiefs up here."*

"You chose well, Gall. The boy's aura radiates loyalty."

"I don't need the sight to judge his worth, Meftah. Soldiers are my business. Is everything ready?" he asked Oakham.

"Yes, sir."

"Let's get this over with," Gallanto said.

Landra, as Oakham, held her breath as the chief took up position at the platform's edge. Gallanto posed in statuesque stillness, surveying his people with an air of admiration and pity. His features suddenly hardened, and he raised one armored fist above his head. He breathed then bellowed, *"Open the portal!*

Chapter 20

As dark swirls formed between the two arching elba trees, the image broke apart. Landra's actions, viewpoint, and emotional pain became entirely her own again.

Part of her railed against the fracturing reality, and she longed for its return. The promise of a magical vortex felt like a wonderful dream, stopping short of its climax. She recalled the rich colors, sweet sounds, excitement, and pain. Now, the gurgling dregs of a depleted power well, hard wood beneath her body, and a dying man in her arms became her truth. She felt deafened by something that was missing. The world felt empty and thin, like there was an absence of Soul.

Her shoulders heaved with grief and emptiness, but there was more pain here than a lost fantasy. This was betrayal. *Utter betrayal.* The broken Templer promises wrenched her guts. She'd grown up knowing of the exiling, but to experience the moment of separation hurt beyond reason. This was personal. Her great-grand-mother had promised to return. Now, Landra carried the entire resentment of Warrior-kind in her heart. She resented Meftah for her good intentions, her lies, and her magic.

Yes, great-grandmother, I blame you for my flaw too.

Pink strands of mist, which had congregated around the Collector, broke loose and drifted free. They gathered beneath the underside of the spiraling path. Had her great-grandfather left with them?

"Chief Gallanto?"

"Find a way, child of my life," the ghost chief replied, and then his presence thinned out of existence.

Hey, wait. Find a way to do what? You can't leave me with that.

No answer came.

Shelk!

She wanted to reach for him again, but Oakham's slipping hand dragged her back to reality. The old soldier slumped against her body, flaccid and scrunched with his head lolling to one side. She felt his rattling breaths on her chest.

"Oakham?" she said, giving him a gentle shake.

His kaleidoscope aura swirled slower now, fluttering weakly at the edge of her blue Soul. A single breath escaped from his gaping mouth.

No, no, no! Don't die.

"Don't do this," she said, rolling him away and settling him on the wooden path. She removed her jacket and folded it under his head for support. The sight of his sunken features hit Landra like one of her father's fists. His skin was grey, but his aura was greyer now, and its swirling slowed with each passing moment.

"Soldier Oakham!"

He cracked his eyes open to slits and turned his weary, blind eyes to her face. Rasping punctuated each of his ragged breaths. "Did you see?" he asked.

Landra hesitated, not wanting to share her experience.

But this is a dying man's last wish. He deserves an answer. "Yes."

"Ah!" Oakham breathed, and his body relaxed. "That was the last… We were supposed…"

She cradled his hand in her lap and stroked the thin skin. "It's time to rest, soldier. We'll sit awhile. Then I'll carry you up to the platform and call for transport. You'll feel more comfortable in the medic barracks."

"No, dear! Leave me here. I'll not desert my post now. This is where I…"

He stilled, as if the energy to speak had departed. His mouth worked small motions as if trying for words, but no sound came. Then another short breath puffed through his lips.

She didn't need a medic's training to see the mantel of death hanging over him, but his end shouldn't be here—not like this. He deserved better. A gurgling sound rattled in his throat.

Shelk.

Landra wanted to tell Oakham that everything would be fine. It wasn't true. *You will die, the power's nearly gone, and we're heading for civil war. Your vision changed nothing.*

Instead, she tugged her uniform straight and set her arm across her chest with the Collector in her hand. She couldn't give Oakham life, but she could show him respect.

"Soldier," she said, her own breathing heavy with emotion, "the execution of your duty has been exemplary, and now it's time to pass the burden along. I can take it from here. Time for you to rest." She saluted with her free hand, trying to still her shuddering shoulders. "Three-bar soldier Oakham, you are dismissed."

His face relaxed and then stilled into a slack smile. His noisy breathing marked out time, but the space between each rasp lengthened until the next one never came. She sat in silence, the soldier's hand resting on her knee, and his aura expanded around her body. In that moment, she knew him again as he had been in his youth, with his passion to serve and dedication to tasks. He'd chosen his duty, and now he'd chosen his moment of death, as if he'd waited until she could share his end.

His aura threads rose in a cloud, but instead of frittering away or melding with the pink clumps they darted about. A few twists later, they arrowed toward the remnants of the magic well and plunged through the surface. A gurgling swell welcomed the addition of Oakham's Soul before the pool stilled.

For all Landra's soldier bravado and Warrior ambition, she mourned the veteran soldier with the raw passion of a young girl. Wiping tears from her cheeks, she wondered at her reaction. She'd known him for less time than it had taken her to visit the overlevel, but he'd touched her enough to awaken grief.

Why should I be surprised.? You shared the torment of our people, old man.

She had to adjust to the last sentry's death, the betrayal of her people, and a magical vision too. What was she supposed to do with that now? The veteran had declared a Soul memory unbreakable. Yet the experience faded from her thoughts, leaving a plundered emptiness in its wake. She recalled the events, but there was no play-like repetition of the scene in her head. She could no more recapture the actuality of each moment than she could recall the physical pain of her father's beating from the night before. She remembered Chief Hux's fists around her neck, her fear, and that it had hurt, but recapturing the sensation of pain was impossible. The Soul memory felt the same.

I indulged in magic, and for what?

Her face crumpled and she felt dirty, as if she'd done

something wrong. Her great-grandfather's permission for the sharing meant nothing. In Landra's world now, a dead chief's order provided no validation.

"Find a way," Chief Gallanto had said.

Bah! Find a way to do what?

She was still kneeling by Oakham and resting the Collector on his chest when noise came from above. Thisk's angry voice came to her ears loudest of all.

"What have you done with her?"

"She's there, Warrior Fourth. I can see her in the pit."

Thundering steps rattled the walkway.

Landra dragged a sleeve across her tear-streaked cheek but she felt too weak to stand. The Warrior charged down the path toward her, his features locked into a mask of worry and the whites of his eyes shining starkly in his bearded face. He stopped a stride short of where she held Oakham and swayed, as if taking in the scene. "What are you doing? Are you all right? Put that knife away," he stuttered out like shot-fire.

"She killed him," another voice said. "She killed the last sentry."

Several robed figures crowded behind the Warrior, and the press of their anger was palpable. Dark lines shot through their auras in a furious collage.

Thisk grabbed Landra's arm and hauled her to her feet.

"Run!" he ordered, and she didn't dare disobey.

Chapter 21

The Warrior Fourth dragged the knife from Landra's hand and replaced it in its sheath. He hooked his fingers into her collar and forced her into motion. She didn't want to leave Oakham's body, but Thisk gave her no choice. He charged up the spiral path with her in tow, barging several startled priests aside.

"Thisk?"

"Run."

Stiffness tightened her thighs, but a strange slackness ran through the rest of her body, like it would fall apart if she continued. The combination made her stumble often, but Thisk's strong grip bounced her up each time and pushed her on with barely a pause. They made it up to the platform, and the sight of Oakham's empty chair flustered her badly. She stumbled to a halt. The Warrior resorted to dragging her past the plaque.

The ramp was clear of visitors now, as if the Templers had expected trouble. It made flight easier, and Landra felt relieved to have few witnesses. This would make prize gossip once word of her undignified departure spread.

Shelk in a basket. I'm in a nightmare.

Thisk didn't slow as he approached a group of priests who barred the way at the ramp's end. He barged past them, careless of who he sent scuttling or whether Landra's face clashed with flailing limbs. One Templer staggered back, catching his boot in his robe hem. Landra's last sight of the priest was of him toppling backward over the guard rail.

They came to the great doors, and it was hard to know what to take in first. Landra glanced at the immense structures, barely believing she'd seen the doors open in her vision. With rusted hinges and vines growing across the center line, it didn't seem like they could have opened in years, but her attention moved to another Templer, who sprawled near the base of the doors. Fiery swellings marked his face, and another priest sat bowed over his limp arm. The limb sagged as if dislocated from its socket.

"What happened?" she asked.

"I happened, so unless you want jail time, I suggest you keep moving."

"Wait!" an order screamed out from behind. Landra's backward glance spotted a chasing Templer group, but they couldn't match the pace Thisk set. Neither could she, but the Warrior dragged her up to his speed. They hurtled along the small path, plowing through the visiting cadets who were making their way out.

More witnesses, and ones with flapping tongues. Great.

Ogling stares followed their passing, and Thisk's bulky shoulder jostled one girl into the wall.

"To the shaft," he growled in her ear. They exited onto the busy concourse. The crowd had swelled again, so they wove their way through, careless of who blocked the way. At a shout from a temple guard, the Warrior ducked them down a smaller corridor and turned several corners.

"What will your father say about this?" he demanded under his breath. "We'll be lucky to stay cityside."

Shelk to the mist and back. What will Father say? Preoccupation with the momentous historical events had left little room for processing the real-world implications of the day's trials. Chief Hux would never understand if she told the truth, but she couldn't face that problem yet. She had an enraged Warrior Fourth to deal with first. The over-level had never seemed like a better place to visit, so she drew up the will to match his pace. She charged for the shaft.

Thisk didn't make for their original entry point but found another narrow corridor to head down. "Festival visitors stay here," he said, "so it should be empty now."

His prediction stayed nearly true. They only passed one soldier before reaching a shaft door. The one-bar soldier turned his head to follow their movements, his cloth poised over a corridor plaque. He watched them depart, his hand rubbing the *Ring 11* sign in automatic movements.

A familiar outline came into view on in the wall. Rather than produce a key to open the shaft door, Thisk booted it, sending it swinging open. A bleary-eyed sentry stumbled from behind the shaft's tree, snuggling a quilted blanket over his padded clothes. The extra wrapping didn't stop his breath from puffing white into the chilled atmosphere.

"Report," Thisk demanded, still clutching Landra's collar.

"What?"

"Are you guarding the shaft or bunking up on duty time? Looks like you've quite a nest back there, and these lights are on daytime settings."

It was true, Landra realized. The shaft was much brighter than the ones she'd used before, but the piercing cold still reached her core. She thought of her jacket and remembered leaving it under Oakham's head.

Thisk dragged Landra to the store rack and released his grip to ransack the shelves. He padded up, as if ready for a novice sword battle, and threw warm-weather garments her way. Already gasping from the chill, she didn't need more urging to dress.

As they changed, the sentry poked his head around the tree to watch, a mixture of fear and bewilderment widening his tired eyes. His mouth sagged open, but his eyes fixed on Thisk's insignia and he didn't ask questions.

"What's this?" the Warrior asked, launching a furious kick at a pile of blankets that blocked the ladder's base. The movement uncovered a sword. The Warrior snatched it, twisted the hilt in his fist, and launched it toward the sentry, point first. "I think this is yours."

The young man ducked, but the weapon planted in the tree beside his head with enough force to hold it in a horizontal position. Landra shuddered, sensing the force of Thisk's temper wasn't meant for the sentry. He radiated fury like an inferno, and when he punched the trap door at the top of the ladder, it slammed open and bounced back. He flung it again. This time it stayed, creating a vortex of swirling leaves throughout the shaft. His disappearance through the hole left her scrambling into the rest of her clothes and chasing after him.

She emerged onto the dismal overlevel. An invading storm carried a deeper cold now, one that made her want to curl into a ball and stop running. Tiny lights twinkled from a nearly dark sky, and if it hadn't been for subtle over-level lighting and the shine of Thisk's aura, she might have completely lost his shadowy silhouette.

"Thisk."

He continued onward. It didn't take brains to work out she should follow. The midlevel priests had labelled her a murderer; without the Fourth's support, her defense wouldn't carry weight. What was she supposed to say if temple guards caught her?

I'm sorry, but Oakham shared a Soul memory and it drained his body of life. Ugh!

Gathering the dregs of her energy, she tracked the Warrior's form, only catching up as he vanished over the city wall. She leaned over the edge and spotted him scrambling down a ladder that ran all the way to the ground. Full night had spread like a smothering ink blot, but frost glistened on the rungs where his aura light touched. She stared after him, mystified as to why he would leave the city. Behind her was trouble, and down the ladder was… she didn't know, but she had to trust Thisk. She edged around and clambered down. Cracking surface ice welcomed her at the bottom, and her boots sank into chilling mud.

It took a moment for her to absorb what that meant. For the first time in her life, she was away from the base that protected her from danger. This was where the council sent soldiers who committed serious crimes. She peered into the gloom, only seeing clouds of white from her heavy breaths. Her Soul sight finally picked out Thisk's shape, so she gathered her courage and followed him into the forest. The route took her down a narrow, winding trail with ice-topped mud slicks framing the path. Even if she lost the Warrior now, there was only one direction to follow. Dwelling on mud slugs, wild animals, and exile, she started out on her trek.

Around one bend, complete darkness waited. Trees rustled and branches creaked, but she saw nothing.

I wanted adventure, but this is ridiculous.

She wondered if she had the nerve to retrace her steps. She'd known trouble in the city, but any fear she'd experienced felt miniscule to what she felt now. She was alone in the remote lands, and it raised a terror in her gut that she couldn't even name.

If Thisk doesn't come back? If…. Oh, gods of the mist.

A glow sprang to life a short distance ahead. Not an aura glow but the flickering spark of true fire. It had to be Thisk. She strode toward the flame.

Stars reappeared as she stepped into a forest clearing, and the source of the light warmed her heart. The glow shone from a window in a small, low building. Of course Thisk would have hideouts here in the wilds; she should have expected that.

She approached the hut, relieved and tired. After working a latch on the odd-shaped door, the panel swung open. Warmth and blessed light leaked out, but she didn't wait for an invitation to enter. She scrambled inside and turned to bar the door against the invading wind. Once the air stilled, she looked around.

Clutter made it impossible to take in the room's contents, but a fired-up stove and two blazing wall torches warmed her heart as much as her body. A single bed on the side wall looked welcoming beyond reason, but Thisk hadn't claimed it. He sat on the floor against the back wall with an unsheathed sword on his lap. His position gave him a view of the door, but he stared at the stove's flames, as if they held all the answers to his woes.

Landra shuddered at his unblinking and emotionless gaze. Her jaw worked, but there were no right words. She made for the bed and emptied a water flask Thisk had left on the pillow. After lugging a dried food sack off the covers and brushing away crumbs, she flung herself down. Still fully clothed, her body started to warm, but her dread stayed cold and deep. *Will my life ever be the same?*

Thisk's piercing words came to her, filling the room. "Quite a first day, Chief Elect Hux."

Of all the ranks he'd used to address her so far, none had sounded so low.

Chapter 22

Exhaustion kept Landra's nightmares away. The smell of burning meat roused her, and she cracked open her eyes. Mid-morning sun rays streamed through the windows.

A need to relieve herself urged her from the bed, but if she'd thought her body was stiff yesterday, today it locked into a solid sheet of pain. She rolled to a stooped version of standing and watched Thisk crack several eggs into a pan. He'd already damped down the torches to two smoldering sticks, but the stove's warmth cozied the cabin's single room.

She tried making sense of the contents, taking in the array of swords and bows, which rested across wires at the ceiling and the heaped clutter on the floor. Shuffling through the mess, she stubbed her toe against a discarded axe shaft. The chaos crowded her like a set of ill-fitting boots.

"Thisk?"

He glanced at her for the first time since the temple visit, his eyes dark with accusation.

"Is there somewhere to wash? I…" There was no easy way for her to say that her bladder was full. "I need…"

He set his pan off the heat, opened the door, and gestured to the forest with an open palm.

Landra sighed. "I guess I'll hold it."

Breakfast consisted of thick porridge, unidentified meat, and eggs. They stood while they ate, the thick silence hanging like a barrier between them. Tension clamped Landra's jaw tight enough to make chewing hurt. She spooned a few scoops of porridge before putting her dish down.

She wanted to explain. Surely, if he knew what had happened, he would understand. Wasn't it him who had told her to experience history? He'd also told her to stay on the temple path, and she suspected he would never forgive her for that disobedience. His simmering anger swamped her with silence and disregard.

"What should we do now?" she asked.

"You're not fit to do anything. I'm going hunting."

He turned aside, slinging his empty dishes into a bucket. As he padded against the cold, Landra sought for an explanation she could share, but the Warrior looked too angry to listen. He slung a bow over his shoulder and started to leave, but he paused at the door.

"Hux?"

"Yes?"

"Stay in the cabin and fasten the latch while I'm gone. Can you manage that?"

"What happened in the temple wasn't my fault. I—"

The door closed, cutting off her words. She folded her arms across her sleep-creased uniform and peered out the window. Thisk disappeared into the trees. With him out of the way, she sneaked outside to relieve herself.

This disobedience was your fault, Thisk. Would it hurt you to give an order I can follow?

As she leaned back in the shrub, with her trousers stretched around her ankles, an animal wail rose in the forest. Tremors shuddered through her body, splattering dark urine on her pants.

"Shelk to the mist and shelk, shelk, shelk!" Not for the first time, she wished Winton would arrive and put her on report. At least *that* would feel like normal trouble. She pulled her soggy clothes to order and chased inside, making sure to set the latch.

"There you go, Thisk," she said as the metal bar dropped into place.

Trying to make sense of the mess in the ranger hut, she scanned the room again. It looked no better in daylight. In her head, she wanted to tidy, but her body disagreed, so she limited herself to rummaging through the storage sacks marked "clothing supplies.". There was little suitable for her, but she found trousers that would have to do. She fastened a belt to hold the large waistband in place, and she rolled up the bottoms to ensure she wouldn't trip. She eased the jacket and shirt off her shoulders to apply Gren's salve. By the time she'd finished, sticky patches covered her body, shoulders, and neck, but there was no way she could reach her back. The ointment gave some relief, but her exhaustion and pain went deeper than any cream could touch, so she replaced her creased shirt rather than dirty a new one and rolled back onto the bed. As she snuggled against the chill, her sleepy gaze took in the dirty dishes and soiled trousers.

"The room will fail inspection, anyway," she muttered to the walls before fleeing awareness.

In her waking moments over the next days, the enormity of events sank in. She'd gained a promotion to chief elect, indulged in a magical Soul memory, met her dead great-grandfather, witnessed Oakham's death, alienated the Warrior Fourth, and left the city. It was enough to send her back to sleep, but dreams of her father's disappointment stole her rest.

She couldn't imagine what everyone must think of her unusual absence. Her friendship with Baylem wouldn't shield her from the girl's gossip, and without facts, the rumors were likely to descend into the absurd.

Thisk came and went, keeping the fire stoked, the water barrel full, and food on the table, all while Landra huddled in her miserable half-sleep. On her sixth day in the cabin, she awoke to find the Warrior looming at her bedside.

"We train today," he said. "It will be outside, so prepare what you need."

Those were more words than he'd spoken since the temple incident, so Landra stumbled out of bed. Her muscles moved easier now, and she guessed her bruises had faded, but there was no mirror to know for sure. She stretched her body, washed it with water from the barrel, and donned a uniform of supple leathers. The double-layered wrap-over style provided surprising warmth, and it allowed her to secure her long trousers tight around her ankles.

"What weapon should I bring?" She chose some outer garments and pulled on fresh boots.

"None."

"Not even the Collecter?" Landra had slept, eaten, and lived with the knife on her back, ever since her promotion.

Thisk ground his teeth before nodding, but the dark glint in his eye said she didn't deserve the weapon. He led her through the forest along animal trails and finally stopped in an open area where the wind sheeted sideways.

She pulled the hood of her newly acquired cloak tighter and peered at the city wall through the branches. Home was closer than she'd realized.

As the Warrior set his weapons down and assumed a fighting pose, his fierce glare silenced any words she might offer. She set her own cloak aside and matched his stance.

Thisk launched a kick to her ribs before she had chance to settle. It wasn't an illegal move, but the manner of his delivery pushed regulations to the limit. Landra fell to one knee, hugged her side, and groaned. She knew better than to protest and considered staying down. Instead, she eased to her feet and found a stronger fighting position to wait for his next strike. Clearly, he needed to fight the anger out of his system.

Strike he did, and with all his Warrior strength. She brought defensive moves into play, twisting free when she could, dancing out of reach, and stepping close if the chance arose. Scrapping could have saved her some hits, but she didn't know how the Warrior would react to her unorthodox style, so she took the pummeling. A kick to the back of her knee brought her down again.

"You're making a shelking awful job of being chief elect."

She reclaimed her feet to face him, her own anger swelling. What would she learn from this training, except how to survive pain?

"And whose fault is that?" she asked. "I said we should avoid the temple."

"If you'd followed orders and stayed to the path, it wouldn't have mattered. We should be home in the hall now."

It was a relief to hear him talk, even if it was to argue.

"Yes, well, I couldn't stay on the path, so it doesn't matter how long you punish me. I can't be sorry."

"What do you mean you couldn't?"

She had no way of answering without admitting her magic. "I just couldn't, Thisk."

A low growl rumbled in his throat. "Great answer. Tell me, Hux, you defied me, killed the last sentry, and invited civil war. Was it worth it?"

Landra had no way to know if her new knowledge would prove useful. "I didn't kill Oakham." It was all she could say.

"I saw him dead in your arms, and you had a knife in your hand."

"Yes, he died and I happened to be there, but I wasn't responsible for what happened. That was his sacrifice to make. Look, it's no good being angry with me. This is your fault."

"Remember who you're speaking to, citizen." His fists coiled in readiness.

Landra dropped her defenses. If he wanted to damage her, she would prefer it was over with.

"I'm sorry, but the temple visit was everything I feared," she said. "That old sentry had magic and the sight. He saw red in my aura and…"

Thisk's disgust-stricken stare silenced her next words. The seed of resentment festered deep in her people, and she was certain her face had looked the same when Oakham had suggested his plan. Sharing a Soul memory was as far from being a Warrior as she could imagine and even further from being chief elect.

She braced, dreading the impending blow. If only he could beat the magic out of her body. She would stay down this time.

The Warrior raised his fist and thinned his lips, as if fighting to contain his horror. They held there for a long time before he roared out a breath. "Hux? Hux?"

He didn't expect an answer.

"You brought the Collector?" he asked.

"Yes, but—"

"Give it to me."

Landra reached for her knife and offered it over. With an expert flick of his wrist, he grabbed it and stashed it in his belt.

Father had given Landra the weapon and had expected her to keep it, so she glared at the carved handle that showed at Thisk's waist.

"Don't share the sentry's words with anyone," he said. "I wish you hadn't told me what he said. Could you have misunderstood his meaning?"

Landra wanted to deny her magic, but she couldn't lie. She shook her head.

"After all my orders, I can't believe you indulged in the darkest aspect of our past, citizen. What were you thinking?"

His words made Landra feel dirty. "You used the Collector for its magical properties."

"I told you before that accessing power and growing magic are different beasts. If I'd known, I would have never shown you the hethra. You shouldn't have spoken to anyone in the temple.

"I'm sorry."

"And how will that help? Magic might be overlooked in an average cadet. The mist knows I probably have some shading myself, but our army will never trust it in a chief elect."

He wasn't saying anything she didn't already know. She could have told him how little red colored his Soul, but it didn't seem like the time. At least her visit with Oakham had allayed one fear: The old soldier hadn't met anyone else who saw auras, so his passing meant she was safe from further discovery. Still, resentment at bearing this burden turned her anger cold. Didn't Thisk know she would cut out the magic if there was a way?

"Don't get me exiled yet," she threw back at him. "I did what I had to do, and you're going to have to trust me."

"How can I, Hux?"

Landra gathered herself to her full height. "This isn't a polite request, Warrior Ranger Fourth Thisk. This is an order from your chief elect."

He tilted his head and moved his mouth as if rolling a sour ball over his tongue. His curly hair hung around his face, hiding his eyes, and she worried if she'd overplayed her non-existent hand. Trust couldn't be demanded. It had to be earned, and who was she to expect his loyalty? Now this course was set, she had to ignore the way her stomach heaved.

It was hard to decide whether her mention of Oakham's vision had been a slip or a desperate need to share the problem. Either way, she'd risked all by divulging a tiny part of her secret.

Will you report me? What if...? There were too many dreadful outcomes to imagine.

After a disrespectful pause, Thisk relaxed his fists and came to attention.

"You are my chief elect, so I will withhold judgement —for now."

It was barely acceptance. She couldn't expect more under the circumstances.

"But do you know just how much trouble we're in?" he asked.

"A lot?"

"I violated an agreement between Chief Hux and the Templers by coming to your rescue."

"I didn't need rescuing."

"Yes, well, you'd been a long time, and I couldn't have known that; however, it happened. There's no way we can predict the outcome or whether they'll bring you up on murder charges for that stunt you pulled. I still haven't decided whether to take you back to base or to the remote lands."

She eyed the city walls, her body loosening at the thought of never going home. Uncertainty had replaced the edge of anger in Thisk's tone, and nothing could have worried her more. What had begun as an adventure had turned into a disaster. She rolled her wind-dried lips together, imagining what it would be like to leave. Dannet filled her thoughts first, and she wished he were by her side. None of this was fair—not for her and not for Thisk.

"If I stay out here, could you go back?"

"Are you trying to save me, cadet?"

She offered a shy nod.

"Nice gesture. Late, but nice. It's still not an option. Death will find you here on the first true winter's day— probably sooner—and I pledged my service to you. Besides, I broke the treaty. Who says I won't be exiled for that?"

Landra had wanted to do the right thing, but relief pushed a thin grin to her face. She didn't want to face her troubles alone. "So, what do we do?"

His answer took longer this time. "We'll train out here as if you're going to compete in the championships as the chief elect. It will give me time to think."

"And a chance for things to settle in the city."

His grimace showed his doubts, and there seemed little else to say. They'd reached a better understanding now, and it was her turn to trust him.

Chapter 23

Landra suffered fewer injuries once they worked toward a single purpose, but that didn't mean that she was pain-free or that the tension between them eased.

Thisk set his palm out, level with his chest. "Your foot needs to reach here."

She kicked toward his raised hand, but her boot stopped short of the target.

"You're moving once my foot gets close."

"Obviously. I don't want my hand damaged, but you're not making the target anyway."

"We've been at this for ages, Thisk. Can we do knife work now?"

"No!"

"But it's my best skill. Didn't you say I should develop my strengths?"

"Fine!" See that tree on the other side of the clearing?" He pointed. "Land a knife in the trunk, and we'll call it a strength."

She looked to where he pointed. The trees here differed from the ones on base. Their slender trunks and

169

spine-laden branches pointed like arrows to the sky. She drew the Collector from her strap and focused on the narrow target.

Settling to throw, she homed her gaze on the target, but a flat-handed blow struck her cheek and snapped her head sideways.

"What the shelk?"

"Where did you find that knife?" Thisk asked. "I'd hidden it."

She staggered, her ears ringing like the mother of all sirens. "It was only under your jacket. I thought you'd forgotten to give it back."

"I chose not to return it. There's a difference." He snatched the knife from her grip and launched it with enough force to plant it in a low tree branch. She'd have to climb to reclaim it now.

"What did you do that for?" She started for the tree.

"Leave it there, citizen. The Collector is dangerous for someone with your… tendencies."

"You want to abandon it out here in the remote lands? Weren't you the one who threw a tantrum when you thought I'd thrown it at a bird? But now it's fine to leave it behind in the wilderness? What happened to it being an irreplaceable artifact?"

"I'm the Warrior Fourth. I don't throw tantrums. Back on the overlevel, I acted like that because I thought you'd risked losing the knife. I know where I'm leaving it for safe-keeping, and there's no one out here to steal it."

Landra's cheek burned in the cold air, and she lifted a hand to the skin where the slap had landed. Winton was a mist-forsaken piece of work, but he'd never hit her outside of a training ring. Not like this. Not in temper and in defiance of protocols. In all her life, no one had done that. Her pride hurt as much as her face, but she wouldn't give him the satisfaction of seeing her react, so she straightened to face him. Drawing a different knife from her belt sheath, she focused on the target. Her burning cheek fueled her outrage, and she uttered a low growl as the blade left her hand.

Thisk came to her side and followed her gaze as the knife arced through the wind. Satisfaction rippled through his aura when the knife dropped short.

"Seems like short-blade work isn't such a strength after all. Good job. We have all your weaknesses to work on, Hux. Can we get back to practicing kicks now?"

Landra pursed her lips, mentally cursing him seven ways sideways. "Yes sir," she said, and the Warrior reset his hand.

"Won't it be more useful to kick here?" She relaunched her leg toward his groin but stopped short of contact.

"That's one option." He edged back.

He'd better believe she'd land that kick one day, and her satisfaction would offset any retaliation he might send her way.

"We have nine kicks to learn if you're going to master the full range of fighting movements."

"Winton called me more of a scrapper, and that's worked so far."

"It depends what you're after. The high kicks score more championship points, but if you want to settle for less, I won't waste time training you."

"Fine! Let's do this." She planned to slam her boot into his fingers, no matter how far he moved. As soon as his hand set in place, she launched her attack with a roar, but her boot missed again—and by a good margin. "Shelk!"

"Flexibility takes time to develop."

"I don't have much of that."

"Flexibility?"

"Time." She couldn't help but dwell on the impending ceremony.

"Worry is a waste of energy, cadet, and I'm tired of your whining. Come here and lean against this stone."

A mossy rock face provided some shelter from the worst of the elements, but when she set her back against the wall, moisture from the rain-sodden vegetation leaked through her clothes. Thisk didn't care. He grabbed her ankle and raised her leg, pushing hard enough to force her back against the jagged rock beneath the moss.

"Agh!" she groaned as he pressed her knee straight.

"You need this work to avoid injury,"

"Then why does it feel like it's causing me injury?"

Thisk ignored her. "If we do this every night before you sleep, you should feel some difference soon."

"Do all Warriors go through this?"

"There are rules in the city, but I can tell you one thing. Whatever hardships Warriors endure, they do it without squealing like spoiled brats."

Landra clenched her teeth and rubbed her bruised cheek, certain that Warrior trainees didn't endure what Thisk was putting her through. He'd admitted he wasn't a trainer, and she was sure he was making this up as he went along.

"Agh!" she groaned as he repeated the lifting action with her other leg. It hurt more than the first side, but she bit her lip to stem her cries. After a minute of agony, he dropped her ankle and left to retrieve his cloak from a tree stump.

"That's enough for today."

Relief surged through Landra. She could settle into the cabin and warm herself against the stove before the evening chill deepened. Gathering her cloak, she set out toward the ranger hut.

"Not yet, cadet," he said. "You have a knife to retrieve, and I don't mean the Collector."

She turned without argument and limped away.

True to his word, Thisk put her through similar agony every evening, stretching both her legs until they went over her head and sometimes settling her into the splits in both forward and sideways positions. Once there, he pressed his weight onto her shoulders and bounced. It was easily the most painful element of her full-body stretching routine.

His training methods for weapons utilized more traditional protocols, and there was no suggestion of employing the hethra.

One rainy day, she stood before him with her sword raised, feeling like a fraud. His aura flashes colored the rain as it fell around him, signaling an imminent attack, so she darted sideways to dodge his blow. Swinging around, she brought her own blade down on his padded shoulder before shuffling out of reach.

"You're improving." Water ran off his hat and trickled into the lines of his baffled frown.

Landra flinched with the guilt of a cheat. He would never approve of her Soul sight advantage, but turning the skill off was no more possible than choosing deafness. If anything, her Soul vision had brightened since she'd shared Oakham's memory. She was glad there were few doors to see through here.

To allay suspicion, she held still for Thisk's next attack, even though she knew when it was coming, and his sword whipped her weapon away. His blade tip settled in line with her nose, and his expression reordered into a mask of weary frustration.

"But your concentration is hopeless. At times, I daren't close in because you read every move. Then, it's like you've gone to sleep. Meditation might help your focus, but we'd be idiots of the mist to add that to your training."

"Why, if it can help?"

"Think, cadet. Soul priests use those training exercises."

"Oh. Maybe I'm just too small for sword work."

"You have decent tactical instincts, but you're flighty. If I sent you into battle now, you might lose your head or risk the Warrior next to you."

He slid his sword away and rolled his shoulders. "I think that's enough for now."

Another session was over, but Landra didn't feel her usual relief. More time had gone by since her flight from the city, and panic over what was to come unsettled her gut more with each passing day.

"Can we stay a bit longer?" she asked. "I need to practice."

"I can't argue there, but I won't be teaching you. As you're keen, grab an axe and fill the log pile before you come in."

"What good will that do?"

"Keep us warm." He laughed before disappearing through the trees.

Landra sheathed her sword, shook the rain droplets from her jacket, and wiped moisture from her lashes. She replaced her cloak, wondering why Thisk had failed to understand her urgency. Competing in the championship took skill, but surviving the remote lands took more. She was sure they had been gone for more than half of their allotted sixty-day cycle.

She stormed back to the ranger house, planning to request a solo training routine to fill her time, but a push on the door found it bolted.

"Thisk?"

When no response came, she leaned on the panel and eyed the log pile. The waiting trunks nestled beneath a makeshift cover, with a freshly sharpened axe and a water skin resting on a chopping block. She claimed the tool and took her position in front of a log. The city wall showed through the trees beyond, and homesickness shredded her emotions as she took her first swing. The axe crunched with more force than she knew she possessed, and aura dots erupted from the gouge in the log. Insects swarmed away to disappear into the stack of chopped wood.

At least I'll have bugs for company. Each heft of the axe seemed to dull her distress more, as if weariness could dampen her misery, so she continued working, even when her shoulders burned and sweat coursed down her back. By the time Thisk called her inside, she only had aura light and a glint from the shuttered window to guide her way back.

The exertion made for a difficult time the next morning, with an unbearable return to stiffness and pain. Staring into her near-empty salve pot, she sighed.

Best keep the dregs in case Thisk discovers even more painful trials.

"You ready to work?" Thisk said.

"I suppose. Are we doing knife training today?"

"The answer's still no." He buckled a sword belt.

"But I'm good with a knife, really. That tree you asked me to hit was just too far."

"I know you're good. That's exactly why we're not doing short-blade work. You can juggle the knife through your fingers with all the fancy flips and rolls championship judges like. Those moves will gain points for looking pretty, even if they have no place in a real fight. Your instincts in close quarters are good, and your aim is ridiculous."

"Sure," she said, assuming he was mocking her.

"Take the compliment, Hux. Seasoned veterans can't match your results. All you need now is more throwing distance."

"So, what are we doing today?"

"We're surviving."

He threw an empty sack at her chest. "We only eat what you put in there today. House stores are off limits."

Landra gripped the rough sack, and chills raised the hairs on her neck. *You've decided to stay remote-side.*

Before she could dwell, Thisk pushed her out of the door and threw cold-weather garments at her back. The door slammed, and a grinding noise accompanied the sliding bolt.

Landra stared at the hut, knowing the Warrior wouldn't come out again, so she wrapped in her gear and went searching for food.

Chapter 24

Chick-birds roosted at the edge of the clearing, so Landra searched in the grass for eggs. Despite the protest of clucking birds, she returned to the hut empty-handed. It didn't take chief elect thinking to realize Thisk had sneaked out early to collect the morning's supply.

Do you have to make everything difficult?

He didn't have to, she decided, but that was his way. She considered her options and decided to forage rather than hunt. Summer fruit remnants lay in decaying mush at the base of bushes, ripened beyond use, but she remembered a brambly hedge out back. The last time she'd looked, its berries had been too green to harvest, so she picked up her sack and trekked that way. A purple mass of swelling berries greeted her as a reward. For every juicy delight she popped in her mouth, she put one in the bag. The sack started to bulge, but before it was completely full, an aura movement stopped her mid-reach. Orange shades scuffled in the undergrowth.

Bird? Rodent?

She eased her hand to her belt sheath and found the

knife slot empty. Thisk had chased her off without preparation time, and now was she alone in the wilderness without protection.

"I'll see you in the demon mist, Thisk," she said into the forest noise.

The aura's orange shades deepened and expanded at her outburst. Before she could react, a flurry of white fur sprang from the bush and scrambled to her chest. Fur brushed her face, claws raked her neck, and orange aura-light flickered through her blue shades.

Not a bird. Shelk!

She flailed her arms and kicked her knees, but the animal latched its fangs into her cloak and wouldn't release. Shaking didn't budge the creature, so she unfasted her neck cord and discarded the cloak. Before the animal could grab her again, she ran away, her breathing heavy enough for any beast to track, but a glance back made her halt. There was no pursuit—only a rodent filling its pouches with berries. *My berries*. It snaffled up the loose fruit, which had spilled from the sack's neck and then stuck its snout inside to empty the contents.

She couldn't believe the vicious attack had come from such a small animal, but there was no denying the pattern of its aura shade. She sighed. Having failed to beat a rodent without a knife, she decided to take meat off the menu. After it scurried away, she retrieved her belongings and went hunting for mushrooms.

She returned to the cabin by midday, her lumbering stride reflecting failure more than weariness. Thisk let her in and claimed the sack.

"What did you find?"

"Not much."

He rummaged through the contents. "Poisonous!" he

said, throwing the mushrooms at the wall before she could protest. "You didn't eat any, did you?"

"No." She wondered if he credited her with any sense. "I didn't know which were edible, so I brought them all back for inspection." Griping awoke her empty stomach, and she eyed the mushrooms miserably. They were by far the bulkiest food item she'd found, and she'd scraped her knee on a tree climb to reach them.

Thisk cleared a space on an upturned crate and set the remaining berries and a bunch of wriggling grubs down. "This is it? Didn't you think to bring meat?"

"I didn't have my knife."

"Hrmph," he sounded, as he shared out portions.

Landra only took one berry, her stomach bloated from her earlier feast. "Shall I cook the grubs?"

Thisk picked up a squirming larvae and pushed it into her mouth before she could argue. Its soft, twisting body squelched over her tongue, and she started to spit it out.

"Don't you dare!" Thisk said. "There's nothing else."

Landra squeezed her lips together. She couldn't bring herself to bite down, so she swallowed the grub whole. *Yuck!* It was disgusting.

With the rest of the day, Thisk took her out and showed her which stones sharpened well into blades and where the best vines hung for binding weapons together. He pointed out edible fruits and which ones to avoid. At the sight of a large leaf growing near the forest floor, he twisted it free, ground it between his hands, and accosted Landra with the remnants. She shied away, but when the leaf juice met her scratched neck, the stinging faded, and she allowed him to continue. For all their discoveries, they ate nothing and returned to the clearing with empty bellies.

"Back to wood splitting and stretching for you," Thisk said.

Landra's mouth fell open. She'd trekked a long way to claim her spoils, and it had taken five attempts before she'd managed to climb high enough in the trees to claim her first mushroom. Having learned not to argue, she headed back to the log pile and picked up her axe.

This time, she couldn't bear to face her city, so she turned to the cabin to finish her work. Her shoulders ached and sweat dribbled down her back. She glimpsed Thisk through the window. He was eating a bird leg, and she thought she saw juices run down his cheek. It had to be her imagination because she couldn't see that well from outside. Her next axe swing splintered her targeted log in one move.

Enjoying your feast, Thisk?

The thought was torment because he was obviously relishing his meal. She finished her jobs before stumbling back into the house, never having known such exhaustion and hunger. She reached for the water bottle, which hung on a wall peg.

Thisk snatched it away. "Did you fetch water?"

Landra didn't answer. She threw herself on the bed, her dry mouth making sleep hard to find. "Shelking mud slug with slime for brains," she said into her pillow. She wasn't certain, but she thought she heard Thisk laugh.

Chapter 25

Landra awoke early the next morning and considered Thisk's devious ways. Before he stirred, she hid a knife, bow, and a water flask under a bush outside, so when he acted true to type and shut her out, she was prepared.

That night, she came back with more berries, a floppy rodent she'd managed to spear, an edible mushroom, and a flask of water.

"Clever," Thisk said and they sat down to a satisfying meal. He sniffed the flask. "Where did you get this water?"

"There's a fall behind the horseshoe rocks."

He grinned and tipped his head back to trickle the last drops into his mouth. "Ah!"

Landra watched, unsurprised but annoyed. She'd taken to expect the worst from Thisk, so had drunk her fill before returning to the hut. "If you try that again, I'll bring some brackish water from the sludge pool." Her smile was as sweet as if she were offering him scute.

He looked at her thoughtfully then rummaged under his clothes for a hidden flask. "Drink this before you do logs tonight."

She sighed and wandered out to perform the evening ritual. It startled her when the Warrior came to stand beside her for the axe wielding. He didn't help but instead folded his arms to look at the sky. As dusk fell, he seemed lost in thought.

"The clouds often clear at night," he said. "It's why the temperature drops. Why don't you stop for a moment, Landra, and look up?"

She did stop, shocked to hear him use her name for the first time. There was no predicting how he would address her at any time, but she'd come to realize "citizen" meant he was most annoyed with her performance. What his use of her given name meant, she hadn't a clue.

She peered along the line of his finger and saw a bright star hanging in the darkness.

"Follow that brighter light, and it will guide you back to the base if you're ever lost," he said.

Lost? You're leaving me out here?

Hopelessness ran through Landra. Thisk was preparing to abandon her in the remote lands. Why else do this training? She gawked at the tiny dot for a long time, her mind travelling far. She thought of her great-grandmother, Meftah, and wondered if she'd been born on one of those stars. Jethra was out there somewhere. A sharp prod brought her back to the log splitting task.

That night, Landra's dreams were lively with Oakham and Gallanto, making her wonder if she'd replayed the Soul memory in her sleep. If it wasn't for Thisk, her visions wouldn't feel so dangerous out here. She went about her routine the next morning and discovered her stash had been ransacked by the Warrior, so she spent the day adapting to her new situation.

She twisted a leaf into a cup for capturing water, but the liquid leaked, so she broke open a large nut and scooped out the contents to make a flask. She stripped vines to make a noose, sharpened a stick into a spear, and bound a stone and a cane into an axe. Her stride home had a spring that day, and her sack jounced on her hip with satisfying weight.

As she approached the hut, she could barely believe the axe was missing from the log pile. A night off was long overdue. She pushed on the door, looking forward to rest. The bolt held it in place.

"Thisk?"

"I'm not here."

"Is that supposed to be funny? Let me in."

Silence.

Oh, Thisk.

She sighed. She could either waste her energy shouting at the Warrior or accept he wasn't going to open the door. She'd already predicted this escalation and had started building a shelter behind the ranger hut.

She found it with the frame still intact. High winds had left broken branches on the forest floor, and she'd used them to form a slanting roof. The vines she'd used to bind the structure were strong, but her knots had worked loose. She pulled them tight, and it didn't take much to weather-proof the hut with vegetation.

Once she was happy it would hold, she collected wood and twigs for a fire, dug out some dried moss and slivers of wood for tinder, and set to work. No matter how many times she tried to make a spark catch, the brightness sputtered out. Making fire looked easy when Thisk did it, even without the use of a Soul bead. She had done this before, but Thisk had always been guiding her actions.

Closing darkness added pressure to her efforts, and she realized she was in trouble. If she couldn't get the fire going, she would have no light to work by, no warmth, and no heat for cooking. The Collector was still stuck on a high branch, and the temptation to retrieve it was enormous. She could see why Thisk utilized magical artifacts now, but she didn't dare do the same. If the Warrior found out, he'd likely beat her into the mist, so she huddled inside her shelter and opened the sack.

A small animal with unresponsive eyes and a bloody chest flopped out. She still felt pride at her speared catch, but now she stared at the furry creature in her lap, wondering how to cook it.

With the blackness closing in and a storm of hunger raging in her stomach, she took out her handmade knife to skin the animal. The fur came away, and guts dribbled over her knees. When she was done, it sat in her hands, a network of sinew, bone, and flesh.

Close your eyes and eat. It's still food.

She bit into the raw flesh, trying to ignore the lumpy chunks that resisted her chewing and stringy tissues caught in her teeth. Even after her stomach protested, she forced down two more bites then set the animal's carcass aside.

Hunkering down in the shelter, wrapped in cold-weather padding, she tried to sleep. It was going to be a long night.

Just get to the morning. Please.

Clouds robbed her of starlight, so the darkness and cold wrapped around her like training skins. Her stomach tossed in alarming ways, and shivering rocked her body. Through the deep night hours, scuffles, howls, and jittery auras kept her from rest. *This is awful. This is going to be my life. I won't survive.*

The morning light found her still sitting in the shelter, but the wind had whipped her weatherproofing into the sky and rain droplets streamed from her hat and uniform. The animal carcass had been stripped clean, and trailing entrails tracked away from the shelter. She shuddered, not knowing what scavenger had come close.

I hope your guts hurt as bad as mine.

Landra had never felt so miserable. She returned to the ranger hut with a hunched-over shuffle. Thisk took one look at her and left her inside all day with a vomit bucket. If she were to be exiled to the remote lands, she was sure this was how she would die.

In the following days, Thisk filled in the skills she hadn't worked out for herself. She made enough fires to keep the entire clearing warm and told Thisk she could do it with her eyes closed. He made her try, but she burned her fingers and vowed to never try it again. She wasn't allowed to use the magic stone.

He taught her about the skipper bunny, which should never be eaten raw, showed her how to make wraps from fur, and drilled her in tying knots. They constructed so many shelters that anyone coming out here would be spoiled for choice. Every day ended with training, log splitting, and stretching.

All the time, Landra's tension built. She absorbed Thisk's lessons with attention to every detail. There couldn't be too many days of the training cycle left, and her fate was drawing near.

Chapter 26

On a return trip to the cabin with a sack full of medical herbs, sparkles covered the trees and fallen twigs crunched underfoot. A white speck twisted down onto Landra's cheek, and she stopped to wipe it away. Thisk halted at her side.

"Well, that's it," he said. "What d'you want to do, Chief Elect?"

"Give me a clue. Are we talking shelters, hunting, or something else because I don't know what you're asking."

"The snows are coming early, so it's time to choose: Do we head city-side or make for the remote lands?"

"I—"

After all her worrying, the moment still took her by surprise. "I thought you would choose. Why are you asking me?"

"Call it a privilege of rank."

"Right," she said, but no trace of condescension tugged at the Warrior's dark features. She licked her dried lips, trying to force some moisture into the cracks. Thoughts of her life back on base came flooding back.

Did you declare undying love before Dannet left, Baylem? And what are you doing right now, Bexter?

Her deep sigh blew white mist into the air. All hope she'd carried of knowing the cadet had dwindled. His straight-down-the-line soldiering and respect for the command chain left no room to date a chief elect. It felt like she'd lost him before ever knowing him, but that wasn't enough reason to run away.

"We go back," she said.

"To judgment?"

"If the ruling council thinks I deserve exile, they can put me on a train and send me themselves. I won't duck out of my duty before it started. You don't have to come with me, Thisk."

The Warrior scratched his beard and azure swirls disturbed his aura, but the only reaction to mark his face was a single twitching eyebrow. He hid emotions better than anyone she knew.

"You think I might want to avoid duty?"

"That's not what… I don't want you to get into trouble on my account."

"I think you know me well enough now, Hux. I can find trouble without help. We'd best get everything ready to move out tomorrow. If that snows develops, both the city path and remote land trails could be blocked soon."

"So, we go city-side together?"

"That's what I said."

It wasn't quite what he'd said, but relief loosened Landra's limbs.

They spent the rest of the day organizing the cabin. By the time Landra finished, the inside was cleaner and the contents more ordered than when she'd arrived. Thisk gouged his scalp once when he cut a rough Warrior mark into his hair. Rather than put the thin blade away, he offered it to Landra.

"I'll wait to see Leo," she said.

They gathered their few belongings into carry sacks, and then she climbed the tree to reclaim the Collector. Thisk watched her, not bothering to keep the disapproval from his face.

"Father will disown me if I go back without the knife."

"I know that, but I don't think you should be the one to retrieve it."

"It's my responsibility."

She wriggled along the branch with an outstretched hand, needle-like leaves scratching her cheeks. A creaking sound stilled her, and she edged along a little farther. Stretching her fingers, she touched the Collector's handle and rolled her grip around the carved bone handle. It was warm, despite its frosty resting place, and heat pumped through it into her body.

The hethra came on her like an invading virus, as if it had waited for her to touch the knife. The forest dimmed from view, and she slipped into a visualization.

Darkness swarmed across her vision and bobbing aura lights twinkled all around. City warmth wrapped around her body, shutting out the snappy forest wind. Landra tracked moving shapes in the gloom, only recognizing the forms as soldiers by their faint auras and whispering voices. Despite the confusion, Landra knew one thing—the last time she'd smelled that musty book odor, she had been standing in Father's stateroom. She was looking at her home.

A sudden explosion lit the scene, and a booming noise shook her body. In the illumination, she saw the true horror of the situation. Bexter stood before her father's desk brandishing a sword. Blood splatters dripped from his blade and shaded his blue cadet uniform. His handsome face contorted in a ferocious snarl as dark-robed Templers closed in on him, their staffs raised in attack.

As quick as the scene had emerged, it faded into darkness.

Bexter! Father? Are you there? What's going on?

She couldn't grasp how Templers could have invaded Hux Hall or why Bexter was the one to face them. Enraged shouts cut through her confusion, and a solitary screech of agony drenched her in fear.

No!

She relied on grunts to make sense of the battle. It was like a horrible dream, but a deep of part her knew the truth: The fighting was happening now, in her home, to the people she loved. As she clung to the branch, the cadet's anguished shout jolted her back into awareness. A blue aura rose in her vision, stretching too thin hold together, before it twinkled out of existence—death.

"Bex!" she shouted.

No one answered. Landra's scrutiny flitted over the remaining auras in a desperate search for ones she knew, but in the real world, her tree shook. She thought she spotted Bexter's even shades, but his edges rolled in uncharacteristic curves, so she couldn't be sure.

He would be unsettled. He's in battle. Where is everyone—the guards, Dannet, and Father?

Nothing made sense. Vibrations rocked through the tree again, and her grip released. She tumbled, her vision receding as if being sucked down a tunnel.

Thump! Her back slammed to the forest floor, and her chest burned with the force of her exhalation. Tall trees and a grey sky came back into focus, but she only saw the Collector. It followed her down, point first. Thisk snatched it before it could strike. He hunkered over her, his dangerous eyes, overgrown beard, and unkempt uniform making him look savage.

"Stand up," he ordered.

She had little breath, and her panicked thoughts raced in confusion.

"I said stand up."

Am I hurt? She clambered to her feet, her body sore but not screaming with deep damage. She couldn't make sense of all she'd seen, but her chest squeezed so tight the next white breath wouldn't come out.

Home invaded. Someone died. Oh shelk!

The Warrior's slap came without warning. His open palm met her cheek with more force than he'd used before. Her face numbed, but she felt the shock of the blow deep in her gums.

"I've tried to train you, Hux. I thought you understood about this shelking magic. It's here in our world, but it terrifies most soldiers. And you? You're the chief's daughter and the chief elect. It's most dangerous for you. I would never have taught you the hethra if I'd known of your flaw. This could bring down our world. Don't you understand?"

Landra did understand. She'd always understood better than anyone else. It was a shock for someone else to recognize her predicament, but the Warrior only understood a fraction of her problem.

She didn't just have a Soul touch; she had Soul sight. She hadn't used the hethra or even sought out magic. The power had assaulted her, leaving no option for refusal, but what did that matter now? A crash of panic lit her anger as she thought of home, the battle, her friend, and death. Drawing herself up with a hand on her cheek, she glowered at Thisk.

"If you can't control magic, you should avoid it alto-gether." His aura pulsed with deep blue swirls.

Landra's head pounded, and all she could do was groan. The blow had shocked her system, but Thisk showed no pity. Anger simmered in her gut like bubbling stew. He'd hurt her more than once in the name of train-ing, but she hid her rage with a feigned stumble.

Seeing no caution in Thisk's aura, she charged and jumped, landing both her boots on target. He hadn't antic-ipated her retaliation and was off-guard, so the blow rammed home. Not in a high-scoring kick to the head or a disabling stamp on a joint, but deep in his manhood. Thisk curled in a ball, emitting a strangled groan.

"I'm not feeling very nice today, Warrior Fourth." She yanked the Collector from his grip. "And that knife is mine. We're not waiting until tomorrow to go home. Get your things together. We go today."

She wanted to explain, but sharing the details of her magical vision would only make matters worse. The kick hadn't satisfied her in the way she'd thought it would, but it had been necessary. Nothing could delay her trip, and she didn't have time to field questions. She stormed away from the Warrior and left him to moan.

By the time he returned to the cabin, she'd shuttered the windows. His face was unreadable, but he collected his things and strode down the path toward the city. Landra paused to admire the log pile before departing. It only had a couple of layers when she'd arrived. Now, the stack reached to the window frame.

She glanced at Thisk, who was heading toward the tree she'd targeted during training. That failure still stung, so she drew a plain weapon from her belt strap and set her sights on the narrow trunk. She hurled the blade into flight and watched it whistle past Thisk's head. It had been weeks since she'd thrown a knife, but the skill lived in her body like an old friend. Her last attempt had fallen short, and she expected the same result now, but this shot planted into the bark and held.

The Warrior whipped his head around to glare, but Landra hid a strained smile. She hitched her sack higher onto a shoulder, and set out with a defiant stride. She was stronger now, and she knew what she had to do.

For once, Thisk waited for her to catch up. They walked past the tree together, neither of them glancing at the knife. There were enough weapons in the city shaft, and she wanted this one to stay in the bark. It symbolized the gains she'd made and for a wonder, Thisk didn't object.

Damn you to the mist, Fourth. You made me strong, but I'll never admit that to you.

She set her shoulders back and faced the city—home. Only the mist knew what trouble brewed inside.

Chapter 27

Standing on the overlevel at Hux Hall's shaft door, Landra felt cold inside and out. Thisk hadn't spoken, but there wasn't anything unusual in that. Sometimes he didn't talk for days at a time.

She stuffed her gloves in a pocket, snatched the hat from her head, and ran one hand over the spiky tufts of her hair. Every layer of her clothing felt grimy, and she understood the ranger's usual disheveled appearance better now. Time spent in the remote lands wasn't kind to Warrior sensibilities, but it was the least of her worries.

"Make sure your insignia badge shows," Thisk said, fastening his own pin to his collar. "Your hair tracks are completely gone."

He kicked a loose snow covering from the trap, and flashes of the ransacked hall wormed into Landra's thoughts. She moved her badge to her outer jacket and drew a sword from her hip sheath.

"Expecting trouble?" Thisk asked.

What should I say?

Her cheek still throbbed from his slap and she didn't

want to invite another, so she eased her sword in her belt, squeezed her lips into a thin line, and shook her head.

The Warrior tugged on the trap door's ring. The panel didn't move, so he dropped to one knee, set a gloved hand to the floor for purchase, and heaved.

"Nope. It's not budging. Either it's frozen solid or locked from inside."

"Are they usually locked?" Landra asked.

"They're supposed to be when a sentry isn't posted, but the rules aren't always followed. And there's always a sentry on Hux Hall. I've roamed in and out for years without trouble."

That was before, when battle hadn't wrecked Father's stateroom.

Thisk hammered on the trap, his fist bouncing frost-stiffened leaves into the air. Just when Landra thought he was ready to break in, the trap creaked open and exposed a sliver of darkness. They both retreated, expecting the panel to fling open. It rattled back into place.

"That's not normal." He nudged the trap with his boot and then flipped it over. They both stared into the darkness. If there was any sound from below, it was swallowed by the howling wind. Thisk rolled his tongue around his mouth and scratched his beard.

"Not normal at all." He reached for the ceremonial sword sheathed on his chest. "Stay here, Hux."

"Thisk!" she called, as he turned to climb down.

"Yes?"

She groped for a warning, but her visons weren't welcome. He'd made that clear. "Be careful." She'd never felt more like a coward.

"Did you… Do you know something?"

"Just be careful."

He clambered out of sight, and the wind sounded louder in his absence. Landra dithered at the shaft's entrance to peek over the edge. The Warrior's blue aura-light shifted in the gloom below.

Shelk, Thisk! I can't leave you to face this alone.

Before the thought completed, her boots were on the ladder and she was heading down.

"Citizen," Thisk growled, and she heard rebuke in his tone. "Pull the trap and bolt it behind you."

The wooden panel fell into place and all light fled, leaving a darkness she knew was wrong.

She fumbled the locking ring into position then followed Thisk's blue aura to the bottom rung. Her boots settled on the midlevel, and she was home.

"Where are the emergency lights?" she whispered.

"Don't know."

Wariness trickled red shades into the Warrior's aura, similar to the ones he'd displayed in the remote lands. What had seemed appropriate for confronting hunting beasts was enough to loosen her bowels here in Hux Hall.

"Draw your sword," Thisk whispered.

"Not my knife?"

"Gods of the mist, no. We don't know who's out there."

Shouldn't Father be out there and the hall guard? Who are you expecting to find? Not Templers, I bet.

She eased her blade free as he cracked open the door. Solid blackness endured and continued into the corridor. She waited for a rush of warmth to touch her cheeks, but the iciness of Hux Hall offered nothing.

"We've been invaded," she whispered, relieved to share what she knew at last.

Thisk stilled, and Landra didn't want to guess what he was thinking.

"Stand behind me," he said.

As she hunkered behind his broad frame, he kicked the door wide and stepped out with his sword raised.

"Halt and identify yourself," a panicked voice challenged.

Bright flares in Thisk's aura signaled battle readiness, but Landra recognized the challenging tones. They belonged to a familiar member of the Hux Hall guard, who had a crimped blue aura.

"Wait, Thisk," she said, stilling the Warrior's arm. "That's a three-bar in Father's guard."

"You sure?"

"Sure. That's Hyana's voice."

She felt Thisk's chest heave before he spoke again.

"Who's in there? This is Ranger Warrior Fourth Thisk. Report, soldier. Why have I been stopped?"

Hyana approached the doorway and pulled out a hand lamp. A bubble of yellow brightness captured the soldiers' forms. Three more battle-armored guards stood firm at Hyana's back with their swords raised.

"Thisk?" Hyana queried.

The Warrior ranger edged forward.

"It is you, Fourth, sir," Hyana said with relief. "We thought you were lost, man. Do you have the Hux girl?"

Landra started forward, but Thisk swatted her back.

"The child is safe."

A cycle ago, Landra would have fumed at the Warrior's insult. She understood his ways better now, but, no, even after all they'd been through together, she bristled at him naming her a child. She'd endured enough in the remote lands to demand more respect.

"What the shelk is going on?" Thisk demanded.

"Hux Hall was attacked sir. They came in through the shaft. Were over us before we knew it."

"Who attacked?"

"Templers is the word, sir. I wasn't here myself, but Vesi saw 'em wearing robes. Once the hall guard woke up, the shelking buggers ran like rats from a flood. Did a powerful lot of damage first, though. We're going to be clearing for days, even when the power's back on."

"Where are the raiders now? In prison?"

"No, sir. They melted like ghosts and took their injured with them."

"Any of our soldiers hurt?"

Landra held her breath, waiting for the answer. She'd planned to harden to trouble, but her world had just shifted beyond recognition.

"Some," Hyana said. "Seemed like they wanted mischief more than killing. They came through the shaft from below, hacking off power roots on their way up. Chief won't let any Templers back in to fix the problem, so we'll not have lights anytime soon."

"And our people?" Thisk insisted, a growl in his voice.

"Yes, well, there was a scuffle in the stateroom, and the chief took a knock. I think they went after him in particular. Baylem went crazy and took them all on without help until a couple of cadets got called in. There's no word on her or the lads yet. We were left here to guard what's left, sir, with special instructions to look out for you and the Hux girl."

"Lads? Was Dannet there?" Landra asked. She was so panicked she nearly gave away her vision and asked who had died.

"I didn't get told details," Hyana said, "but I'm sure he's fine. I saw him leave with the others."

Not Dannet. That's good, but who? She didn't dare let herself think about it.

"Where's the chief now?" Thisk demanded.

"Warrior Hall, sir. Said it could be secured better. I'm

supposed to take you there. Sorry about the challenge before. Thought you'd arrive through the front door, and we're all on edge."

"Don't be sorry for doing your duty, Hyana. Take us to the chief now."

"It'll be a march, sir. There's battle armor in the guard room, and a detail will take you."

"Changing can wait. My conversation with the chief is long overdue."

"Might not be safe, sir. I can't guarantee your safety if you march through the base in ranger getup. It's bound to cause a stir."

"I'll take the chance."

"Groke, Fen, take up shaft guard positions," Hyana ordered. "This way, sir." He gestured toward Thisk.

The Warrior sheathed his sword and reached for Landra. "Come on."

She'd listened to the conversation with building despair and couldn't think of her father or Baylem's smiling face without descending into guilt-ridden anguish.

Thisk tugged her to his side and gripped her collar possessively.

"Did I cause this?" she asked. "Is this retaliation for what I did in the temple?"

"Probably not," he whispered next to her ear. "It's more likely my fault. Don't say anything until we know more. Admit nothing."

They stepped out of the shaft into the swell of light from the guard's hand lamp, but the waiting soldiers froze when they saw Landra. She nodded to Ellis, a soldier she'd known for years, but he snatched his glance down to his feet rather than offer a greeting. An unfamiliar girl stared openly and set her jaw dangling.

"Do I look as bad as the guards think?" she asked.

"Worse," Thisk said, "but it's nothing a bit of scrubbing won't cure."

Landra knew that wasn't true. No amount of washing could hurry away the darkening of her cheek or her scars, just like no amount of reassuring could convince her the hall would ever be the same.

"If you won't wear battle armor, at least pick up a fresh cloak for Citizen Hux," Hyana said. "It's a way to Warrior Hall, and she'll cause a riot looking like that."

"There's a good city cloak in my room," Landra said. "If we drop by on the way, I can pick it up."

Hyana sucked air through a gap in his teeth, and his aura juddered.

"Problem?"

"Like I said, citizen, there's been a powerful lot of mischief. Can't be sure your cloak's still there, but we can look if you want."

He led them through the narrow accommodation corridor, which led to Landra's room. She could have navigated it with her eyes closed, but the narrow space looked different in the patchwork of bobbing lights. Every soldier's breath and boot stamp sounded louder in the dimness, echoing in a strange and dreadful song. Snatches of light captured the damage. Pictures hung askew on the walls, and broken furniture littered the floor.

She spotted her door swinging at an angle on a single hinge. So, her room had been violated. As she touched the door panel with one finger, it whined on a screw as it rocked.

"Sorry, citizen," Hyana said. "Guess it wasn't good to have the Hux name during the raid. Good thing you were topside, if you ask me."

"Can you give me a minute?" she asked.

Hyana nodded. "Here, you'll be needing this. He

backed away, but Landra stopped Thisk's retreat by grabbing his sleeve.

"Can you wait? This doesn't feel like home anymore."

"Welcome to a ranger's life. We're never any place long enough to feel like we belong."

"That's not what I mean."

"I know. I'll be here 'til you've finished."

She climbed over the door corner and raised her lamp high enough to take in the room. Her furniture remained in place, but the drawers hung open and her bedding and clothes formed a heap on the floor. She searched for the puzzle Dannet had given her but without success. The oddments, which usually rolled around the bottom of her room's planter, had gone too.

Just as well I took you with me. She reached back to touch the Collector.

The chaos made her want to run, but she rummaged in the heap of clothes in search of a cloak. The one she remembered was there, and she settled the blue cape around her shoulders, draping the hood down her back. Before she left, a mouse scurried through the pile.

Landra stilled her new instinct to kill the creature for food and offered it a small bow. "It's all yours," she said. "There's nothing left for me here." After a final glance around, she left the room she'd grown up in, not knowing if she would ever return.

Chapter 28

Their departure through Hux Hall brought more anguish. Landra peeked through an open door to the armory and saw empty racks where weapons used to rest.

Hyana spotted her glance. "The chief ordered the armory, stores, and kitchen stripped."

It was another change, and every discrepancy from the home she remembered fed her misery.

If I hadn't gone with Oakham, none of this would have happened.

The main exit was deserted now, and she recalled her last trip this way, when she'd chased Thisk to the overlevel. It felt like a long time ago and in a different life.

Hyana held the exit door open. "Warrior Prenderman will take you from here. I'll supervise the clean-up crew. After, we can barricade the shaft and close the hall."

"Thank you, soldier," Thisk said, pushing Landra into the main corridor.

She refused to look back, preferring to remember Hux Hall as it had been in her youth.

Their new escort party looked tired, as if struggling

through the final hour of a double-duty shift, but when their stares fell on Landra, interest broke over their features. Warrior Prenderman removed his glasses for cleaning and balanced them on his nose to scrutinize her appearance. Tiny pops in his aura betrayed his fascination.

"Lead the way, Warrior," Thisk ordered, tugging Landra's hood over her face. His glare told Prenderman to mind his own business.

"Yes, Fourth, of course."

The guard herded his team into position with Landra at the center of the group. On their trek across Central City, she glanced from beneath her hood once, when their route took them through the main concourse. A glimpse of the ceremonial dais sent her blood racing. She recalled the same gold drapes and blue bunting from pictures of Chief Hux's investiture. Warrior statues framed the stage, larger than life and with sword tips raised in salute. There'd not been such preparations in her lifetime, and she couldn't reconcile the grandeur with the troubles her world faced. Full-powered lights bathed the empty stage in yellow beams.

Draining the magic well. A deep sigh pushed breath from her lungs. *Is this real? Will I be the new chief elect?* It didn't seem likely after her misadventures, and she was torn between disappointment and relief.

A sudden feeling of displacement wobbled her stride. Hours ago, she'd been foraging for food and battling the elements. An unexpected part of her wanted that simple, dangerous life back. Her glance shot to Thisk. If he was having problems with the transition, he hid it beneath his dark features, but there was a definite stiffness to his ranger aura when the grand façade of Warrior Hall's entrance came into view. Depictions etched on the wood around the wide doorway showed hard-fought battles, violence, and blood.

Thisk shared a word with the immobile Warriors who guarded the entry. From their expressionless faces, perfect insignias, and ice-still auras, Landra could have taken them for mannequins. They didn't sport many achievement ribbons, but their azure cloaks fell in sharp pleats. As Thisk spoke, the guards' gazes turned on Landra with widening eyes. She tried to bury herself in her cloak, but there was nowhere to hide. Once the conversation ended, Thisk pushed Landra through the entryway. Ceremony usually accompanied a soldier's first passing through the door in recognition of a graduation to elite status.

Not this time.

She was through without fuss and facing a large depiction of her father's sword emblem on the facing wall. It made the place belong to him as much as Hux Hall ever had, but there was no time to dwell. Thisk moved with a purpose, leading her through the maze of tight corridors without need of consulting wall maps. He finally halted in front of an identical door to the one outside Hux Hall's command room. Despite outward calmness, his aura swirled with dark shots of anxiety. *This has to be Father's room.*

"Surely we're cleaning up before seeing the chief," she whispered, trying to keep the door guards from overhearing. She wanted to look her best to face judgment.

"Some problems don't improve with time. Best we face this sooner than later, and the chief will want our report at once."

Landra had experienced her share of nerves, fear, and anxiety in her short life, but the dark shades swirling through her aura represented all three varieties of dread. She hadn't seen Father since her fight for the Collector and couldn't guess how his anger had built during all that had followed. Her knees weakened as if ready to buckle.

"Name and business?" a female door guard asked. At the ranger's glare and a lift of his collar badge, she disappeared inside.

"Take your lead from Chief Hux," Thisk said, running grubby fingers through his unkempt curls. He looked ready to say more, but the door swung wide and banged against the wall. Chief Hux filled the frame, his thunderous grimace making Landra wish she'd bolted for the remote lands. He summoned them inside, and the door closed.

This was a smaller room than the Hux Hall stateroom, and Father's furniture crowded the space like it didn't belong, but his grand desk still formed a focal point for business. Without bookshelves, his dusty volumes formed uneven stacks on the floor, but the base's history record had travelled complete with its stand. A man with beady eyes, shocking white hair, and a slender frame sat next to the desk.

Chief Hux sat down and signaled for them both to face him. "So, you decided to come back."

When neither of them responded, Chief Hux opened a drawer and removed a trinket. He set Oakham's insignia pin on the desk, folded his arms, and glared.

Not Father anymore. Today, you're my chief.

Chapter 29

Chief Hux retrieved a sling from the desk and threaded it over his head. He grimaced as he rested his arm in the fabric.

Landra worried as a daughter. Enduring years of neglect hadn't destroyed her love for the man. *You were attacked and driven from your home. Are you injured, Father? Dare I ask?* She started forward.

Thisk's firm grip tightened on the back of her jacket. "Dignity, Chief Elect."

She remembered her situation and followed the ranger's example, settling her hood back and coming to attention.

Chief Hux's gold-flecked eyes speared her and then slid to Thisk, scrutinizing them both, as if taking in every nuance of their filthy, worn appearance. Whatever injury he'd taken, it didn't affect his sharpness or the spiking intensity of his aura. She waited for him to ask a question or for Thisk to explain.

"Well, aren't you two just a pair," her father said. "Hux Hall was attacked, the treaty is failing, unrest threatens to collapse Warrior rule, and you two turn up six days before the chief elect ceremony looking like a couple of exiled criminals."

Six days. Landra couldn't believe how long she'd been in the remote lands.

"I can explain," Thisk said.

"Stand down, Fourth. I want your report, Chief Elect."

Landra snapped a glance to Thisk and then to the man at the back of the room. She'd tried to keep the promotion a secret, so Father's mention of her new rank set her off-balance. The pale man didn't look like a Warrior, but the length of his hair told a different story. He crossed his legs and examined his fingernails. Elegant curls spun through his thin, blue aura.

Chief Hux offered her a reassuring nod. She stepped forward, looking her father in the eyes, rather than focusing on Oakham's insignia badge. She opened her mouth to ask what he wanted to know, and the nail-primping soldier jumped to his feet. The man stood at the podium behind the chief's desk, opened the history tome to a blank page, and picked up his pen. It hovered over the sheet.

Landra's hand flew to her mouth. There wasn't any part of her tale she wanted shared, let alone recorded, but her father nodded his insistence.

"Tell me everything you've done since we last met," he said. "Lyster will record your words. Pay him no attention."

"A revised training schedule arrived under my door," she started, and the historian's pen scratched as he penned her words. She gaped at him, bringing the report to a pause.

"Carry on," Father prompted.

"Yes. Yes," she said, trying to get back on track. She glanced at Thisk, who stared forward.

No help? Thanks.

"Anyway, Thisk was outside my door, and he wouldn't let me down the corridor to see you."

"Thisk?" Chief Hux interrupted, turning his attention to the ranger.

"There was a schedule," the ranger answered.

"That's not what I mean. She calls you Thisk? Not Warrior Ranger Fourth?"

"I… Yes."

Chief Hux's eyes narrowed. He turned his gaze back to Landra, and she felt like her Soul was under scrutiny. "Carry on, Chief Elect."

Without training, Landra's report jumped between events and tracked back in repetition. She skipped Soul-related events, and when her story reached the temple incident, her eyes flickered to Oakham's badge. Her knees weakened, and her thoughts scrambled. She gathered herself and explained her descent into the pit as aiding a veteran. It wasn't a lie, but it didn't come close to the full story.

She found it hard to decide which parts of her adventure were pertinent, so useless tales spilled out, like descriptions of the cluttered contents of the ranger's house and which berries tasted good. She didn't brag about her successes, figuring he didn't need to know that her personal high point had been when she'd learned to piss and shit in the forest without soiling her clothes. Her tale wandered aimlessly until she ran out of words. Then, she just stopped.

Chief Hux rolled his lip under his teeth. "Hrmph. Sort that out, will you, Dolan?"

"Yes, Chief Hux. We had a lot to get through.

Teaching our chief elect to report didn't come high on the list."

Griffin nodded and closed his eyes. He took a cup of green liquid from his desk and sipped from it, grimacing. "Holy shelk. I'm sure Gren's medicine is worse than any injury."

"What happened, Father?" Landra asked. She wanted to know the details of the attack. *How badly are you hurt? Who died?*

He waved her concerns aside but answered Thisk's inquiring frown.

"Really, it's nothing, Dolan. Well, it's not nothing, but I'll make a full recovery, so you don't need to look concerned. Pass me that bottle, will you?"

Thisk retrieved a half-empty scute bottle from the top of a chest and handed it over. The chief swigged three good gulps.

"Ah, that's better. Now, Dolan?"

"Griffin?"

"Relax, will you? Your stunt caused me no end of worry, but I'm glad to see you both safe. Tell me everything."

Stunt? Landra's misadventures and training had felt far from a stunt.

Thisk reported on events in order and with detail. The first interruption came when the ranger described punching out several Templers, breaking a treaty, and invading the temple on a rescue mission.

Thisk had beaten Landra, allowed her to half-starve, and trained her like a prisoner on punishment duty, but his indiscretion had been her fault. Despite everything, she didn't want him to suffer. She held her breath, wondering if she would have to admit her magic to save him.

"Did you really have to do that, Dolan? I had the worst time straightening things out with the priests."

And there it was. All Landra's worrying and sleepless nights had been for nothing. There wasn't even a mention of Oakham's death. It felt like someone had pulled a plug and drained the energy out of her body. She'd held onto her dread for so long that it felt exhausting to let go.

"I didn't know what had happened to the child," Thisk explained. "Did you want me to leave her there?"

Child? What happened to chief elect?

"She shouldn't have visited the temple alone in the first place. Why else would I post you as her guard?"

Why did you do that, Father? Surely, there was someone else.

"Yes, sir," Thisk said, his words staying tight, but the limits of his aura relaxed, as if his worst fears had fled.

Chief Hux sighed. "I know the job I gave you, Dolan. My daughter goes her own way and finds trouble in unexpected places. I think you're realizing that now. Thankfully, it came out all right. Her attentions to the dying sentry helped me smooth things over. Seems like the priests were fond of the old man, and she did see the plaque, so it's not all bad."

"Yes, sir," Thisk repeated.

Chief Hux waved a hand toward him. "Continue."

The ranger launched into the rest of his story, and Landra saw gushes of relief flow through his aura. The second interruption came at mention of their trip to the cabin.

"The remote lands, Fourth? Really?"

The Warrior took his cue from the change of address and pulled to tighter attention. "I did what I thought best to keep the girl safe and let the fuss settle, sir. And it wasn't the remote lands. We barely left the city perimeter."

Griffin stared at him for several minutes and then

relaxed. "Don't get huffy, Dolan. I suppose she was safest there, especially with everything that's happened on base."

"What has happened?" Thisk asked.

Yes, tell us what happened. I want to know.

"It's a long story for another time." The chief twisted his neck and signaled for the historian to leave. "Report back tomorrow."

"Yes, sir," Lyster replied. He blew on his newly written words, collected his pens into a bag, and left.

Once the door shut, Chief Hux took another swig of scute. "Now, Warrior Ranger Fourth, report on Citizen Hux's suitability to fulfill the role of chief elect."

Landra stiffened her shoulders. She didn't want to be in the room for this. In fact, she would have been happier if Thisk and her father weren't in the room either.

The ranger stared at the wall to deliver his verdict. "Citizen Landra Hux is immature."

The chief nodded, leaned an elbow on the desk, and cupped his chin in his palm.

"She acts on impulse and allows her heart to rule when strategy is required. It's clear she's incapable of keeping information secure. Despite effort, her lack of height and bulk leave her below championship fighting standard. Her education is limited to textbook explanations where real-life experience would be of more use. She doesn't give orders naturally and chooses to ignore clear rules. Hux has little desire to be chief elect."

Landra wanted to sink into her boots. She hadn't sought a glowing report, but Thisk's direct reciting of her faults was worse than anything Winton had ever delivered. All she needed to cap it off was for him to report on her responsibility for Oakham's death and that he considered her Soul-touched.

Where would that leave me? The answers running through her head didn't get better than exile to the remote lands.

"Some of her ideas are misguided." Thisk continued. "At first, I thought she was stupid, but I changed my mind. She learns quickly and retains information. I came to realize she sees problems as a challenge and looks for unconventional solutions. She cares about people, sometimes to the detriment of wider problems. Landra Hux is…"

Don't say it Thisk.

"She's nice."

It was impossible to comprehend the criticism delivered in that one word without hearing the ranger's tone. It struck Landra to the core, but she had no time to recover because his litany continued.

"She has some fighting skill and works hard to maximize her abilities. Her hethra is developing, but we've terminated instruction for the moment. There are signs she will be able to command, given time. She is proficient with some remote land skills and might survive the warm time alone. Despite her ambitions lying elsewhere, I believe she will fulfill the chief elect duty to the best of her ability."

Chief Hux's eyes had narrowed with each condemnation, until now when they closed. He scratched his stubbled chin. "So, you think her an appropriate choice for chief elect?"

What? After that?

"Yes, sir," Thisk answered.

Landra listened for doubt in his voice and was shocked to hear none. Only his aura showed his concern.

"And you would follow her?"

That's a bigger question. Darker streaks tracked through Thisk's aura, and she guessed the main source of his doubts. *Will you tell Father I'm Soul-touched?*

211

"Yes, sir," Thisk said. "I will follow her."

Chief Hux eyed his Fourth. "But you think she'd make a better ranger?"

If Landra had been shocked before, now she was stunned. It felt like Thisk was eternally disappointed with her performance. She hadn't expected him to say anything good. Winton certainly hadn't. She now wondered if her time with the ranger had been about training or if it was a test.

"This is your decision, Griffin," Thisk said, "but if you change your mind about how best to use the girl, I'd consider taking her on as a trainee. It would be a shame to waste the gains she's made."

Chief Hux gave a small smile. "A waste indeed. Thank you for your report, Fourth. You are dismissed."

Thisk snapped to attention and saluted. Once he left, Landra felt more vulnerable than if she were naked. Jagged azure strips shot through her father's aura, signaling more trouble to come. Now, she had to face it alone.

Chapter 30

Chief Hux sipped more of Gren's medication and followed it with a slug of scute. "Takes the taste of that swamp slime away. So, you managed to impress Dolan. That's not an easy achievement."

"I didn't think I had, sir."

She enjoyed a rare smile from her father.

"Not known for sharing, our Fourth. Most Warriors take on cadets as runners, but you're the first Dolan's shown an interest in training."

What Landra remembered most was Thisk sharing his fist with her face. Accepting a position as his runner didn't sound safe or enjoyable.

"But I need you here," the chief said. "You do understand that, right, Landra? I can't spare you to roam the remote lands."

"Yes, sir. So, you plan to go ahead with the promotion ceremony?"

"Of course. Your appointment's been written into the new treaty."

Of course. She shuddered, readjusting to the future she'd given up hope of seeing.

"We need to regroup and confirm our authority," the chief said. "Otherwise, it's war. We've kept it quiet, but a guard died in the raid on the hall. Protesters march every day, and this—"

"Guard?" *Not Bexter then. Baylem?*

"Focus Landra. Thisk was smart taking you to the temple. What did you make of the plaque?"

She wanted to admit that she'd done more than see the plaque, but how could she explain meeting Chief Gallanto? *I'm Soul-touched and shared a vision with the last sentry. I have orders from your dead grandfather. Shelk.*

"I'm not sure, sir," she said.

"You understand we can't close the temple."

Landra nodded.

"If my talks go well, we can come to an agreement everyone is happy with, secure the power supply, and ensure peace. I can't tell you how vital a successful chief elect investiture is to the process. You have six days before the ceremony."

She wriggled to feel the Collector between her shoulder blades, barely believing she was back on the course Father had set into motion the night of their fight.

"I have something to show you," he said. "Come sit beside me."

Landra's world skewed another notch. She'd never sat beside her father, and now she took a place beside him, looking like a vagrant and smelling worse.

"This is an invitation list." He dropped a file in front of her without opening the top cover. "Memorize the names and some facts before the investiture eve party."

"What facts?"

He flipped the top cover open. "Personal things. Like

Warrior Second Tasenda has three husbands and five children she never sees. She will be important to you when you're confirmed as the elect. An ally, if you like. The more you know, the less likely you are to offend."

Landra looked shocked. "Three husbands? How does she manage that?"

"Tiredly," Chief Hux replied, and they smiled at each other. "No one at the celebration will know who the chief elect is going to be."

"Mostly no one," Landra said.

"True. There will be speculation, and you have to join in. Any hint that you're the new chief elect will bring risk. We don't want objections or attacks before the ceremony completes and your elite protection guard is in place."

"What will happen at the ceremony?"

"I'll walk you to the platform. Watch those steps up to the stage. They're bitching wide, and I tripped at my investiture. Make sure to polish and sharpen the Collector before the day. It's an important symbol, and everyone will look out for a glimpse of the handle. Tradition dictates you wear it on your hip."

Landra's mouth dried. She remembered pictures of Father wearing it in the same place, and the truth hit. *This is real.*

"There are speeches and testimonials," he said. "Thisk will speak on your behalf. Will that be a problem?"

"I don't think so, but you'll have to ask him."

"Once the words are over, I'll drape your new cloak around your shoulders and fasten the chief elect insignia pin into the collar. Then you head to the chair for your haircut. I asked Leo to perform the honors. I hope that's all right."

Landra smiled. *A familiar face.* "Where will Dannet be standing?"

Chief Hux's face tightened. "In the crowd. He doesn't know yet. I'm sure he suspects the position hasn't gone to him, but he doesn't know you're stepping up."

Landra's relaxed disposition fled. Her good intentions to share the news with Dannet had been lost on the over-level. "You have to tell him."

"No need for a fuss. He can find out at the ceremony like everyone else."

"Not with me as chief elect. You can't do that to him, Father. Promise me you'll tell him before the day."

"Enough Landra! I'll do what I think best. Now, you should go and clean up before rumors spread of you going feral. It's hardly what soldiers want from their leader. There's more to the job than having fun in the remote lands."

Fun? She hadn't the energy to argue.

"Dismissed," he said, and there was nothing to do but leave.

With her boots barely outside the door, she heard her brother's voice.

"Where the shelk have you been?"

"Dannet?"

Her brother stood there, a sharp new haircut framing his angry features. Bexter stood at his side.

"Bex," she blurted out. Her gaze tracked over his body looking for damage. "I thought you were hurt."

He didn't shy away from her scrutiny. "You heard what happened? I'm fine. That rumor spread when Baylem's blood sprayed over me. I took a few blows during the battle, but nothing serious. Gren's declared me fit for duty."

"Yeah," Dannet said. "He's quite the hero, our Bex, charging in to fight the invaders before the guard arrived. He has to get an achievement ribbon for this. If I hadn't been tinkering with Barthle's ovens again, that might have been me." He straightened and glowered at Landra. "But what about you?"

She returned his scowl, wanting to tell him her news. "What about me?"

"Where've you been, Lan? No one knew, not even Chief Hux."

"Field trip."

"And what are you wearing?" Dannet gaped as if unsure what to criticize first.

Landra realized she still wore the outdoor cloak from her room around her shoulders. She swung it off but was dismayed at what lay beneath. Her dust-shaded trousers and tight-fitting jacket looked worse. Dannet stared at the crust of dried mud breaking into crazy patterns over her boot caps.

"Don't look at me like that," she said, her face heating. "These are cold-weather clothes. I told you I've been on a field trip."

"To the remote land bogs? You stink worse than Bex's socks."

His guess wasn't far from the truth, and she was certain her hot cheeks must be glowing brighter than Bexter's red ears.

"I don't need your opinion," she said, mortified to be seen in such a state. Bexter's presence made it worse. She'd not bathed properly for weeks and hadn't looked at a mirror in a cycle. The young cadet's turnout was entirely the opposite. Only some Jethrans fulfilled their soldier destiny with style. Raven Bexter carried his athletic frame with dignified confidence.

"Why were you both even in the hall?" she asked, trying to change the subject. "I thought you went back to the academy."

"We did," Bexter replied. "For most of the cycle. They closed for the chief elect preparations, so we were sent back to the hall. Everyone knows how that turned out."

"The staff decamped here after the attack, and we were ordered to come along," Dannet said.

"Ordered?"

"Anyone with the Hux name is on strict security lockdown. I'm surprised you managed to stay out on your holiday for so long."

She let that pass. "You sound cheerful for someone who's homeless."

"Look where we are, Lan. Warrior Hall. I thought it would be years before I came through those doors. There are Warriors everywhere, and you should see their achievement ribbons. I even got to spend time in their group training sessions."

"Sounds fun, but I really need to clean up and find Baylem. Is she bad?"

"No word yet," Dannet said. "She came in with another injured guard. I think they're still with the medic."

Landra caught Bexter staring. "Is something wrong?"

"You're looking very—"

"What?" she snapped. *Dirty? For sure. Battered? Accurate too. If rumors are back from the temple, add Soul-touched and murderous to the list.*

Bexter and Dannet gaped at her outburst.

"Don't be like that, Lan," her brother said. "We're all feeling stressed with what happened back at the hall, but that's not Bex's fault."

Guilt kicked Landra like a mule. She wanted to snatch the words back when she saw the cadet's stricken expression. She'd been through more trauma in the last cycle than in all her years before, and her emotional walls were shattered. She took a steadying breath.

218

"Sorry. I've had a hard for few days, and it got to me. What were you going to say, Bexter? I'm looking very…"

The cadet hung his head. "It doesn't matter."

"No, go on," she prompted.

He still didn't answer.

"Please?" Landra said.

"I was going to say that you look very athletic."

Holy mist. Landra had tried to attract Bexter's attention for years without success. He'd offered polite conversation but nothing more. Now, she saw him staring at her newly muscled shoulders, and his blue aura pulsed into deeper shades, inviting her to touch its boundaries. *Why now, Bex, when there's no time left, and my life is such a mess?*

"Athletic!" Dannet snorted, breaking the mood. "You've got to be kidding. Landra's a pushover." He shoved her and gave a surprised laugh when she didn't waver. "Maybe she's been working out, but she's never pinned me down in a wrestling match and never will."

"I need to head to the showers," she said, wanting to save them all from the embarrassing moment.

"Enjoyable as this has been, we should go too, Bex. The Warriors don't like it when we block their corridors."

"Not me," Bexter said, and Landra glanced up.

"I'm not family, so I have to work to stay here. I'm assigned as your duty guard, Citizen Hux."

Thisk's doing. Got to be. Had she mentioned Bexter to the Warrior? She was sure she hadn't, but it was just his style to post the object of her infatuation at her side. The man had a twisted sense of humor. No, she was certain Bexter's name had never come up, but she had dreamt about the cadet most nights. *Did I talk in my sleep?*

"I'll catch up later then," Dannet said. "I have a dozen things to sort out. Don't do anything I wouldn't do, Bex."

Landra stared after her brother, convinced he had no

idea about her attraction to his friend. *Just as well. You'd only make a joke.*

"Where's my room?" she asked.

"In the barracks, I'm afraid. Space is tight this close to the city hub."

"Makes sense," Landra said. "Lead the way."

Chapter 31

Six days. Landra didn't feel ready for the ceremony. Whatever training Thisk had provided didn't seem like preparation for what was to come. She had so much to do, but she decided to take the next few days one step at a time.

"Which way to the stores?" she asked Bexter.

"This way." He tugged her down a narrow side corridor. "Store Chief Dell is a bit stern, but you get used to him. By all accounts, he's good at his job."

They ended up at a counter facing a man who looked too young to be a Warrior, never mind a department chief. His permanently downturned mouth, stiff cheeks, and unblinking eyes made Landra nervous to speak.

"We only stock Warrior uniforms here," Dell said, glaring in disgust at Landra's condition. "Try on base."

"Citizen Hux has a billet here for security reasons," Bexter said. "Did a parcel arrive from Hux Hall with her belongings for laundering?"

The quartermaster narrowed his eyes, as if not quite believing such a low-ranking soldier should stand in his stores. There was an order to the man's aura that made

Landra understand why he wanted her gone. Without a new uniform, Landra's appearance had no way to improve, so she held her ground.

"I'll check," Dell said before heading into his back room. After a few minutes, he returned and dumped a large parcel on the counter. "This seems to be for you, but if you need more uniforms, take a trip onto base or send a runner. We don't have room to store kits for every rank here."

If it wasn't for her Hux name, Landra was sure Dell would have called guards to escort her away. "Thank you, Stores Chief Dell," Bexter said, snatching the parcel. Landra grabbed it off him.

"I can manage my own kit, Bex."

They made a brief stop at her new bunk, and she was relieved to find her roommates absent. Seeing them before she'd showered would hardly make a good impression. It was a six-bed bay, but only four looked occupied. She sorted through her kit for a change in uniform and hung the rest of the clothes on a rail. Her pale blue citizen uniforms looked at odds with the darker Warrior blue garments on the other racks, and she spared a moment to let that sink in. She'd wanted this, to be in Warrior Hall, but her manner of arrival felt more wrong than she could explain. A deeper regret stayed with her too. Every soldier on base wanted to reach here, but she'd glimpsed the possibility of more. She didn't need to see the homeworld to keep Oakham's longing and sadness in her heart. It was part of her now. *Maybe I'll share Dannet's excitement later.*

They headed for the showers next, and Bexter waited outside.

Not awkward. Yep, not awkward at all. I really saved us from that one.

She found an empty cubicle, hung her new uniform on

a wall peg, and locked the door. With each layer of remote land garments she removed, more dirt dropped to the floor. An intermittent water stream sluiced the gunk away. Her discarded clothes went into a laundry bag, but she suspected Dell would throw them away rather than attempt to clean them. Her knife strap went on a peg, and the Collector's pink blade gleamed in its sheath. She stared at the weapon.

Can I do this? Can I assume the chief elect role and broker peace?

She still stared at the knife as she turned on the shower and stepped under the hot stream. Lathering soap over her head made her spiky hair soften. Clumps of filth twisted in the water. She rubbed soap over her body, accepting that it would never be the same. Her frame was more muscular than she remembered, but there were scars too—silver reminders of falling on rocks, scrapes climbing trees, and nicks taken in battle. The magical scar still tracked down her arm in a series of spider web patterns, more faded now but still there. She rubbed soap into the lines, wishing they would disappear altogether.

Once she felt clean, she leaned against the wall, let the water cascade over her body, and thought of Bexter. A range of lustful scenarios played in her head. *Are any of them possible? Chiefs take partners, don't they? And female soldiers are expected to bear children. Shelk Thisk to the mist.* Sometimes his humor was beyond understanding.

A flicker at the edge of her vision made her turn. Her pale blue citizen uniform swung on the wall peg, its crisp fabric making her anticipate looking like a soldier again. She dismissed the light show as imagination and gave herself a break. *Who wouldn't be on edge after returning to find her home ransacked?*

It had been a nearly a cycle since her last hot shower,

so she squirmed against the stinging sensation and enjoyed a brief respite from the of turmoil her life.

Hot bolts of light exploded in her vision. Landra grabbed at the wall, her hands scrabbling on the smooth surface. Her heart jumped when she recognized the assault. Naked, and with Bexter standing outside the shower room, Oakham's Soul vision overtook her like a like rampaging sickness. She'd just had time to recognize her worst fears were materializing before she became Oakham again, checklist in hand.

Templers manned their trees, Meftah stood with Gallanto on the platform, and the greeting party gathered at the bottom of the ramp. She set about her tasks as Oakham, repeating actions like doing drills on a loop, but inside, she screamed in protest. It was the anguished plea of a trapped creature, desperate and shrill. Without any control, she yelped in the real world.

Drum-like thumping intruded on her completion of Oakham's checklist.

"Citizen Hux?" Bexter said from outside the shower door. He sounded concerned.

Landra's senses shared a dual reality. In one world, she performed as Oakham, reliving her people's defining event. In a smaller part of her mind, she felt the water on her back and heard Bexter's worried shouts. The cadet was thoroughly Warrior-born. He smelled like a Warrior, walked like a Warrior, and acted with a Warrior heart, regardless of current rank. There was no place in his world for Soul magic. If he discovered her secret, she would lose him forever.

"Landra?" His plea sounded more urgent.

She couldn't answer. The grip of the vision had her in its power, and she went about her tasks as the old soldier. She was Oakham, torn apart to see Gallanto say goodbye to his wife, broken to see the portal come alive for the final time.

"No!" she wailed in the real world then pushed. The shove wasn't a physical action but a mental rejection of all that appeared before her eyes. She threw her fury into repelling the magic. She rejected her magical flaw, the unwelcome promotion, the loss of her mother, and the violation of her home. Her frustrations coalesced into a single mental shove, and the scene pixilated. Encouraged, she thrust again until the vision shattered into a myriad of fragments. They spun past her face like shards of ice, each bearing a slither of the fake reality. As the travelling pieces thinned, she slumped to the floor and felt water running down her body again. She hid her face in her hands to block out the world, but a deeper dread set in. She wanted to deny what she saw, but with her eyes closed and her hands pressed over her face, she could still see the world. This wasn't the Soul memory coming to play tricks on her reality. The shower room came into focus as clearly as if she looked at it with wide-open eyes. A pile of blue-tinged towels filled the rack in the corner, a low wooden bench was spotted dark with dampness, and her uniform still hung as a reminder of her soldier heritage. The door shook from louder banging. She shivered, trying to deny the worst of her nightmare and the awful truth. She couldn't just see the world. She saw Bexter and his aura through the wall.

Give me a break, world. Just give me a break.

Thisk arrived to pound on the door, with Bexter dancing in agitation at his back.

"There was a scream," Bexter said. His words came to her ears as clearly as if he were standing beside her in the room.

"Hux!" Thisk shouted. "Open the door."

She couldn't respond. Her magic was still growing, despite all her efforts to keep it in check. She was turning into a Templer, and shock controlled her now. Her body slumped, too exhausted to move. She wanted to tell Thisk not to worry and that she would be out soon, but the lie wouldn't come.

The door burst open, and she couldn't move. Thisk stormed into her cubicle. Bexter leaned his head past the door but ducked back at the sight of her nakedness, a healthy dose of embarrassment overriding his concern. She wanted to hide, but that wasn't possible. She had nowhere to go and no strength to move.

"Fetch a medic," Thisk said, unabashed by the scene. He switched the shower off, tore the ceremonial cloak from his shoulders, and threw it over her body. Decency restored, he hunkered down at her side.

Bexter's aura shrank as he headed down the corridor.

That's good. Don't witness my shame.

She was alone with the Warrior now and couldn't help sharing his panic. Blue darts coursed through his aura. He pried her hands from her face, but she looked away, misery in her gold-flecked eyes.

"Can you walk?"

She didn't answer, so he bent down and scooped her into his arms. She huddled into his chest to hide her face, his forest-smelling jacket reminding her of the cabin. His roaming blue aura filled her Soul sense, offering blessed blindness to the rest of the world, so she gripped the fabric of his shirt and pulled herself closer.

"What happened?" he asked as he charged through the corridors.

Tipping her face up, she worked her mouth until words would come. "A nightmare." It was both the truth and a lie.

His knowing stare didn't ask for more, but she knew he would want an explanation later. Whatever gripes they'd brought from their trip were forgotten now.

"I made the wrong choice," she said in a small voice. "Why didn't we disappear into the remote lands?"

"Because we wouldn't survive the winter."

"I know, but we should have gone anyway."

She felt his grip tighten around her body.

Medic Sturton met them halfway to his infirmary and shuffled alongside as they kept walking. "What happened?"

"Not here," Thisk growled.

Landra wanted to shout at gawkers who watched their progress, but she hadn't the energy to make noise. Thisk settled her into an infirmary bed, and Sturton shooed him and Bexter away. The soft mattress, thick blankets, and warm air stream provided more comfort than she'd known in a cycle. She didn't want to find sleep in case her fears tagged along in her dreams, but an unnatural weariness pulled her down, deep enough for the world to fade. As she slipped into sleep, Gallanto's voice whispered, "Save our people, child of my life."

Chapter 32

After an excessive amount of prodding and poking, Sturton declared Landra a splendid physical specimen and fit for discharge. He tutted over her bruised cheek, which was too shaded to have come from falling in the shower, and he prescribed physical activity to relieve stress. Then he ordered her away before second siren with the comment, "And a good haircut will make the world of difference."

Landra stared at the wall and wiggled her fingers before her eyes, checking she couldn't see through to the space beyond. The action pulled an odd stare from Sturton, and she guessed the man had her pegged as an idiot.

That could prove interesting once my promotion's announced. Here comes Landra, the idiot chief. A weak smile found its way to her lips.

She wore a brand-new uniform, but the Collector hadn't arrived with the fresh supplies. A memory flash from the previous day saw it hanging on a peg in her shower cubicle. She went rigid before deciding Thisk would have sorted its safekeeping. At least, she hoped he'd taken charge of the knife.

With things on her mind, she didn't step out of the infirmary right away. Of the two other patients under Sturton's care, one was a Warrior with a slash to the leg, taken in service on the Warrior's Run. The other was Baylem, who slept behind a wafting curtain.

Landra lifted the screen to peek inside. Tightness squeezed her heart at what she saw. Her friend sprawled over the bed as if no bones supported her body. Yellow-stained bandages wrapped her head, spasmodic breaths broke through her pale lips, and her lidded gaze seemed to drill the ceiling.

You survived, you're in the right place, and you're not as bad as you look.

It was easy to think but impossible to believe. Baylem's aura stretched thin enough to resemble an almost-white shroud.

Sitting beside the bed, Landra stretched a hand over her friend's delicate Soul, and a strand of blue light drifted loose from the aura. She reached for the thread, only to see it dissipate into particles between her fingers. As the Soul strand winked out, Landra felt the loss in her gut. *Oh, Baylem, you're leaking away.*

A sob caught in her throat. She lifted the girl's slender hand into her lap and was surprised by its coolness. Training calluses ridged the palm.

"You're supposed to be dead," Baylem whispered, opening her eyes to slits.

"You're supposed to be asleep," Landra countered.

"There'll be time enough to sleep soon."

Landra controlled her short breaths, but silent tears tickled her cheeks. "What do you mean I'm supposed to be dead? Is that what everyone thinks?"

"Only the gossips."

Landra smiled. "How are you?"

"Sturton says I'm recovering, but it doesn't feel that way. Seems like it's a bad idea to duck under a falling hammer and take a sword slash. I can't get my strength back. Every time I wake up, more weakness washes over me." Even as she spoke, another twist of aura-light drifted free.

What can I say, Baylem? You're right. You're leaking away. Not useful.

"From what I hear, you saved my father from raiders," Landra said. "Don't let him avoid giving you a ribbon for this."

"I wouldn't go that far. A couple of guards were there and Bexter too." Her grip suddenly tightened. "Rednet— he took a blade through the guts. Innards spilled every-where. Did he make it?"

A shape formed in Landra's memory of the invading hethra, a soldier dying, and an awful scream. *So, that was Rednet, and he'd been impaled by a blade.* She hadn't known the quiet guard, but his death felt wrong. *A sword wound on a Templer raid?* That didn't make sense. She couldn't bring herself to answer the question.

Baylem broke the silence. "I hear Bexter came with your family to Warrior Hall. Have you seen him yet?" A sly twinkle lit her eyes, lightening the mood.

"Maybe," Landra answered, and they both managed a laugh, but Baylem's chuckle led to a coughing fit. More aura strands drifted loose until a sip of water settled her shaking.

"What are people saying about the raid?" Landra asked.

"How would I know? I've been laid up in this bed, and

Sturton's strict about visitors. I was hoping you'd have the goss."

"No gossip, just a sore head from my fall in the shower."

Baylem groaned and contorted her face enough to make Landra laugh. "Best go before Sturton comes to check. If I don't look asleep, he'll throw poison down my neck."

The girl looked like sleep would descend, even as she spoke, and Landra knew she should let her rest.

"I'll check in tonight," Landra said, but she wasn't truly certain she would see Baylem again.

"With an update on Bexter?"

"To see how you are," Landra answered.

"Boring! When you come back, be sure to bring Dannet."

"I'll try," Landra said, and another tear rolled. "I'll set you up on a date."

Baylem couldn't manage a response, so Landra eased away. Threads of the girl's aura attached to her uniform, and a solitary strand tangled with her own blue shades and melded. By the time she drew the curtain back into place, her friend was already making convincing sleeping noises. Sturton witnessed her tearful goodbye, and they locked eyes. He didn't offer any words; there wasn't anything to say. Landra was grateful he left her to her grief.

She wiped her sleeve across her face and left. A mass of blue Warrior auras confronted her in the corridor. She glanced each way to see who would approach, but no one took notice. For the first time since her chief elect appointment, she was free to roam around. With the Collector missing, too, she felt a release, along with a side order of panic.

Warrior Hall turned out to be a lot like Hux Hall. It

contained a condensed version of all that was on offer in the city. She found the barber's shop without much trouble and sat behind a queue of five Warriors. Gripping her citizen pin, she met their stares. *What? Not seen anyone in such a mess? Is it a crime to have a low-ranked soldier here?*

If there was anything Landra wanted right now, it was to feel like a soldier in the Jethran Army. She needed this haircut and refused to leave. The barber's seat freed up, and all five Warrior heads turned her way.

"Go ahead, citizen," one of them said. "You need this more than us."

She took her place in the chair and saw what they meant. Gold-flecked hair tips covered her ears, and her insignia mark had vanished. She put her pin on the table and waited.

"Citizen Landra Hux?" the barber asked.

"Yes. How did you know?"

The barber took out his scissors, rather than clippers, and trimmed the ends from her lengthening strands. Then he put his scissors down and indicated for her to depart.

That's it? I know you cut Warrior hair, but have you forgotten how to do soldier cuts?

"Shouldn't it be shorter?" she asked.

"You're down for a partial trim."

"I am?" This never happened with Leo. "And what about my insignia?"

He pursed his lip and shot her an impatient glance. "That's it. Like I said, you're down for a trim."

She stumbled out of the chair bewildered, but the seated Warriors exchanged knowing glances. A reflection showed them making signals behind her back.

What the shelk is going on?

At home, she was familiar with every aspect of her world and the people who worked there. Here, she was lost. She wandered back into the corridor and wondered what to do next. The extent of her freedom became clear when she strolled through the corridors and found herself near the Warrior Hall exit. The guard on duty snapped to attention but barred her way. At her puzzled expression, he cleared his throat.

"Citizen Hux, I have orders from Ranger Warrior Fourth Thisk. You're not permitted to leave."

She goggled, surprised at being recognized again, but not by the order. *This is Thisk at his best, but does everyone know who I am?* She was used to being recognized in Hux Hall, but here she should be nobody.

"He said it was for your own safety, citizen," the guard said, mistaking her reaction.

Landra nodded, taking comfort from Thisk's security, even if he wasn't around. This arrangement was preferable to having a guard shadow her every step.

She turned in the opposite direction, wondering what to do. A baking smell reached up the corridor, and she had her answer. When had she last eaten? She followed the aroma, and her route took her past the stores. Dell opened his desk-panel and chased into the corridor. Blue stars of excitement danced in his aura.

"Citizen Hux, may I see you for a moment?"

His tone was more respectful than on her last visit, and she followed him into stores. A cautious frown knitted her eyebrows together.

"I received more orders regarding your uniform requirements," Dell said. "Please, can you stand over here, so I can take your measurements." She followed his instruction, still puzzled, and Dell set a tape measure around her chest.

"I've never been measured for uniforms before."

"This is a special one-off. I don't ask questions, citizen. I just supply whatever uniforms are ordered."

"Who ordered this one?"

"Like I said, Citizen Hux, I don't ask questions."

And then Landra knew this was Father's doing. A special uniform could only be for the promotion ceremony. She suddenly realized Dell knew exactly what he was preparing. She stood in silence as he turned and adjusted her body. He measured each aspect of her form, but his knowledge of her chief elect status made the experience surreal. Thisk's appearance in the doorway came as a relief. At least with him, she could be herself.

"There you are," the Warrior Fourth said. "I've been looking all over for you. Sturton wasn't supposed to discharge you until a guard was in place."

And with that, Landra's freedom ended.

"How are you feeling, citizen?" he asked.

It was interesting how he used her official rank, now they were back on base. Out in the remote lands, he'd used whatever honorific matched her behavior.

"Much improved, thank you, Ranger Warrior Fourth Thisk."

His face offered polite satisfaction, but blue waves of scorn roamed through his aura. He looked smarter than she'd ever seen, like a shaggy, wild animal after shearing. A band controlled his unruly curls, and his clipped beard hugged his face, revealing the hint of a short scar across one cheek bone. The clean lines of his insignia declared his high-ranking status, but his calm, rangy aura was the most reassuring thing Landra had seen all day.

Here in Warrior Hall, he wore his best cloak—with its abundant display of achievement ribbons—a ranger uniform cut from Warrior blue fabric, and his usual sword. Only his boots showed wear, and she suspected he rotated a few sets without taking new ones from stocks. *Understandable.* By the time she'd come back from the remote lands, her foot blisters were just starting to heal. *This new pair will tear my skin to shreds.*

"I'm pleased you're doing well, citizen," Thisk said. "You nearly done, Dell? I need the girl to run some errands."

"I've got what I need, Warrior Fourth."

"Good."

Thisk grabbed Landra by the arm and walked her out.

"What's this job you've lined up for me?"

"No job. Where've you been?"

"The barbers, but I might need to go back because he didn't cut my hair properly."

"He did exactly what Chief Hux ordered him to do," Thisk said. He glanced each way down the corridor, making sure no one could hear. "Your investiture is days away, and the proceedings involve a ceremonial haircut with your new insignia. How can that happen if you're cropped short and have a citizen mark? It could delay everything."

"Oh," Landra said. "So, the barber knows about—"

"He wouldn't have been told, but it's easy for anyone with eyes to guess."

"It's overwhelming, and I'm not even sure I should follow Father's plan. Not after... You know. My... incident."

Thisk yanked her to the wall and shot another glance around. "Now that we're here, you have to go through with it. There's too much at stake to duck out. Just don't do that thing again."

Landra knew what he meant, but if he had the impression there was a way to control her magic, he was deluding himself.

"You eaten? The food hall is down this way." He walked away, but Landra called him back.

She did her own check of the corridor before speaking. "What happened to my kit from the shower room? There were certain items I left behind."

"You mean, one certain item?"

"Yes, well, what happened to one certain item? Do you know?"

"I do, and don't worry. It's safe."

He led them into a long room filled with trestle tables and benches. Landra had never seen so many Warriors together in one place. Most of them ignored her and continued eating, but some stares followed her movements. She picked up a juice flask, roll, and a bowl of hot oats before finding a spare seat. The soldiers at the next table pointedly didn't look her way. Thisk joined her with a plate full of meat and spiced vegetables.

"Does everyone know about me?" she asked.

"That depends on what you're asking. Some of them know that we're sleeping together."

"What!" She pushed back her chair and jumped to her feet.

"Sit down. The soldiers not gossiping about us as a couple think you've lost your mind. They're watching in the hope you'll throw another wobbler. Please don't give them reason to spread that rumor further."

She reclaimed her chair and eased back down. No one was looking at her now, but the food hall had fallen quieter than Gren's waiting room. As if things weren't bad enough, Winton appeared. He strode in, gloating to be accompanied by a two-bar Warrior. He paused at her table to make sure she noticed, and his tight, ordered aura glowed.

"Good day, Warrior Fourth, Citizen Hux. I heard you

fell in the shower. That's some nasty bruising you have there. I hope you have a speedy recovery." His textbook politeness barely covered his delight at Landra's recent mishap.

"Thank you, Trainer Winton. That's very kind, and I can assure you I'm fine."

"You want to join us?" Thisk asked in a leave-me-alone tone.

No, no.

Winton considered a moment, not hiding that he would enjoy the prestige of sitting with the Fourth. Landra wondered if he would change toward her when her new status was announced.

"I would," Winton said, "but I came with a friend today, thank you."

Once he disappeared, Landra stabbed a knife into her roll. "All this talk can't be good news for the ceremony. Father will be furious if he finds out."

"I think he already has. We're both due to face him on report."

"When?"

"In about"—he glanced at the world clock on the wall —"ten minutes."

"Great!" She wasn't sure she wanted to eat now, but an aroma drifted up from her roll that was impossible to resist. She gulped down as much food as possible before Thisk cleared their dishes.

"Come on," he said. "Let's not be late."

Chapter 33

"Everyone else out," Chief Hux said when Landra and Thisk arrived. The pair stood before him, as sure of their innocence this time as they had been of their guilt at the last reckoning. The chief made them wait until he finished unpacking his sword collection. The bandaging supporting his arm had gone, and he stretched his fingers with a wiggle, as if they tingled.

Finally, he turned to Thisk. Even Landra flinched at the fierce shine in his gold-flecked eyes. His long hair hung around his shoulders today, the gleaming strands radiating a healthy shine. His loose training outfit didn't detract from his business-like manner, and despite being a fraction shorter than the ranger, there was no mistaking who held the authority in this encounter.

"Warrior Ranger Fourth Thisk," Chief Hux said, and the ranger's spreading aura tightened, along with his spine.

"Sir."

"My son has come to me with concerns."

Landra twitched, annoyed that her brother would

bring tittle-tattle back to Father. If he'd heard the rumors, he should have asked her about them.

"Concerns, sir? What has Dannet said?"

The chief sneaked a glance Landra's way. "He visited my daughter in Sturton's surgery and noticed fresh bruising on her face. He believes you've beaten her."

Landra's mouth fell open, and she shared a shocked glance with Thisk. It was true that he'd hit her, but he did have reasons and she'd done worse in return.

"This is ridiculous. Dannet shouldn't come telling tales," she said. "Have you told him about the promotion? Is this a way of getting me back?"

"He still doesn't know of your new rank," Chief Hux said, taking her face in his hand and tilting her head sideways. He checked out her mottled cheek. It was the kind touch of a father. Landra's thoughts churned, concerned with Dannet's ignorance rather than his complaint. She opened her mouth, but her father's snapping aura stilled her protest.

"You deny this happened?" His eyes narrowed to bring the evidence into focus.

Landra flattened her lips into a line, not sure what to say.

"It's true. I hit your daughter," Thisk said.

Chief Hux turned his focus to the Warrior and confronted him face-on. "Explain!"

The ranger didn't flinch. He squared his shoulders and said simply, "I was annoyed with Citizen Hux and struck her."

Teeth ground behind the chief's stiff jaw, and he settled all his attention on Thisk. Bright slivers of purple fury shot through his aura.

Landra hadn't seen those before. "He did but—"

"Not now." Chief Hux raised his hand to silence her

protest. "I hadn't believed it when I heard the gossip, Dolan, but it was the least ridiculous story to cross my desk about you two. Is the rest true as well? What have you been doing out there in the remote lands?"

Thisk's aura held the calmness of an innocent man, mostly. "Chief Hux, sir, you tasked me with protecting and training your daughter. That is what I have tried to do. In the process, I believed she was putting herself at unnecessary risk, and I lost my temper. So, yes, I did hit her."

"Against all protocols and rules?"

"It wasn't on base, sir, so technically no regulations were broken. I'm no tutor, and you know that. I just did what I thought right."

"Right? Any soldier following your example will think it's acceptable to hit our chief elect."

"Only if they are stupid, sir. I wouldn't recommend it to anyone."

"And what's to stop them?"

"The chief elect will stop them, sir. She packs an exceedingly painful retaliation." He shuffled uneasily, as if remembering the kick to his groin.

The chief glanced at his daughter, his gold eyebrows stretched. Landra couldn't believe they were being grilled on this when their temple escapades had passed with little comment.

"We settled the matter, sir," she told him.

"So, you have no complaint, Landra?"

The memory of Thisk's blows would take longer to fade than her bruises. His training methods had been brutal at times, but she'd learned a great deal under his guidance. Now that she had the opportunity to share her grievances, the desire ebbed. "No, sir. I have no complaints. Any differences we encountered have been resolved."

"With fists?"

"And boots," Landra said. "I'm a soldier, sir, not a delicate Templer to be coddled."

Amusement twinkled behind Chief Hux's gold eyes. His glance shifted between them. "Hrmph. We'll call this matter closed then, but is there anything else I should know before the gossip-mongers beat a path to my door?"

Landra exchanged glances with Thisk. The remaining tittle-tattle was nonsense, but her magic would always be a dangerous secret.

"No, sir," they said together, almost too synchronized.

Chief Hux sighed. "Good, because our future's in the balance. The Templers are holding ransom over the power supply, and Warriors are fuming. Another Templer faction has demanded vengeance for persecution. Both sides would like to see the promotion ceremony derailed. Secret talks have secured an agreement, and we need this truce to side-line extremists. Your appointment is vital, Landra. Everyone needs continuity and the succession line secured. Your promotion will come as a surprise in many circles, but securing peace is going to require a different path."

Landra sank into her boots, feeling the press of responsibility shrink her aura. She wondered if Father would follow this route if he knew how different her path might be.

"Now that I've shared our strategy, I ask you again, are you both certain there's nothing that could jeopardize our plan?"

"No, sir," Thisk said.

Landra took a moment longer than she should before answering. If she was going to admit her growing magic, now was the time. A warning glance from Thisk convinced her to stay quiet. "No, sir."

Chief Hux's questioning gaze flicked between them, as

if he sensed deception, but he scratched his head and expanded his chest in a sigh of acceptance. His aura stilled, but tiny darting lines betrayed his nagging worry.

"That will have to do," he said. "I'll put an end to this gossip. Make good use of your final days to prepare, Chief Elect Hux. I have a busy time ahead, so I probably won't see you until the investiture party. Remember, careful conversations will serve us best, and you should save any painful retaliation tactics for the championships or if we end up at war. Am I making myself clear?"

"Yes, sir," Landra said.

"Dismissed."

By the time she found her room, she discovered her belongings had been moved to a single cubicle with a locking door. *Snug.*

It was smaller than her room in Hux Hall, with furniture crowding the space at odd angles because of the tighter curving walls. A ridiculous flower-patterned mirror hung above her bed, and diagrams of fighting maneuvers covered the remaining walls, as if the previous occupant had left in too much of a hurry to take them down.

Someone had draped her clothes over a hanging rail rather than suspend them from hooks, and the Collector rested on the desk, along with the puzzle ball Dannet had made. She recognized Thisk's less-than-subtle touch and wondered how he'd made it through the academy. Pulling a chair out from the desk's footwell, she slumped down. The puzzle ball rocked gently on the wobbling desk.

She picked it up and turned it in her fingers, admiring Dannet's soldering of the wire cage. *Will you ever make me a gift again once you know what I've done?* Her teeth scratched together as she considered her deception. She'd meant to tell her brother everything, even before Thisk had taken her to the overlevel. Chief Hux should have never kept him in the dark. Now, it felt too late to tell him the truth, but he would know she was going to be chief elect soon enough.

Shelk in a slop bucket.

Tipping the cage, she watched the bead roll through its center and along the wire channels. Whichever way she angled it, the ball ran into a blocked route.

"Thanks, Dannet. Just what I need—a problem I can't solve."

She retrieved the Collector, meaning to stow both the objects beneath her bed, but the bead came to purple life inside its metal cage.

Her breathing quickened, her thoughts whirled, and her mood plummeted. "Of course," she said with resignation. "Magic." The Collector always brought her power to life. Without rolling the cage, the ball rose inside its metal trap. Her blue aura encased it, and her mental desire for escape sent it twisting through the channels. Wires distorted with a whine to allow the bead's passage and then creaked back into place. Finally, the bead of purple magic dropped through the center channel and out of a hole. It settled on her palm and made her skin tingle. *I'm about to become the first magic-possessed Chief Warrior Elect in Jethran history.*

"Fantastic," she said to the wall. A relieved sigh parted her lips when the wall didn't answer back.

Chapter 34

Fear of discovery had nagged Landra since her magical visions had emerged. Today, it squeezed like a tightening noose. She practiced a gritty smile and waved at her reflection. This was how she used to look, not with shaggy hair, gaunt cheeks, and gaudy party clothes, but auraless and dull.

A glance down to her flesh-and-bone hands stiffened her smile into a pained mask. Auras might cast no reflection, but a flip of her palm sent eddies swirling through her real-world Soul. *This is my truth.*

She heard a noise outside. *Rap, rap.*

"Guard detail here, Citizen Hux."

"I'll be out soon."

"Make it quick. We're on a schedule, Lan. We're to accompany several guests to the investiture party tonight."

Brennan's voice. The three-bar's service to Hux Hall had begun well before Landra's arrival from the junior barracks. His familiar voice was unexpected but welcome.

"I won't be long," she said. "The world won't end if the party starts without me."

Might be worse if I do go.

With every important six-city Warrior and Templer scheduled to attend, Landra couldn't imagine pulling this off. Just because Oakham hadn't met any Soul-sighted soldiers didn't mean there were none on base.

Not shelking likely. I should have said something sooner. Why did I hide?

The knock came again.

She slipped the Collector's strap over her tight under-bodice, covered her knife with a flouncier shirt and jacket, and arranged her trousers. Dell's custom design of floating panels barely covered her thighs and showed a ridiculous amount of skin.

Rap, rap. "Is everything all right, Citizen Hux?"

Deep breath, Landra.

"Coming."

A compliment of four household soldiers from Hux Hall waited outside. *A nice touch.* She knew them all—Brennan, Cleaver, Harp, and Dobbs. Much as she liked them, she tugged the back of her overgrown hair, wishing she had Thisk for protection.

"Hey, Lan," Dobbs said, beaming. His gaze fixed on her legs. "We get to walk you through Warrior Hall and on to the party."

"Everyone in place," Brennan ordered, and the group formed a loose ring around Landra to head down the corridor.

"Who d'you think they'll announce tomorrow?" Dobbs asked, edging alongside Landra.

"Not our place to guess," Brennan answered. "Youngsters like you don't know the way of things. Part of the excitement's in the surprise. Ain't that right, Lan?"

She took a deep breath, added bird-like grace to her

bearing, and felt ice in her heart. "That's the way I heard it."

The quizzing brought home her situation. *This time tomorrow, I'll be the new chief elect—or in jail.* Anything between felt impossible.

Dobbs nudged her elbow, feasting his gaze on the peep of her thighs. "But surely you have an idea who it is, Lan. I bet it's Dannet. Did he say anything to you? Go on, you can tell me."

"It's supposed to remain private until the ceremony," she said, swallowing hard and trapping her trouser panels in place beneath her hands.

"I know, I know. But—"

"Dobbs!" Brennan snapped. "Stop your whining and keep watch. Citizen Hux knows the rules, like you should. Taking you on a job is like dragging along a junior barracks brat."

The young soldier leaned in close and winked. "Share the news with me when the others have gone."

Landra's stiff smile made her cheeks ache.

"Can I have a dance when my duty finishes?" Dobbs asked.

The floor seemed to rise to her next step, making her stumble. Dobbs caught her arm. At only four years her senior, his one-bar rank and a posting to the Hux Hall guard put him on a Warrior track. He'd be a good catch for any girl, but his thin aura dissipated against her own strong shades. The mismatch doused her interest. She'd already planned to search Bexter out for a dance.

Still, why limit myself to one partner on my last night of freedom? Dobbs will likely salute me tomorrow rather than ask for a date.

Chanting sounded as they neared the Warrior Hall exit. Not a soothing temple chant, but angry tones riding a stream of hateful shouting. Landra's heart thudded against her ribs.

"Attention," Brennan ordered, and everything changed. The guards halted in a tight circle around Landra, swords drawn. She reached to her hip for the sword Thisk had given her in the remote lands, but bunching, soft fabric filled her grip.

Shelk! Defenseless.

As the chanting mounted to a persistent chorus, phrases stood out, making sweat break on her palms.

"End Hux rule! Templer for elect!"

Back off and you'll get your wish, Templers. Half of it, anyway.

She strained her neck to see through the exit and saw a female Warrior striding to meet them. Light bounced off the woman's bevel-edged sword at odd angles, and muscled shoulders spread her battle-spiked epaulettes wide.

"Templer protest outside," she said. "Leave the back way."

"Is it bad?" Brennan asked.

"It's nothing," she answered, but gyrating flashes surged through her aura, exposing the lie.

So, it begins.

From her vantage point, Landra saw a line of helmeted Warriors, holding still behind a row of positioned shields. Their massed auras formed a heaving ball of roiling blue light.

"Hold, Warriors," the order went up from the commander in charge. An arcing firebolt crossed their line, flying over their heads like a comet trail.

The bolt landed in the Warrior Hall entrance. Red, molten tongues spread from the impact, licking the walls as they raced through the corridor.

Landra jolted back, recovered her balance, and

charged forward, sure the missile had hit the supporting soldier ranks. *Fire in a wood-built base—criminal, unconscionable.* Rage set her ready to battle.

"Easy, tiger." Brennan moved to block her path. "We have Warriors to deal with this, and my duty is to keep you safe."

"But no." She edged to pass him. Her Hux Hall guards shouldered together, blocking her progress. Their combined auras gelled into a warning barrier she was loathe to touch.

Not fair.

"Brennan?" she asked, a pleading note to her voice.

"We know our job, Citizen Hux, and that's to protect you. It's time to go."

"This way," Cleaver said, dragging her back down the corridor. The wood beneath her feet shuddered.

"Run," Brennan ordered, as a rolling ball of fire chased them down the narrow hallway. "The magic's after us."

"Shelking demons of the mist," Cleaver swore.

Landra's terror soared, equaling what she felt from her guards' auras. Her legs pumped, her heart banged out a staccato rhythm, and her thoughts froze. Fire filled the corridor behind to form a blazing trap, and flaming tongues chased after them. Harp paused to drag old Brennan up when his legs failed, then resumed his flight, but the old soldier buckled again not three strides further on.

"Shaft," Landra said, as she remembered Thisk's lessons on evacuation routes. "Where's the shaft?" Her eyes darted around, but she couldn't recall the hall's geography. Her reclusive stay in Warrior Hall felt like a mistake now. Heat from behind reached her aura, rippling her blue shades in wavy patterns and softening their edges.

Brennan went down again, so she turned back and ran

toward the inferno. There was no smoke or natural coiling flames. Red magic rode arrowing tongues of fire down the corridor. Heat blasted her face, and she knew they were going to die.

The magic fingers aimed for her with precision. She couldn't imagine how anyone would know who to target, but she was sure her secret was out. *These men will die with me. Not fair. Can't...*

Her aura surged into action in an instinctive response. The blue shades expanded into an immense bubble, which encompassed her guards. *Yes. Yes. This might help.* She focused enough to harden her aura edges into a shield, but heat still seared her skin. Sweat poured down her neck and back. *Hard to breathe.* Each second the shield remained in place, her energy drained more. It was exhausting, debilitating. Her body shook, her teeth rattled, and she wanted to sleep.

Can't rest now. Surely, this is what it means to be chief elect— giving all to save my people. So, I'm using magic. Doesn't lessen my courage or devotion.

Her knees wanted to buckle but she edged forward, her aura ranging with a will of its own. It grew again, enveloping and suffocating the flames. The fire crackled and snapped, fighting the constriction, dwindling in size, and fading in color. Her aura's edges closed tighter, squeezing, squeezing. The blaze licked at her limits in search of fuel, but an inner bubble of stronger color protected her soldiers. Her outer bubble left no gaps.

Splutter. Spit. The fire stalled. It twisted, dwindled, and popped out of existence, leaving a stench behind—and the trace of a Soul.

Who's there? Shelk.

Harps's rough grab at her collar woke her to the world again. "What were you thinking, citizen?" He pulled her away from the smoldering section of corridor, and the aura contact broke.

She glimpsed a wisp of pink thread shrivel and twist away down the passage, and her own blue shades wound in like a sucking whirlpool. It felt like there was no room in the narrow corridor, and her chest heaved as she tried to reclaim her breath. Warriors charged down on them, their fury battering Landra as their volatile auras spun with outrage. One insistent Warrior herded them to safety, and her guards settled into a close group with her at the center.

"You all right?" Brennan asked.

"Right," Dobbs and Harp answered.

"Shelking shit balls," Cleaver added. "What happened there?"

Landra knew but wasn't about to explain.

"You, Citizen Hux?"

You asking me if I happened? Or if I'm all right? The guards' stares made her cringe, and trembling ran through her entire body. "I'm fine," she said, remembering the Soul touch and feeling far from well.

"Take it easy, dear," Brennan said, and Landra could have sworn it was in Oakham's voice. "The fire's out, and everything's under control."

In whose world?

"A party's not worth this," the old soldier said. "We'll stay in the hall tonight."

Landra grabbed his arm. There was nothing she wanted more than to hide in her room. "No, Brennan. I still need to go."

"Come on, love, there'll be other parties."

"Not true," Harp said. "Investiture parties don't come more than a couple of times in soldier's lifetime."

"Well, I might not see another, but that means you

whippersnappers have another to look forward to. I'm ordering you to stand down."

Landra's grip tightened, and she leaned toward Brennan.

"D'you need to see Medic Sturton?" he asked.

"No, Bren, I need to go the party."

"I don't think so."

Landra breathed deep, taking air into her strained lungs and steeling her determination. "Brennan, I don't want to go to the party. I have to go, and that's an order. I…"

He turned wise eyes on her and took in the shaggy cut of her hair. His half-cut, half-tattooed insignia showed his experience. With floppy jowls, age-spotted hands, and bowed shoulders, he was old enough to command them all, but he pulled to attention. He stopped just short of giving a salute, but whirling thoughts showed behind his lively blue eyes.

"And you have to go to the ceremony tomorrow?" he whispered beside her ear.

Landra took longer this time, but she nodded.

"Guard detail," Brennan shouted, the command returning to his growling voice. "Head for the back door. There's a party to attend."

Chapter 35

After a quick stop to clean up, Landra tracked through the City's deserted corridors with her guards. "Where is everyone?"

"Dancing," Dobbs said, the mischief in his voice carrying no trace of their recent ordeal.

"Of course. It's a big occasion," Brennan said. "There's not been a night like this since Griffin stepped up. Funniest thing I've ever seen. We could tell he was getting promoted cause he looked ready to mess himself. Begging your pardon, Citizen Hux."

Landra wondered if he was trying to help her relax. Did she show the same look now her father had worn then. For shelk's sake, she had more reason to feel nervous. Her stomach heaved as if she'd swallowed a skipper bunny raw. Whoops of excitement came from the leisure sector concourse, unsettling her more. Soldiers were celebrating a chief elect appointment, and tomorrow they would know it was for her. She gripped her belly, thinking the skipper bunny had started a party in her guts.

"Just party noise," Harp said in a reassuring voice.

Great. Can everyone tell I'm shitting myself?

They turned the corner, and an unprecedented celebration greeted them on the concourse with acrobats contorting into unimaginable shapes, musicians plucking cheerful melodies, and dance troupes coordinating practiced moves. Every light ball beamed at full brightness to illuminate the ceiling's bunting.

"Holy mother of the mist," Dobbs said. "I've never seen anything like this. Don't they know there's rioting back at the hall?"

"Doubt they do," Brennan said.

Landra dug her heels into the floor. *Surely this can't be for my promotion. It's too much.*

Casually dressed soldiers spilled out of every bar and food hall, laughing as if oblivious to the troubles of their world. A sparking liveliness to the aura mass held her attention, and she couldn't look away. *Don't you know civil war is coming?* An image of the scenes back at Warrior Hall flashed into her thoughts. *Gods. It's already here.*

"Can't beat one night off from duty and worry," Harp said, as if reading her Soul.

She glanced at him then turned away from the pink tinge in his aura. *Shelk! Nothing makes sense tonight.* She didn't know who to trust, who to follow, or who to believe anymore. *Why isn't Thisk here?* He was more confusing than any soldier she'd met, but he was a protector she trusted.

"Let's get you to this party," Brennan said. "Guard detail, Grekko's bar is on the other side of the concourse. Stay close as we make our way through." He drew his sword before nudging the group out into the heaving throng but held it point-down to forge a path.

Landra stayed in the middle, barely accepting the surreal event. The gold walls, decorated ceiling, and spattering of pink auras overwhelmed her senses.

"This is fantastic," Dobbs said. "Do we have to wait for the chief to die for another holiday and free drinks?"

"Dobbs, I'm gonna give you a kicking all the way back to the hall if you don't shut it."

"Don't mind me," Landra shouted over the party noise. "Dobbs is right. Everyone is happy. I wish it could be like this all the time. Knowing my father's constitution, we'll be waiting decades for another party."

"I pity the ones left on duty," Cleaver said in his usually dour tones.

"There's not many working," Harp said. "It's a skeleton watch tonight."

The conversation stopped when they reached a queue snaking out of Grekko's door.

"Shelk," Dobbs said. "Will I even get in this place? There's more high-ranking insignias here than on the honors board. Nothing below a two-bar Warrior in sight."

"Probably not," Brennan said, pushing past the queue to the front.

"You sure Landra's allowed in?" Harp asked. "She's only a citizen."

Brennan answered with a snort. "I'm sure."

"Name?" The door guard snapped out with tired efficiency.

"Citizen Landra Hux," Brennan said.

A perfectly proportioned Warrior at the front of the line pushed him aside. Casual-cut sleeves showed off the definition edging his biceps, and his stature made Brennan look like a child. "Hey, can't you see there's a queue?"

"Sorry, sir." Brennan stiffened to attention but held his ground. "Citizen Hux has priority security."

The Warrior scratched his angular jaw and narrowed his eyes at Landra. "Hux, eh?"

"Yes, sir," she answered. wondering if he knew her true

rank. Her gaze slipped hopelessly down the line of waiting Warriors, and she wondered the same thing about every soldier there. *You'll know tomorrow, and won't it be fun?* Now, she was certain she had that shitting look Brennan had talked about.

"Soldiers with priority security jump the queue," the door guard said.

The Warrior threw up his hands in disgust. "Shall I say I'm called Hux?"

Landra didn't want special attention, but she had no control here. The door guard checked her off his list, as if her name meant nothing, and opened a barrier to allow her through.

"Any weapons?"

"No, sir," she lied, certain they wouldn't confiscate the Collector if they found it on her back. The discovery would cause a scene, though, so she offered her most innocent smile.

"Citizen Hux," Brennan shouted, making her look back. "Enjoy the party."

Landra's aura quivered in response. It wasn't a normal feeling nor a comfortable one. She hesitated, trying to steady her legs, but weakness hit her from nowhere. *How can I be this fragile? Lead a Warrior faction? Yeah, right.*

She strained for a breath, which wouldn't come, and widened her legs to firm her stance. Her head drifted as if unable to hold a thought, so she leaned against a wall. *I'm an embarrassment. I'm...* A pale blue thread twisted up through her aura in front of her face, and the truth hit her like one of Thisk's blows. The aura wisp didn't belong because it was a slither of Baylem's Soul.

She'd caught it before and intertwined it with her aura, but now it wanted to drift free. The body weakness, the struggle for breath; it belonged to her friend. Recognition of the sharing strengthened her connection to Baylem. She knew the girl's fragility, sensed her drifting to thinness, and shared her pauses for breath.

Landra hung her head, trying to hide her shock. *How can this happen? Magic, leave me alone*

She licked her lips against dryness that wasn't her own and grabbed the wall for support. This was her experience with Oakham all over again. Baylem wasn't in her arms, but they were still linked. One more breath came and then one more. The next breath never arrived. Fading, emptiness, ending—Baylem broke apart.

No, no, no. Baylem?

She felt the girl die, just as she had felt the old sentry's passing. Landra wanted to shout, cry, or scream, but she couldn't release her emotions in this place. Not surrounded by Warriors she was supposed to lead. *What should I say? Give me a moment to deal with my magical connection to a dying friend?*

She thought of all her training sessions with Baylem. This wasn't like saying goodbye to Oakham, who she'd barely known. This was parting from a friend. There'd be no more gossip, no friendly banter, and no more confiding secret desires.

Don't cry, don't cry, don't cry.

She gasped and nearly sank to the floor. This didn't seem possible. Landra's aura roamed, as if searching could reclaim her connection, but there was nothing to latch on to. Deep grief crumpled her against the wall, and trapped tears stung her eyes.

"Citizen Hux?" the door guard asked.

Landra came back to herself and saw soldiers staring, but not at her Soul. Her decorative-paneled trousers draped artfully over her exposed thighs, showing skin right up to her waist. Most stares showed more desire than embarrassment, but her glare of desperation sent them scuttling. She closed her legs, flattened the panels, and set her face into that non-committal mask she was becoming used to wearing. "It's been a long day," she said to the door guard with a weak smile.

Another lie, another pretense. Will deception define my time as chief elect? No doubt.

Before continuing to the party, she willed her aura to reach for Baylem's drifting thread. It hung close, spreading and tattering, but she captured the light strand into her own darker shades. Laughter, the joy of a shared meal, boy secrets, a training partnership, trust, friendship—it was all just a memory of Baylem now. Not wanting to lose those parts of her friend, Landra trapped the spirit that wasn't her own, entwined it with her essence, and nodded to the guard. The door to Grekko's opened.

Grief colored her Soul with shards of light, which darted painfully like exposed nerves, but she fixed a smile of serenity on her face and walked through the door. Dobbs shouts came from behind.

"Enjoy your cocktails and posing, Lan. I'm off to get shelk-faced."

Chapter 36

The party boasted a more impressive array of insignias than the queue outside had. Warrior auras and leisure outfits blended with the wall drapes, bathing the room in a mass of azure shades, but odd dots of color splashes made Landra feel less exposed.

Riots, magic, death, and I'm supposed to celebrate?

She dragged a sigh up from her belly and looked around. The Second and Fifth City chiefs hunched together over a tall table, engaged in deep conversation and balancing untouched drinks between their fingers. Warrior Third Preston stood to one side, arms folded, and silver eyes glaring at a line of temple singers. The chief barber circulated amongst the guests, grinning like he'd gotten into the scute two hours before everyone else.

Landra lifted her foot from a sticky patch on the floor, and a heavy stench of fermenting vegetable matter drifted up. *Fun party. Should have gone with Dobbs.*

It was a smaller room than she'd expected, with conversing Warriors occupying every tall table and others spilling onto the tiny stage and dance floor. She looked for

Thisk first but couldn't find him in the crowd. The ranger would fit in with the political posturing and disingenuous conversations here like a clown at a wake, but she couldn't help feeling abandoned. It had been days since she'd seen him, so she guessed his duty to her was done.

It's my duty that's the problem now.

She scanned the crowd to pick her first conversation, but an arm linked with her elbow and whisked her forward.

"Allow me to introduce myself," the swarthy-skinned young man with a pinched nose and buried eyes said. He spun her around on the dance floor, scattering Warriors to the walls. Tight trousers hugged his thin hips, but ruffles billowed out of his yellow shirt. His short-cropped hair showed off a chief tailor insignia.

"I'm Jeffro," he said, hinging at the waist to form a bow. "I created your outfit for tonight."

So, you're to blame.

"I thought Dell got me this."

"Ah, well. Dell supplied the measurements, but I crafted this beauty."

Landra wanted to kick him for her outfit, but she held her peace and feigned delight.

"Let me look at you." He held her away at arm's length. "I've so few opportunities to create casual wear for the female form. I want to show you off."

Landra wanted to hide, but Jeffro spun her around.

"Gorgeous," he said, with unexpected lust glinting in his eyes.

Thanks for making me the center of attention. Was one last night of anonymity too much to expect?

"I knew the bronze and gold shades of that blouse would complement your flecked hair and eyes," he went on. "The fabric's really hard to source, but it makes those trousers flow beautifully. Shame your dance slippers are hidden.

She automatically poked her toes out and glanced down at the sequined creations. Of course she stood out. So much had happened Landra only now processed that her outfit was intended to be a golden beacon amidst a sea of blue. So much for secrecy. She inwardly squirmed under the attention but outwardly smiled with the diplomacy of a chief elect. "My outfit is wonderful."

"It was a close thing. I finished off the celebration outfits weeks ago and then new measurements came in for you. Have you been working out, girl? Come on, tell me the truth. You and I can't keep secrets."

"Everyone works out ahead of the championships," she said, determined to keep her remote land training with Thisk to herself.

"Are you entering?"

"I'm not old enough," she said, and by normal rules, that was true. "But every soldier likes to join in the preparations."

She remembered her father's instructions about careful conversations and tried to think of a specific aspect of her loose outfit to compliment. It wasn't going to be the trousers. Their flowing panels were highly impractical and showed a ridiculous amount of skin, and she'd nearly tripped once when the fabric caught between her legs. A return to uniform skins couldn't come soon enough, and her feet needed to be in boots rather than soft shoes. "I love this blouse," she said. "The sleeves are so delicate." The design truly was to her liking, but not because of the intricate floral patterns. The sleeves were long enough to hide her spider rash, and the firm under-bodice and flouncy fabric hid the Collector at her back.

Chief Hux approached. "May I cut in? I'd like the first dance of the evening to be with my daughter."

"Of course, Chief Hux, we weren't going to dance,' Jeffro said, dropping Landra's hands and backing away. "I was just showing her off."

Griffin grinned at the tailor then scooped Landra's arms into his. As if in response, Templer musicians set their fingers to stringed instruments and strummed out a forgetful melody.

It was strange for Landra to hear Chief Hux call her his daughter in public, and she cautioned herself against feelings of warmth. Soldiers would look back on this tomorrow and see this moment as the Chief presenting his nominated successor. This was all business, and he certainly looked official, with his gold-streaked hair banded back to show his Chief's rank and his blue uniform looking crisp, practical, and almost black

"Am I doing well, Chief Hux?"

He whisked her in a circle without giving an answer. "Are you wearing your birthday gift today?"

"Yes, sir. I don't have a safe place to keep it, so I wear it all the time when I'm out. My new room locks, but I'm worried a Warrior might spring an inspection."

"I should have thought of that," he said, swaying to a halt and spinning the other way. "You should call me Father for this evening."

She always thought of him as Father, despite rarely using the word to his face. The promotion ceremony would likely change their relationship to chief and chief elect forever, so she relaxed into the dance, determined to enjoy the moment of closeness. He stopped them in the middle of the floor and sighed.

"How are you feeling, Landra?"

Exhausted, depressed, determined, nervous. Memories of

Baylem ambushed her mood. *Grief-stricken. Can I say that? No, no. I shouldn't know she died.*

Her father ignored the over-long silence and gazed at her. "There's something I've wanted to tell you, Landra, and it won't be appropriate after tomorrow."

She looked into his broad face, uncertain, and relieved to see his skin glow with health. They locked stares, and it seemed like neither of them knew what to say.

"I'm sorry," he said eventually.

She stood, mouth agape, and her father let her go. As another dancing couple spun toward them, his mouth framed into a sad smile and he backed away.

Emotion shuddered through her body. *Sorry for what? Being an absent father, not finishing the conversation, or for making me chief elect?*

Maybe it was all three. She gazed at his receding form, but her brother maneuvered into the space and grabbed her arm. His gaudy, rust-shaded suit marked him as another of Jeffro's victims.

"Dannet!" she said. "I didn't realize you'd arrived. Is Bexter here?"

"What? You'd rather spend time in his company than mine?"

"Obviously," she said with a skittish laugh.

"Well, you're going to have to wait. Bex is arriving later. Come over here, will you?" He dragged her to a quiet corner, away from the dance floor. "Landra, I have something to ask you. With the ceremony tomorrow, Chief Hux should have spoken to me by now if the promotion was mine. Has he said anything to you?"

Oh shelk. "Like what?"

"Like who's going to be chief elect?"

Landra worked her mouth, hoping a good answer would come.

"You look surprised!" Dannet said. "I knew it. You have no idea why he hasn't spoken to me either. I feel so stupid. Anyone here could be the chief elect and I wouldn't know, but people are congratulating me as if I've got the job. I blurt out the official line, about no one knowing who the chief elect is, but they don't believe me."

Landra's mouth worked, an admission dancing on her tongue. It carried a bitter taste. She should have shared her news before Thisk had taken her from the city. Now, it felt too late, and her hands trembled like overlevel leaves in the breeze. Dannet had practically raised her and deserved better. Store Chief Dell knew of her promotion and the barber too. Shelk, even Brennan from Hux Hall knew. She glanced about to check who was near.

"Dannet," she said. "I have something to tell you." She swallowed against her tight throat. "There was a night last cycle when Father called me to his stateroom and asked me to take his knife."

"What's that got to do with anything?"

"It was a big thing."

"I suppose. He did the same to me a couple of years ago."

"What?"

"Sounds the same," Dannet said. "He told me to fight for his knife and then beat me stupid. Did he hurt you, Landra?"

Confusion muddled her thoughts. "Well, he did hurt me a bit," she said, underplaying her injuries. "What happened when you took the knife?"

"Are you crazy? He half-killed me, and there was no way I was getting that blade out of his hand. I had an engineering exam the next day, so I stopped fighting when he drew blood and walked out. Expected punishment duty for a cycle, but he never said a word. I lost a lot of sleep waiting for that report to drop, I can tell you."

The crowd noise disappeared for Landra and she swayed, too stunned to speak. Her brother had faced the chief elect challenge first but had left the test unfinished. She knew he'd been trained to become chief; it had been obvious throughout their lives. But his failure had left her with the turmoil and pain to deal with. A seed of resentment worked its way into her thoughts, and she wanted to scream at her brother.

"So, what do you think, Lan? Should I talk to Father?"

Betrayed by the person I love most—you.

"Is something wrong? Lan?"

"Wrong?" Her front teeth bit down on her lip, stemming the rest of her tirade. She steadied her breathing and waited until she could trust her tone. "Do what you want, Dannet. You're old enough to make decisions; that's clear. So, if you want to talk to Chief Hux, you should just do it and stop moaning to me."

"What?"

She wanted to tell him about the promotion, but now it wasn't to ease her conscience or do right by her brother. She wanted Dannet to know how he'd destroyed her life. Raw as her emotions were, her dreams of anonymous travelling through the cities, becoming a Warrior on merit, and finding someone to love felt like as great a loss as Baylem's death. She ground her teeth to stop her resentment from spilling out and stormed away. Her flouncy outfit fluttered in her wake.

Can this evening get any worse? Why didn't you just take the knife, Dannet?

The partygoers divided before her angry stride. There was nowhere to hide, and the job she'd come to do still weighed on her thoughts. What was the point of staying up half the night to go through the files if she didn't mix with the partygoers? This was her duty now, however she'd come by it, and she couldn't shy from the task. She slowed her stride, breathed herself to calmness, then actively searched out Warrior Second Tasenda.

The woman leaned against a wall and stared into the crowd. A tight band secured her blond hair behind her head in ratty tails, showing off her ranking insignia, and deep alertness shone through her blue eyes. The report Father had supplied said she trained relentlessly and ignored her three husbands for the sake of work. True to form, she was one of the few people in the room still wearing duty uniform. Training tiredness showed on her lined features, ageing her a decade beyond her thirty-nine years.

Landra bit down her resentment and forced herself to make an approach.

"Warrior Second," she said, "you look as if you're on duty. May I bring you some refreshments?"

"No time for eating. I have to keep everyone safe." Her words sounded like more of a boast than a complaint.

"Good to know you're on duty," Landra said. "Are you expecting trouble?"

Tasenda frowned. "I'm always expecting trouble." She set her eyes on the crowd again in a clear sign of dismissal.

"If you change your mind about the food, let me know. Even our guards work best on full stomachs." She smiled at Tasenda, not knowing if this was what Father wanted. After a salute and a small formal bow, she turned aside to look for her next conversation.

"Hux," Tasenda said, drawing Landra back.

"Warrior Second?"

"You're a woman."

That much seemed obvious, but Landra had never been called a woman. Citizen, cadet, chief elect, girl, and nuisance, but never a woman. The Second's blue eyes held her attention, and she wondered what the woman wanted.

"Here's a piece of advice, Hux. When the Warrior class was exiled, they brought muscle and might. There's never been many women here, so we're expected to breed like skipper bunnies. Don't let anyone bind you to that future. If you want to be a Warrior, work harder and for longer than the men around you."

"Thank you, Warrior Second. I'll keep that in mind."

Tasenda favored her with a sly smile. "If you're passing the food station, you can bring me something back."

Landra nodded and moved on, hoping she'd made her first ally. The Second's advice didn't relate to her life, but listening had formed a connection. She worked the room with bitter efficiency, talking power shortages with Bairstow, the problems of tallying credits across six cities with Altur, and family feuds with Hagen. It was tortuous, and she longed to be elsewhere.

"Our district is arguably the most important," Henderson told her. "The animal pens and hydroponic units supply all six cities with food."

Landra was about to agree when a tingling power brushed her aura's edges. She turned, moments before an influx of robed Templers set everyone else staring. Five male Templers swept into the party room wearing tailored robes of vibrant burgundy. Their robes looked spectacular, with weighted hems, pinches at the waist and cuffs, and a split up the front to show fitted trousers. They weren't anything like the formless sacks most Templers wore.

The party noised damped down, and uneasy mutterings rumbled until Chief Hux marched across to greet the

Templers with a warm shake of their hands. The festivities set in motion again, as if a switch had flipped.

Landra wandered apart from Henderson, even as he still talked, and she made a circular path away from the new guests. She'd been given no files on Templers, so Father couldn't mean for her to talk to them, but her eyes tracked the new arrivals. They split up and circulated through the crowd.

Four of them boasted soldier blue auras with dashes of red, but the one bearing a Chief Templer insignia had a swirling crimson Soul with dashes of blue. It swelled out from his form, roaming the crowd as if searching.

Hide, run.

She veered away, only to bump into a soldier—Bexter.

As Landra staggered, she soaked in the sight of the cadet. His rolled shirt sleeves and rough trousers contrasted with his sharp haircut and flawless skin. She didn't know why the combination aroused her so much or why her passion should flare now. He was beyond reach and the least of her concerns. Her body disagreed, and she used the staggering to cover her weak legs.

"I'm sorry," Bexter said, offering a steadying hand. Their palms touched, and the world dimmed.

Chapter 37

Only Bexter felt real. Landra's Soul writhed inside his aura, delighting in the touch points and connections she found there. Fleeting impressions of his compassion and strength enveloped her, and she couldn't take her eyes from his green eyes and dark features. He met her gaze, and an untimely emotional surge quivered her next breath. Her unwanted promotion, the Templer threat to her freedom, Baylem's death, and her anger at Dannet all faded in importance. She sensed more and relaxed her aura to admit him into her Soul. Virgin she might be, but that was about to change. Not with a physical joining, but with something more, and in front of everyone. She was bare to his contact.

"You knew!" her brother's raised voice intruded, a world of accusation cracking his voice as it had in his teens.

What?

Dannet barged her away from Bexter, snapping the contact. The world refocused in stages for Landra, and she wobbled back on her heels. She stared at her brother, taking a long moment to adjust and understand his words. Her breath came fast still, and the lust of her connection took longer to dispel than the vision.

She focused on Dannet's bunching fists and recognized his anger.

"I spoke to Chief Hux," he said.

Oh shelk.

She stepped apart from Bexter, taking a moment to assimilate all that Dannet's words meant. He'd spoken to Father and knew she was to be chief elect.

"Aren't you going to say anything?" he demanded.

"What can I say?"

"An explanation might help, but forget an apology. It's too late."

"I've nothing to apologize for."

"Really? All this time…"

Landra couldn't refute his unfinished accusation. The bite of his anger inflamed her own resentment. "I'm not happy with this, but you failed, Dannet. You left the test." Her sharp words caught the attention of the closest soldiers.

"Maybe this should be saved for back at Warrior Hall," Bexter said. "Your loud voices are causing a stir."

"Stay out of this, Bex," Dannet told him.

"Leave him alone," Landra said. "This isn't his fault."

"No, it's yours."

"Not true. I never chose to be ch— I don't want this. You're better than me, but I have no choice. You made sure of that."

Dannet's gold eyes flared, and his bared teeth shone beneath the bright party lights. "Not better, Lan. D'you think that's why I'm angry? You're strong, focused, talented… You'll be great. But why didn't you tell me? How could you leave me to find out like this?"

Pain tightened her chest, and words wouldn't come. Her secrecy clawed at the heart of their relationship, raking doubt into what they'd thought was unbreakable.

Dannet's arms flailed his distress to the world. He turned with a glare at the staring crowd and stormed away.

"Where are you going?"

"Home. I'm going home."

Landra saw him barge through the partygoers without a care for their shocked stares. She plunged into the crowd after him.

"Excuse me, sirs," she said, elbowing her way through. A red-robed figure stepped sideways to block the route, and her anxious gaze lifted. She readied to unleash her frustrations on the stupid man but stopped when his glittering gaze locked on her face.

"Chief Templer Vellion," the smooth-cheeked priest said with a gentle bow. "I've been looking forward to meeting you."

Not now.

She spared a moment to take in his glossy skin, oversized dark eyes, subtly long hair, and knowing smile. The Templer wasn't on the list of important people Father expected her to meet, and she'd hoped to avoid the man altogether. Now his aura invaded her space, and power thrummed through her being.

"I'm busy!" she said, pushing him aside with a sweep of her arm. She darted around the startled man, leaving him tottering.

Gods of the mist. How furious will you be, Father? What am I thinking?

In truth, Landra knew exactly what she was thinking. The Chief Templer was a problem for later, along with Father's Soul-breaking anger, but her confrontation with Dannet was long overdue. She made the exit in time to see her brother weaving through the concourse crowd outside, but the door guard barred her escape.

"Citizen Hux, are you leaving? Shall I call a security team to escort you home?"

Think.

"Yes, please," she answered, trying to control the tremor in her voice. As the guard turned to his duty roster, she flattened her body to squeeze behind him. His insipid Soul shades buffeted against her solid boundaries, but he never flinched. By the time he turned back, she'd gone.

Landra ducked between two queuing Warriors and flung their cloaks high to hide her escape. She plunged through the milling crowd, keeping Dannet in her sights. Her brother didn't have the ranger's height and bobbing Warrior hair, but the rust-red party suit made him easy to pick out.

The leisure district party raged in excess, so she willed her brother to stay close and soak his sorrows in scute, but he peeled away from the crowd to turn down a corridor.

Going home, Dannet? Not to Warrior Hall. Not that way.

She followed until a soldier staggered back into her shoulder. Spray shot up from the scute tankard in his hand.

"Outta my way," he said, spinning around. Once he saw Landra's athletic body and over-exposed flesh, his eyes sprang open and his face brightened.

"Oh, sorry, love. Want to party?"

She shoved him back, her hands sinking into his fleshy belly. "No, and neither should you. That gut needs exercise more than scute."

"Charming." He lurched back. "Has anyone ever told you that you look like Chief Hux?"

"No, and you're drunk."

"Yeah," he said, with a laugh deep enough to wobble his paunch.

She heaved him aside and forged a path toward the corridor. A drifting trouser panel caught on a guard's sword hilt, and it stole another moment to untangle the fabric. "Ow," she said, as a thick heel dug through her slippers.

By the time she reached the spot where Dannet had turned into the corridor, he was nowhere in sight.

"Shelk!"

A ring of armed security Warriors guarded the concourse exits. Their attentive stares roved the crowd for trouble, so they barely noticed her slipping by into the empty corridors beyond. A faint footfall ahead gave her a clue to Dannet's direction.

That's the way to Hux Hall.

She dithered, undecided whether to follow or return to the party. This wasn't a child's decision to make. The situation forced her to choose what sort of a leader she intended to become. If she went to Hux Hall, there'd be no return to the party and chief elect duties tonight. But Dannet had made her world right more times than she could count. She sucked in a deep breath and went after him.

Her feet padded silently down the corridors, and she was grateful for the soft soles on her slippers. She put the evening's troubles out of her thoughts, and her mood calmed in stages. Dannet's failure might have doomed her to take on the chief elect duty, but it wasn't his fault. His drilling in combat techniques was good enough, but he'd never been a true fighter. He preferred building things to whacking them. If Father had told him the significance of taking the Collector during the trial, she was certain he would have found a way to claim his destiny.

The echoing sound of Dannet's boots faded, so she checked a wall map to stay on track. At a familiar intersection, she heard hushed voices coming from the narrow corridor, which led to Hux Hall. Her steps slowed when she heard Dannet's name.

"Turgeth, you sure that was Dannet Hux?" The voice sounded too clumsy and full of delight to show caution.

"No mistaking that hair and stupid gold flecks. It's like shelk gone bad. Huxes wear it like a crown. Was Dannet, for sure."

Landra flattened herself against the wall to listen.

"Snatch him now," the voice said. "I want to make that shelking son-of-a Hux suffer."

She held her breath, certain her pounding heart would burst. A gasp escaped in a noisy puff, and an automatic stretch of her lungs drew in more whistling air. Her senses amplified, turning her breaths into sirens, the voices into shouts, and wooden grain beneath her fingers into canyons. This fear surpassed what she'd felt during her fight with Father. She pressed her back against the wall, pushing the Collector against her spine.

Attack.

It was a stupid idea. She and wasn't sure where it came from, but the idiot Templers were threatening Dannet.

"Let's go inside and grab him," the clumsy voice said.

"Don't be stupid, Mendog. We can hardly charge into Hux Hall."

"Can too. The guards left with them Hux bastards after the raid. Everyone else is at the party."

That's true. I bet you're alone, Dannet. Will you guess I followed? Did you lock the door?

"If we're caught inside, there'll be the worm-infested mist to pay," Turgeth said. "At least out here we can say we're heading to the Tally Hall. The boss said to leave no trace. Do you really want to face him if we mess this up?"

"No," Mendog sulked.

"Neither do I. Explaining how you let the boy escape will be hard enough."

"It wasn't my fault," Mendog said. "The boss told us to watch him, and I did that good. I watched him run through the corridors and into that door."

"That's your problem, not thinking. No one could have guessed the chief elect would leave his protection detail, especially the day before the announcement ceremony, but you should have adapted."

Landra listened in alarm, an array of hideous outcomes running through her head. Would they kill Dannet or snatch him? Worse, what would they do if they took him and realized he wasn't the chief elect? For all she knew, these were the same Templers responsible for the Hux Hall raid and Baylem's death. A suppressed ball of grief nearly broke a sob loose, but she held it tight.

If Thisk were here, he'd know what to do. He'd take his six-foot-three mass of muscle out there and arrest the Templers or pummel them stupid.

She tried to think her options through. Father would want her to find safety. The treaty came first for him, and there was more at stake here than her brother's life. Dannet had always been her protector, so he would want her to leave too. *I have to run.*

"What do we want the boy for, anyway?" Mendog asked.

"Not our place to know, but if you ask me, the boss should ransom him back to the chief a piece at a time, all in the name of the temple. Let's see a treaty working then."

Horror tattered the edges of Landra's aura. She peeled from the wall and turned into the smaller corridor, putting herself in full view of… *Oh shelk. Not Templers.*

Chapter 38

Landra clamped her lips together, caught in panic. Her gaze tracked up the forms of two soldiers. Both topped Thisk's height by a good three inches.

Huge.

Their bulked muscles strained the seams of their uniforms, and broadswords dangled from their grazed fists. Her entrance brought them around, their blades swinging into position. She sucked in a breath, stricken.

Momentary panic flared in the soldiers' eyes and nostrils, but as they took in her stature, ridiculous clothes, and lack of weapons, their mouths twisted into amused smirks.

"Party's on the leisure concourse, darling," the thick-spoken soldier said. "Be off!"

Mendog. Has to be from that voice.

Her scrutiny took in his pinch-tight uniform, mangled face, and hair insignia, but she couldn't match his catering specialization mark with his distorted features. No angled nose and drooping eye came from tossing pancakes, but his pale aura disturbed her more. Its ragged edges broke in places, as if improperly formed. He lumbered toward her, his wonky eye glaring from beneath his drooping lid. His lips parted into a snarl of crooked, yellowing teeth.

"Let me handle this, brother," Turgeth said, settling an arm across Mendog's chest. "You lost, girl?"

Landra's attention flickered from one soldier to the other. The men resembled each other, but Turgeth was the unspoiled version. His uniform molded around his muscled frame, and his small aura glittered a brighter blue. He had the same long nose, but straighter, and his matching brown eyes shone with a brightness denied to his brother. His calculating stare filled her with more dread than any amount of Mendog's ogling.

What the shelk am I doing?

Landra knew exactly what sort of a leader she wanted to be now, and it didn't involve sacrificing her brother.

I stole your future, Dannet. Now, I take your death. She shuddered, determined in her decision, despite her gut-curdling dread.

Shouldn't Father have realized the choice she would make? Thisk had warned him; she was nice. The time had come for her to own the title.

"You have to come to security with me," she said, tremors putting a squeak in her voice. *Shelk.*

"What you talking about, girl? We're on guard duty." Turgeth flashed a straight-toothed, evil grin.

"Can't you see she's another Hux?" Mendog asked.

"Easy, Men. I see."

The brothers stared at her short-cropped hair, loathing showing in their differing features. Turgeth rolled his sword hilt over in his fist and settled into a fighting pose.

"So, you're not coming with me?" Landra said, humor covering the paralyzing fear in her heart. She'd chosen this, but it didn't mean she could be brave. Misting shelk, she couldn't hold her hands steady. "As chief elect, I order you to stand down and report to security."

Mendog snorted a laugh.

"I don't think so," Turgeth said, tilting an eyebrow. "D'you think we're stupid enough to believe you're anything but a citizen."

She'd expected them to doubt her. Hadn't she doubted herself? But for this to work, she had to make them believe her true rank, or what would stop them from dispatching her and then taking Dannet anyway? She had to make her brother worthless to them.

Landra reached a trembling hand behind her head. She'd pulled the Collector from her strap before, thoughtless of the consequences. Now, she grabbed it with exact knowledge of what she was doing. The handle felt warm, as if ready for action, and the knife slipped free, a tinging sound echoing out as the blade cleared the sheath.

"Woah!" Mendog said with a chuckle. "Fight!"

"The Collector!" Turgeth hissed, an entirely more calculating expression darkening his features.

Thank the mist. "Yes, it is the Collector, and I am the chief elect." She pointed the pink blade toward Turgeth and swished it before her body. Her father had used a similar move, but it was a slither of Gallanto's Soul which urged her to action. She felt his shape now, inside the knife.

Collector of Souls, indeed.

How could she have not realized the knife's nature before? The name should have given it away. More Souls than Gallanto's rested here, but her great-grandfather pushed them aside to fill Landra's awareness with his heroic presence.

"Fight, girl," he ordered. "Fight for your life."

Landra gripped the Collector, her body pumped, and her attention honed to a crystalized point.

Turgeth's brows creased together. "My mistake. I believe you now. This one's for you, brother. Take her down."

The misshapen man ambled forward, his overbuilt frame swaying. Landra stabbed the knife forward. Deep purple flashes shot down its blade as Mendog's heavy sword swung toward her head. She ducked like the scrapper she'd always been and raked the Collector's blade across his cheek. The big man howled with anger rather than pain. Red dribbles leaked from the thin line that marred his face.

"Bitch!"

I'm in for it now. She settled a safe distance away, eyeing the magical rash on the thug's cheek. Purple lines crawled into his ear and burrowed down one side of his neck. The more he raked at his earlobe, the further the web pattern spread. Its lines stood proud in purple streaks.

Serves you right.

Turgeth's aura flared, warning her to move. His raised sword committed to the path of a downward sweep, so she darted aside and spun into one of Thisk's high kicks. Her foot shuddered into her attacker's chin.

Not just for championship points. Thank you, my friend.

The big man shook his head, as if freeing himself from the blow. Whether she wasn't heavy enough, hadn't landed the kick true, or her slippers had softened the blow, she didn't know, but Turgeth grinned as if untouched. He seemed to grow as he straightened.

Gods

She flashed the knife toward his gut, but he was quicker than Mendog. He shouldered aside her attack and landed a fist in her face. Landra staggered sideways, rocked seven ways from the mist. The pain didn't register at once, but her ears buzzed and flashes darted across her vision. She shuddered down to one knee, refusing to release the Collector. She couldn't stand. Couldn't think. All Turgeth had to do was swing his sword, and it would be over. *Dead.*

"I am the chief elect," she said again, fainter then before and with more of a tremor, but she to be sure they had no use for Dannet. "I order you to stand down."

Laughter rang over her head like a victory fanfare.

"We won't kill her," Turgeth said. "We'll take her and the boy."

No, no, noooo! I'm the one you want.

"Get up," Gallanto's deep voice rang in her head. "Fight!"

"I can't. I tried." Tears of failure leaked down her face. She was done.

"Fight," Chief Gallanto said again. Landra couldn't respond, but the mist answered his call.

Chapter 39

Magic was Landra's enemy. It had always been her enemy. Now, her aura thrummed with awareness of the incoming fog. The wisps connected, twisting to cognizance in the high corners of the base. Shreds of disembodied Souls rallied to Gallanto's call, swirling at first then darting through the city corridors in a path toward the Collector.

This was everything Landra despised. She was a Warrior, not a Templer. She knew that much in her heart. Isn't that why she'd fought her growing flaw?

But now? To save Dannet?

She set aside dread, like putting her uniform in a drawer. It was there but hidden. She accepted no restrictions on her sacrifice and puffed out her chest, opening her Soul to the magic. Raising fresh eyes to the world, she saw beauty to the incoming threads. They raced toward the Collector, faster, faster, thickening, as they reached the blade.

Landra found her feet, and her voice. "To me. To Gallanto."

The knife shuddered from the impact of incoming Souls. They twisted together, sacrificing existence to amass as one single aura. It broke free of the Soul-laden knife but refused to disperse. Instead, it congealed into balls, grew limbs, a torso, and a head. A wraith-like figure formed, towering at Landra's side.

"Gallanto?"

Am I dreaming? Or have I already died?

The brothers' gaping told Landra she'd lost her mind. Maybe she had, because she recognized her dead great-grandfather from Oakham's vision. His chief's insignia, flecked eyes, and gold-streaked hair brought her memory into focus, but this wasn't a recollection come to life. This misty character had individuality; it was impossible to deny.

The vision morphed through several outfits until settling on toughened battle armor with protection for the torso, forearms, and thighs. A long sword grew out from Gallanto's hand. He scrutinized it with a creased face and bounced it in his fist until the blade grew another finger's length. "Better."

Wavering like an overlevel fog, the ghost chief turned to Landra. "Good to meet you, great-granddaughter!"

Holy shelk and son of the mi...!

His body might have formed from pink fog, but Gallanto's aura pulsed with the deep azure shades of a Warrior. Magenta traces played around the edges, but he was soldier at the core.

"Do we fight?" he said, a mischievous smile lifting the corner of his mouth. All Landra could do was nod.

Mendog grunted. "What is the girl doing?"

"Don't know," Turgeth said. "Think she's lost her wits."

Landra could barely comprehend what was happening. As Mendog stepped forward, readying his attack, Gallanto blocked his path. The chief roared, his misty form disassembling as Mendog strode through his shape. He reformed on the other side, turned, and hefted his sword high. His blade swept down onto Mendog's back in a mighty pink flash.

"Agh!" the man screamed, dropping to one knee. His coarse uniform fabric remained unmarked and there was no blood, but true pain showed on his face.

"Stop messing, Men," his brother said.

"Not messing. Something hit me."

Gallanto grinned at Landra. "Will that help?"

Her father had none of this levity, but maybe Chief Gallanto had lived in easier times. He gazed at her with more love than Griffin Hux ever had, and he was here for support. Could she just hug him? "It will help, thank you."

"These are better odds," Gallanto said. "Not right, two grown soldiers picking on a girl."

"I wasn't doing that bad."

"Oh my. If you act any more like Sonlas, you're going to make me cry."

Faced with Landra's bizarre behavior and Mendog's inexplicable injury, the brothers' attack had stalled.

"To battle!" Gallanto bellowed.

Landra felt better now and took advantage of Turgeth's confusion. She dodged inside his defense and slashed his chest. At the same time, Gallanto swept his weapon down on Mendog again.

"Bastard!" Mendog screamed, slashing his own sword through empty air.

The next time Landra darted in, Turgeth was ready and furious. He landed a heavy-handed fist to her gut.

No breath, no strength.

She crumpled but refused to fall. Raising the Collector again, she thrust it forward. The more she thought of her great-grandfather, the more the knife's color deepened—from pink to lilac then to purple—and the more her magical strength grew. There was a connection she had no time or desire to explore.

"Joining in?" Turgeth asked, snarling at his brother.

Mendog dodged the next strike by luck. He twisted in and grabbed Landra's hands.

"Unleash your power," Gallanto ordered.

"Power? What power? I don't know how."

The ghost-chief's hand brushed her cheek. It was tender and so powerful that Landra thought she would burst. She couldn't say how it happened, but an explosion of energy broke around them, forcing Mendog to release his grip and stagger away. The magical effort drained her physical strength, and she slumped to the floor. In her weakness, the connection with Gallanto tore apart.

The Warrior chief's wraith-image thinned, twisting in on itself before spreading wide. "Save our people, child of my life," his echoing voice called as he dissipated into pink floating twists.

"Don't go! How can I save our people? I can't even save myself."

Turgeth saw none of it. He darted in to grab her arm, pinching and twisting with expert skill. He nipped the pain points and pressed her face into the floor.

Landra sprawled there, squirming in futile defiance. A slight movement tore an agonized scream from her throat. Gallanto had gone, and the fight was lost.

One loud shout and Dannet would come, but she couldn't do it. Wouldn't. He was the reason for her sacrifice. She refused to fail now.

Fat fingers wrenched the Collector from her grip, and

the world faded by another degree. She wriggled, clenching down her cries. She wanted to scream again. Instead, she slid into the hethra.

Chapter 40

Landra's agony diminished when she visualized her surroundings. The walls wavered to nothing, and her consciousness slipped through, taking her inside Hux Hall. It was dark apart from a light in the training room. Dannet stood on the mat, thrashing a sword in a vent of frustration. She wanted to hug him and tell him everything was fine, but she knew it wasn't.

This feels like goodbye.

Sorrow drenched her, nearly ejecting her from the moment. She clung to her magic, refusing to break her trance. Her Soul sense wrapped around her brother, smothering him with the love and the gratitude she felt. He was her strength, her confidant, and her friend, but she couldn't hold onto him.

If I'm going to save you, I need to let go.

She forced her consciousness away, and knew in the real world, she sobbed. That final goodbye was impossible to admit, so she flung her Soul out in a heart-rending sending.

Unerringly, she darted to her father's side and joined

with his panicked mood. He barked orders in his sharpest tones, and soldiers jumped to action. Greece's door guard flinched before his wrath, and Landra knew she was the cause.

"Find her!" Chief Hux flung at the world, but she knew that was impossible. The guards didn't know where she'd gone, and there was no time for a full search. She sensed fury, despair, and grief welling beneath her father's hard shell, and she recoiled from his disappointment. He'd put his faith in her as chief elect, and she'd failed before starting the job.

Didn't I tell you I wasn't fit for the role? Why didn't you listen? I'm sorry Father. I'm sorry.

Thisk arrived, looking worn and anxious. Landra touched him briefly, making him glance up. Somewhere deep, she'd known he had magic, but the thought had been too dangerous and difficult to grow in her mind. His intensity was unbearable, and she threw herself away from him, her consciousness flitting amongst the party guests until she snagged on Bexter. The cadet's green eyes searched, as if hunting for a lost partner, but he wasn't aware of her presence. She had no solid connection to him. Not yet. Not ever. He was the promise of a future, which would fade from memory.

Too much loss. Too much pain.

The hethra visualization was unbearable. She cast her consciousness toward the temple, where no one would know her, but one final contact seized on her thoughts. She roamed the high reaches of the trees, the demonic swelling of the magic well, and the lifeless space of the platform, picking up the sweeping pink strands of mist in her wake. Solitary threads twisted and writhed, coming together in knotted strands. Oakham's essence trailed behind Landra's Soul like a comet's tail.

Pain intruded, drawing Landra back to her body. She screamed, her stomach ablaze and Turgeth's grip clamping her neck—squeezing, squeezing. Mendog stepped up, sword sheathed, but his fist balled. Raising his huge arm, his eyes fired with hatred, and his Soul paled to white streaks of nothing. Landra couldn't move or duck. The fist powered down, carrying disaster, oblivion—failure.

Oh, Father, I wanted to make you proud.

Epilogue

The terror of raised voices welcomed Landra back to reality. Burning spasms coursed through her body, and warm blood welled from her gums. Misery found her immediately.

"You were supposed to watch the boy. Why in the history of the mist did you kidnap the girl?" someone asked.

"But she's the chief elect, boss."

"Really?" The sarcastic tone rang thick with disbelief.

Landra listened, her predicament seeping into her consciousness, one dreadful, pitiful facet at a time. Numbing bindings constricted her wrists, and agony crunched her into a ball of panic. *Prisoner.*

Earlier events crashed back into memory, her wordless dread building when she recalled Turgeth's plan. "Ransom Dannet back a piece at a time," he'd said. Her shuddering response invited more pain. It coursed through her body in an all-encompassing wave. She clenched back her screams, terrified of drawing her captors' attention. *Too much. Can't survive. I should be dead.*

"I gave clear orders, and you failed," the boss said. "If you were going to bring anyone back, it should have been Dannet."

Wait. You don't have Dannet?

Landra ran over the words in her head, checking she'd heard right. If they hadn't taken her brother, some part of the plan must have worked. She relaxed from her tight ball, but even that small movement hurt, so she stilled and probed her puffy cheek with her tongue. She let the tip roll over the tender gums and cracked her eyes open. A vast, rugged cavern came into focus, too different from the base's manufactured labyrinth to offer hope of escape. What was she thinking? There'd be no way out.

"What are we supposed to do with the girl now?" the boss asked.

Something about the clipped tones set Landra on edge.

Without moving her head, she turned her swollen eye on the man they called their boss. A blue uniform of Warrior issue swamped his wiry frame, and a ceremonial cloak draped down his back. His scrawny neck disappeared inside a stiff collar, and his sandy hair showed a full maturity of Warrior growth. Landra couldn't breathe, didn't want to believe her eyes.

That face, that voice—it was Warrior Third Preston. Horror compounded Landra's torture as the level of betrayal became clear. One of her father's trusted generals had plotted to kidnap his son. She needed to do something, but she had no power. Her broken body could do nothing. She was useless. Nearly dead.

Failure, failure, failure. Chief elect. Blah!

"We made a decision," Turgeth said.

"*You* made a decision," Preston corrected. "Everything we'd hoped to achieve has failed. The announcement ceremony went ahead, and everyone watched that dratted Hux

289

boy get promoted to chief elect. The treaty with the temple was signed by all parties. Tell me, Turgeth, how did your decision benefit our cause? Now, we'll be pandering to those mist-ridden Templers for years to come. If you'd taken the boy like we planned, Chief Hux would have cancelled the ceremony or named me as elect."

"But she had the knife," Turgeth said.

Wait a minute. What? The ceremony went ahead with Dannet. Holy shelk!

Landra couldn't help herself. The news was the best outcome she could have hoped for and a fine reward for her sacrifice. An evil chuckle shook her body, which turned into a noisy groan. The pain seemed more bearable now that she knew Dannet's fate. And then it wasn't. *Gods, this hurts.*

"Let me see that knife," Preston said.

"Here," Mendog replied. "Hey, boss, I think the sleep syrup is wearing off. She's awake."

So, you know I'm listening. Don't care.

A kick crunched into her ribs, catching her bound hands. The jolt sent searing bolts of pain into her shoulders, and a shocked roar ripped from her throat. Startled gliders flurried from high roosts and settled back in a flap of wings.

Shelking mist balls, so I do care. Just kill me and get it over with.

She sensed the next kick before it smacked into her side. Expecting the blow didn't lessen its damage, and she writhed on the floor. Hard, cold rock cradled her face, and jagged corners dug through her flimsy party outfit. A sword swung over her head, so she prepared to die, stricken with terror and all courage gone.

"Stop that," Preston said. "Don't damage her yet."

Yet? The thought of more suffering was too much to bear. *Show mercy. Finish this.*

Preston swished his cloak over his shoulders and kneeled at her side. She viewed him through narrowed eyes, unable to move. The Warrior's slate-blue aura touched her richer shades, sharing more of him than was bearable.

Jealous, cruel, hateful. Not fit for the uniform, bastard. The mismatch made her retch.

Without warning, Preston yanked on the tethers and hauled her to a sitting position.

"Agh." For a moment, pain filled her world to the exclusion of all else. *Can't last. Mist, take me.*

The scene faded, then reappeared for Landra, bringing the Collector's carved handle into stark view. She longed for death, but her body refused, sentencing her to teeter on a sword edge of suffering.

Preston twisted the Collector's blade before her eyes, fury contorting his lined face.

"You!" he said. "Why do you have this?"

Landra couldn't have formed words, even if she'd wanted to speak.

"Of all the soldiers the chief could have chosen for elect, there's no way he would have given the knife to you," he said. "I expected him to insult his generals by passing it to family, but to give it to a girl short of cadet age… What's special about you?"

Landra had already considered that question and never come up with an acceptable answer. She rolled her jaw, preparing to speak. "I stopped your plot." Swollen lips made the words thick.

Preston's grip tightened on the knife handle until his knuckles stretched white. He

shot her a venomous glare. "Stupid girl. I should kill you now."

Not the worst thing. Do it please. I give up.

"Save our people, child of my life."

The words stilled Landra's twitching. She wasn't certain whether the call to fight came from Oakham's memory or was an echo from Gallanto. Either way, the penetrating instruction bored into her Soul. Chilling dread turned her stomach as she considered bearing this agony rather than submitting to fate. She'd come to terms with her mortal end, but this...

Wetness spread between her legs, and she screamed inside. "Do you know what you ask, Gallanto?"

"What?" Preston asked.

Landra didn't answer the Warrior traitor. She groaned, railing against her promised future of pain and fear. The Collector twisted before her face, offering no escape. Dannet might have been announced as chief elect, but the knife bound her to a responsibility that wouldn't be denied. She squeezed her eyes, ignored her pain, and roared, "I will, Chief Hux." It signaled her full submission to the role of chief elect in fact, if not in name.

The look Preston gave her suggested he saw madness. She considered for a moment and decided he might be right.

"So, you were really meant to be chief," he said with disgust.

It didn't feel true. It had never felt true, but she didn't feel like a Templer either. A realization broke into her consciousness, and agonizing, wound-tearing laughter bubbled up from her gut.

"No," she said through gritted teeth, but with absolute certainty. "I wasn't meant to be chief elect. I was supposed to become a ranger." It was the greatest truth of all, and her hysterical laughter rang around the rocky crevices like a peal of bells.

Key to the Library

You are at the doors of the Hux Hall library.

If you enjoy this world as much as I do, gain free access to documents, maps, world building notes, and army personnel files by joining my Fantastic Worlds Book Club.

Enrollment on my mailing list will keep you up to date with book releases, new library material, exclusive offers, and inside information.

Subscribe at

www.amandastwigg.com

About the Author

Amanda Twigg is a geeky grandma who loves fantastic worlds.

She was training to be a journalist when circumstances changed her life. She became a tennis coach at the age of thirty and has worked in that profession ever since. In 2014 she was awarded the title of Aegon Children's Tennis Coach of the Year.

Throughout her career, Amanda has never lost her passion for writing. Now, she devotes more time to creating fantasy worlds from her home in Wales. The rest of her life revolves around her husband and family.

The Absence of Soul is Amanda's first novel.

Don't be afraid to say hello. You can connect by sending a message to amanda@amandastwigg.com

To my husband Philip, who deals with the mundane so I can live in a fantasy world

———

With thanks to

Adam, Emily, Sharon, Madeline, Shirley, Cruncle, and Fozia

Alex should have a special mention, as I have tormented him over the years with early versions of every story I've written

———

Editing - Cayleigh Stickler at Black Cat Edits
Cover - Richi the best at 99designs

By Amanda Twigg

The Sentience of a Stone

━━━

SOCIETY'S SOUL

The Absence of Soul

Corrupted Soul

Printed in Poland
by Amazon Fulfillment
Poland Sp. z o.o., Wrocław

55879615R00181